THE
PERFECT
WORLD

A Journey to Infinite Possibilities

THE
PERFECT
WORLD

A Journey to Infinite Possibilities

By

PRIYA KUMAR

EBD

EMBASSY BOOKS
www.embassybooks.in

THE **PERFECT WORLD**

By **PRIYA KUMAR**

© Priya Kumar
First Published in India: 2011

Published by:
EMBASSY BOOK DISTRIBUTORS
120, Great Western Building,
Maharashtra Chamber of Commerce Lane,
Fort, Mumbai-400 023, (India)
Tel : (+91-22) 22819546 / 32967415
email : info@embassybooks.in
Website: www.embassybooks.in

ISBN 13: 978-93-80227-93-1

Printed and Bound in India by
Repro India Ltd., Navi Mumbai

"The only way you can really postulate any kind of a goal at all is imagination. And if you don't postulate high-flown goals - if you don't hitch your wagon to a star - it's a cinch you're not going to get up to the top of the pine tree, because it takes that much to get this much.
"You know, in Alice in Wonderland it says you have to run just to keep up. You have to run twice as fast if you want to get anyplace."

L. Ron Hubbard

"We choose our families, we choose where we will be born. We choose the people we will serve, we will love and we will grow with."

My family has been my choice, the best choice I have ever made.

My mother is my good-fortune-maker. She is my life-support. I chose her for her courage and compassion.

My father's pride and encouragement keeps me humbled. I chose him for his strength and passion for all he does.

Kapil, my brother will always be the first love of my life. I chose him for he is an angel in disguise. I will love him till eternity.

Suchita, my sis-in-law, I chose her for the fun soul that she is.

Aarya, my god-daughter is my twin soul. She is my equal. I can't wait for her to grow up.

Myra, my god-daughter, I chose her so I can have a hand in being a part of her purpose.

Coco, my Yorkshire terrier, she is a bundle of all the goodness in the world. I chose her so she could have the life she deserves.

"The solution to all problems lies within. The answer to all questions lies within. The key to greatness, the key to prosperity, the key to love, the key to success, heck, the whole universe, lies within." – *The Perfect World*

My coaches, Gisela Gunter and Karl-Heinz, allowed me to reach that place of power within, where all that I have and don't have, is of my own choosing. I have never been happier. I have never been cleverer. I have never been so certain about who I am and what I am here for. They have had the greatest role to play in my success, my sanity and my spiritual freedom.

Gisela, Karl-Heinz, I share you with the world.

www.life-improvement.net

"There is no 'one' creator. However, there is 'one' purpose for creation – freedom. Freedom from the illusion of mediocrity, scarcity and compromise. There is a better world, one that you first create within. There is a Perfect World, a world where truth, love and spiritual evolution is the code of honor of all." – *The Perfect World*

The Perfect World is a co-creation of like-minded people. My publisher's belief in my purpose made it his purpose to publish the book. Varsha's passion has been contagious all through. The support of my team, the power puff girls, Aarti and Priyanka, made writing the Perfect World possible.

And you, the special being, who has turned to read this page, created The Perfect World to be read.

The Walk

'How does one define success? What does success really mean?' I pondered as I walked down a muddy track kicking at loose pebbles in the way. The pebbles landed with soft thuds in the bushes a few feet away. Nature is amazingly accepting of our misplaced emotions. If someone had kicked a pebble my way, I would have answered with some rocks. The emotionally loaded pebbles landing in the gracious lap of nature, took some steam off my foul mood. The question, *'what is the meaning of success'* had been haunting me, keeping me up at night, making me impatient for an answer I could agree with. I worked at a local newspaper in the sales department. Selling newspaper space was my job and I hated it. I still haven't figured out how I got the job. I suspect that my boss thought *she looks good and so she can sell.* I found no joy in my work and my discontent found its way out in my words, my thoughts and my attitude. My cynicism however, was an asset to my team. I had the ability to find faults and they drew on my perspective to better their projects. Finding fault with others helps justify one's own shortcomings, but my colleagues used my shortcoming as their strength. This was becoming a growing problem for me; I soon became a critic of everything, including my own life.

I looked down at my white canvas shoes, spattered with the wet, golden brown mud of the track and I knew that the stains would permanently dim the shine of the white fabric, just as Danny had predicted.

Danny dealt in real estate. He worked for the largest real estate broking house in the Canary Islands. He was meticulous, organized and a perfectionist. I, on the other hand, was messy, scattered and really didn't care about the small stuff, er, which means I cared about nothing. Danny believed in security, job security. I believed I needed to quit my job. Danny loved me, and I had never loved. I had loved the attention Danny gave me and he misunderstood my acknowledgement as love. Danny had his whole future planned. I could not even dare to envision myself in his. Whoever said that opposites attract had no clue about relationships. Danny and I had been dating for over two years, but our 'opposite' attitudes were the major cause of the dipping attraction between us. And last night we had mutually agreed to 'take a break' from each other.

"Would you be back in time Niki?" Danny would ask me accusingly when I wanted to go off alone into the forest. "You seem to drift off when you walk."

Of course I 'drifted' off in my walks. What else do you expect from a person who by her own standards was 'wasting' her life on a daily basis? What else do you expect from a thirty year old sales executive who really really wants to write books? How do you expect anything sane from a person who hates her job but does it anyway because it pays the bills? She is unhappy to the point that she makes everyone around her unhappy. She is confused and dejected to the point that she contaminates everyone else's clarity and enthusiasm. It's not about what others tell you about you, it's about the truth you know about yourself. The truth you dare not confront and the truth you cannot change; the truth that your life sucks!!

I walked on aggressively.

I was afraid this was going to turn into one of the walks where you don't know where you are going. Danny hadn't called since last night and my boss had called several times this morning. Though taking a break was my idea, I suspected that Danny would use this break to break free from me. I did not go to work. I wanted to call my boss and tell him that I needed a break, but I didn't dare make that call. Looking at my performance and my attitude, I am sure that he too would use the opportunity to break free from me. My eyes flickered mechanically over the green bushes ahead, a sign of my 'deadly introversion' as Danny described it.

I was introverted and didn't speak much, quite contrary to the quality that you would seek in a sales person. And when I did speak, you would wish that I hadn't, and to be honest, I too wished that I hadn't. If only my life could be different. If only I had the courage to do what I loved; to write. If only I had enough money, to do that. If only I had the ability to love a man for who he is and not punish him for who I am not. If only I could be happy with myself, with my work, and my life. What had happened to me? How did I land up here? I was not always like this. Then where did I lose myself?

My feet were treading forward but my mind was looking backwards.

I stood still under the darkening sky gazing up at the stunning mountain range that lay ahead of me. The sky was scattered with clouds moving hastily along. I often looked for pictures in the clouds but today they were as dispersed as my thoughts. The walk from here on would be uphill, leading to a large clearing about a mile into the alluring forest. It had the largest tree stump I had ever seen. I had always imagined sitting on it and writing my books. That was my dream. Though I had often ventured there to write but with so much frustration in my head the only words that would emerge were, "My life sucks!"

I bent down and tightened my shoelace. My jeans were still muddy from last night's walk after Danny had packed and left. I missed him. I walked uphill hesitatingly. Wet mud is usually quite slippery. Just last week I had taken a nasty fall and had twisted my ankle. The initial climb was steep and I had to shut down the chatter in my head to stay focused on my foothold. I wanted to get to the tree stump to 'write my book', or, at least to think about a plan to turn my life around.

How does one write a book under so much pain and pressure? How does one think constructively with so much frustration and negativity looming in one's soul? Pressure is good when it is a driving force, but when pressure breeds self-doubt, then creation is almost impossible. My compromise with my work was putting my career under pressure. My compromise with my reality was putting my ability to relate with myself under pressure. Every time I came for a walk, my mind came alive with all the conversations I had never had, with all things that I wanted to do that I never did, with all the opportunities that came my way that I never grabbed. I carried this baggage of things undone and words unsaid up the mountain, hoping somehow to get rid of it and walk back free from the load that constantly haunted me.

I wanted to think about my life, about what I really wanted to do. I wanted to think about my dream. I wanted to write books. I wanted to be an author. I wanted to make my own start and my own mistakes. I wanted to fail if that is what it took to succeed. I wanted to learn and find out for myself the meaning of life and the meaning of success. I didn't want the urgency of paying the bills steering my life. I didn't want everyone discouraging me that 90% of authors never get published, that I should be grateful that at least I had a job and that it was time I got married and made babies. I wanted to be in love. I wanted to feel free. Maybe my vision of how I wanted my life to be was misplaced, but I wanted to experience my own wrong and discover my own right.

Half an hour seemed like a good time to make it to the clearing, have my share of the universe sitting on the tree stump and make it back. Maybe Danny would be back home tonight. Maybe he was gone forever.

I was a good climber. I took the last step off the steep rock and looked ahead into the dense forest. It was dense but inviting, the sky was still light above and the chirping of the birds returning home brought a sense of peace to the place. I parted a branch and stepped into the forest, and to my dismay the branch swung back right into my face leaving a small bruise on my left cheek. My cheek stung with the sudden impact.

"Darn," I muttered. If Danny would be back, he would make a big deal about this bruise tonight. I shook my head. Danny made a big deal about everything, no matter what the situation. Whether I bruised my cheek, sprained my ankle or had a headache, it was all a big deal.

"I love you more than you love yourself," he would say as if that self-acclaimed declaration gave him unwarranted control of my life. I had no doubt that Danny cared, I had no doubt that Danny loved me, but in a stupid kind of way, I did not want so much love. It was suffocating me.

If Danny were back, I knew the rest of the evening would be about the bruise on my face and about how careless I was. Danny clung with such idiotic obstinacy to his idea of what was best for me that he failed to see how his every attempt at that was only hurting me. Just the thought of it hastened my pace in frustration. Maybe I didn't want Danny back.

The forest had a whole range of creatures, mostly friendly. I loved the birds; they had colors that could defy any painter's palette. I took a deep breath and challenged myself to walk ten steps ahead without thinking about how miserable my life was.

I guess one level below misery is when you don't know what you want. I wanted Danny to come back and I also wanted Danny to go away. I didn't want to work another day at my job but I needed the money I earned from it. I wanted to write a book but I didn't have the time for it. Misery comes from being stuck in this vicious duality.

There went the ten steps.

I stopped, grit my teeth, made a fist to the sky and swore that the next ten steps would be in utter peace. I guess peace is not a decision one makes; it's a state one acquires. But heck, I decided to walk in peace.

"Why? Why me!!!!" I spoke to the tree on the left.

I walked on muttering. I guess my walks brought me no peace, but sure helped me release my frustration to make me peaceful enough to swallow another day of a life that I did not want to live.

"Help me out of my own trap. Someone help me get out of this rut that people call life. Someone help me, please." I begged to no one in particular. I didn't want to be ordinary. I didn't want to be average. I wasn't like this; this mean, nagging, insensitive humanoid. I had talent, I had aspirations, and I had a dream. I needed someone to help me find the courage, the passion and that winning edge that was needed to make it big.

A sudden sweet smell filled the air. I sniffed, raising my head. It was a smoky sweet smell of some mixed spices. Where was the smell coming from? I had walked in the forest for twelve months and I had never smelt anything like this. It was induced. The smell was coming from the clearing ahead, I suspected.

I hastened my walk. Mystery is a great distraction. Until now my head was filled with the misery of my life, and this mysterious smell had my attention off my world and in the direction of its source. What was this smell?

It was too late for walks. I knew that people did not come strolling up the forest at this hour, and that is why I liked being here, away from people. Danny would make a big fuss about it, and it generally ended in an argument, the result was that I found my way up in the forest, almost every evening.

The smell only grew more pronounced as I walked forward. I could see the trees give way into the clearing, just a few feet away. I could see the tree stump standing majestically, holding in it the setting sun and a thousand best sellers, and there, from behind the tree stump emerged a thick line of smoke. It was the smoke that was emitting the smell of burning spices. What in the world was going on?

I broke into a sprint and I stepped off the track, into the clearing. The tree stump obscured the base of the smoke and the heavy smell of spices stung my nostrils. I darted towards the stump, alarmed.

"What are you doing here?" A voice shrilled and I could have had a thousand heart attacks in one second as my feet froze on the ground. I spun around and standing right behind me was the old, hunched back, Thelda, the Sorceress.

"Thelda!" I heard a *gasp, gasp, gasp, gasp* of air dragging through my lips but I could not stop it. It felt like the forest was shaking, like there was an earthquake, but I knew it was my own trembling that was causing the illusion.

"Thelda!" I rubbed my eyes in disbelief.

"Aren't you supposed to be dead?"

Thelda was a Sorceress. She lived in the forest and was known in the Canary Islands for her witchcraft, her dealing with spirits and everything crazy anyone could think of. She died last week at a self-acclaimed age of two hundred and fifty years. The news of her death had made it to the headlines of my newspaper. And here she was, alive and kicking, doing some of her mumbo jumbo in this forest. If this was a dream, then I had to urgently wake up. I slapped my hand over my face but I was as awake and alive as Thelda the Sorceress who stood before me. I kept staring in disbelief.

Thelda was dressed in an orange robe, her silver white hair scattered in all directions. She wore a neckpiece of broken bones made of bird legs. Her face was not as shriveled as it appeared in the pictures but her hunch was steeper, giving her a very wicked aura. Her eyes were grey and held mischief in them. She held a large bird leg with claws as big as her hands. She smiled and her lips seemed to be quivering in a silent laugh. Her pearly white set of teeth defied her age.

"What are you doing here?" She demanded, raising the bird leg and obstructing me from going towards the tree stump.

"You must not inhale the incense," she said furiously tugging at her bone necklace.

"What's going on? Aren't you supposed to be dead Thelda? I have already been smelling the incense for the past few minutes by the way," I tried to get a hold of myself. The initial shock had passed. I was not afraid of Thelda when she was alive and I was not going to be scared of a dead Thelda either. Danny lived in mortal dread of her powers but I did not share that fear. I did not believe in sorcery, I did not believe in black magic and I did not believe in ghosts. I wonder what I really believed in though? Maybe I was a non-believer; non-believer in anything that was to be believed in.

"I was er, dead, but now I am back," Thelda hesitated for a second. She broke into a smile and winked, waving her hands animatedly to demonstrate that she indeed was alive.

Danny had told me about Thelda. He had told me stories about how she had the power to bring the dead back to life, cure people of terminal illnesses, curse evil people to leprosy and some other crazy stuff, which I just brushed away. Danny was emotionally weak. He believed in destiny, he believed in security and he believed in his fixed way of thinking. But no matter how much I had turned a deaf ear to sorcery and witchcraft, Thelda was in front of my eyes alive.

"If I can bring the dead to life, then do you think I can remain dead for long," she chuckled wickedly, her lips quivering again as she did.

"Then why did you die at all?" I did not buy Thelda's theory of coming back from the dead. That was impossible. She had been buried six days ago and should have been decomposed. But she looked younger than the pictures I had seen of her. Her death must have been a hoax to create a greater following of believers I guess. When people would find out that Thelda rose from the dead, it would create a strong impression and faith in the paranormal. Maybe she had gone into hiding and planned her come back.

"I needed a break." Thelda walked towards me and looked into my eyes. Her eyes had sagging bags of skin around them and in an eerie way, she had earnestness about her. 'I needed a break' was the last thing I expected her to say. Now this was something the Sorceress and I had in common.

"Well, you don't believe me and you don't believe in me so it won't hurt to tell you. Sorcery is hard work. Didn't you see the endless queues outside my house? People kept coming, night and day. There came a time when people just stopped taking responsibility for their lives because Thelda was there to set it right. And Thelda did set things right. I was tired. I needed a break. I didn't want to be a Sorceress anymore. So I decided to die and think about my life and what I really wanted to do. My tenders announced that I was dead and I stayed in my death pit waiting, er, to die." Thelda spoke from her heart and left me totally baffled.

She rubbed her eyes and twitched her nose. I could not help but think about the beauty that lay concealed under the wrinkles. Thelda peered into my eyes and my thoughts, estimating whether I understood what she said.

In the ancient times, the Canary Islands had strange ideologies around death and dying. Here, dogs were considered sacred animals. There were gods with dog heads. It was well-known that the natives still treated the dogs with their medicines and supposed magical powers while they were alive, to rejuvenate them so that they could live longer. They also mummified dogs after their death. I also knew that some ancient cults treated and mummified their leaders in the same way. If the leader wanted to die, that is if *he* had decided to die, then sometimes their ceremony to treat the body for mummification started days before he actually died. So supposedly if the leader would announce 'I think I want to die', then they would start treating his body for mummification before he physically died. This practice, where the leader would lay in his death pit immobile, awaiting his spirit to break free had not been heard of for centuries. So that explained the hoax about Thelda's death. She took *a break* in her death pit while her tenders treated and tended to her, preparing her for her willed death. The public declaration of the death was important to make the decision to die irrevocable.

I shuddered at that thought. The natives had weird ways and Thelda was evidence of that. She had brought the ancient myth about dying at will into practice again.

"And now I am back!" She said with childish glee. Her face lit up like that of a school girl excited about her first dance.

This was madness. Utter madness. The scary part was that I could relate with this madness. A madness that gave me comfort that I was not alone in my turmoil. Even though my partner in sentiment was a supposedly dead witch, I found myself smiling.

"You must leave now!!" Thelda raised her hand and the bird leg again in an attempt to scare me, in vain. If you don't believe in something, then it no longer has any effect on you.

I shifted my gaze to the smoke. It was emerging in thick spurts from the bottom of the tree stump and moving up in a straight line towards the sky about ten meters in height and then disappeared abruptly. I found that very strange.

"What's going on?" I asked ignoring her and walked around her towards the tree stump. Thelda followed me, her back bobbed up and down as she did.

"I am purifying the place for their arrival," she spoke in whispers, darting a glance behind her.

"Whose arrival?" I was aghast. There was a bundle of spices at the foot of the stump. There was no visible fire but it was emitting a constant thick smoke. The smell of the spices was very strong. It stung my eyes, making tears flow and causing my nose to run. Thelda however was unaffected by the smoke.

"The evolved souls from Zedius, from the planet called the Perfect

World. They are arriving at midnight. I am preparing for them. They are highly evolved souls, mind you." Thelda smiled, the creases on her face smoothened as she did.

I could not believe my ears. First it was the sorcery and black magic and now some alien creatures of her imagination that she described as 'evolved souls from Zedius'. This woman was hallucinating and probably better off dead.

"This is madness," I muttered, totally ignoring Thelda's hysteria.

"I was in my death pit..." she said, bending down towards the little bundle of spices emitting smoke and plucked out from it a smoking piece of clove. She held the clove in her trembling hand and a thin streak of smoke emitted from it extending up to the sky.

"But I had to come back for them." Thelda whispered on the word 'them' as though they were sacred beings. She toyed with the smoke and then waved the clove around in circles.

"What are you talking about?" I asked, my eyes searching the clearing and the forest pathway for any further evidence of Thelda's madness.

"The evolved souls from Zedius, the Perfect World, are arriving at midnight. They are on a mission, a mission to take me to Zedius. Planet Earth is going to witness the presence of two evolved souls from another faraway world." Thelda spoke excitedly.

I guffawed. I could not help but laugh. How in the world were people so naïve to treat her the way they did? The con woman had them convinced that she was dead and was now preparing her return with some 'aliens from outer space' story.

Thelda continued despite my disbelief, "They," she whispered, "have been signaling for a long time now. I had not made up my mind totally about what I wanted to do. Finally when they made me the offer I could not refuse and so I decided to come back."

Who would ever believe that I met Thelda? Who would ever believe this conversation that I was having with her? Even the reporter who did the story about her death would not believe me.

"The Perfect World, Zedius, is in trouble. There is too much perfection. Everything is right. And you know how devastating that can be? It's like sleeping with the enemy," Thelda chuckled, "On the Perfect World, I would never have a job. I exist because things are not how they are supposed to be."

"Zedius will be destroyed if it cannot be saved because no one wants to live there. It's too perfect. So in their last attempt to save it, they have been communicating with different planets to help. While in the grave I received their communication. They want me to come to Zedius and add some intellectual flaws in their perfection so that it would become an interesting life of struggle, overcoming and victory for the inhabitants. With my kind of experience in dealing with people's flaws for over two centuries I am one of the most wanted candidates in the universe." Thelda explained sprightly. My mouth was open.

"I had been considering their request for a long time but finally when they made me the offer, I jumped right out of my death pit. And look, the treatment has actually rejuvenated me," Thelda looked around and whispered the last sentence.

"What was the offer?" I was curious. Thelda was a good storyteller and she had me eating out of her hands.

"If I went with them," Thelda raised her hands to the sky to symbolize the superior souls, "to Zedius, The Perfect World, and helped them set it right, er, wrong, er slightly wrong, then I could have the power all the beings of Zedius have," Thelda said as she bent towards me as though letting me in on a very confidential secret.

I raised my eyebrows in anticipation.

"I would have the power to be, do and have anything I want." She whispered so softly I literally had to read her lips to understand what she had just said.

I let out a long breath and I straightened up.

"You should not be here," Thelda concluded as I stared at her. She paused, held my cheek with her skinny fingers and stared directly into my soul.

"Niki Sanders," she said looking into my eyes.

I leapt out of my skin. She said my name! My full name! How the hell did she know my name?

"Ah, by the way it's best you break up with Danny. He will never let you grow. He will convert you to his mentality and you will soon forget your dream of being an author. You will kill your spirit with him, and you will kill him with your spirit. I suspect you have done that already, to each other. You were meant to be an author. The world will change as your thoughts will first change you. Your purpose will find its way in your life. Danny is not your choice. He is your excuse. Free him. Free yourself. Your freedom lies a few hours away, choose wisely. Your chance to your desired destiny will be given to you," Thelda spoke, making circles of smoke around my head with the smoking cloves in her other hand. Her eyes fixed on me.

My hair stood up on the back of my neck and a chill ran through my spine. I jerked my face free from Thelda's hand. I could digest Thelda's return from her well-publicized death. I could digest the story about her being treated in her death pit to prepare her to die. I could digest the story about the aliens she called evolved souls from Zedius and Thelda's departure into outer space. I could accept all that psychobabble without much concern. But this!!! This was about me!! How did she know my name? How did she know about Danny and me? How did she know about my dreams? How did she know the secrets I had not even told myself? For the first time in this whole encounter, I had freaked out.

My stomach began to churn uncomfortably. My head began to spin. I needed to get back home. This was not happening. I shot one horror struck glance at Thelda and she was smiling a sinister smile. I spun around and my trembling legs began to carry me hurriedly back to the forest.

"You should not have come here Niki Sanders. But you did." She yelled as I hastened my strides.

"I can see your soul. You will come back. For it is your destiny..." I heard her words over the frantic beats of my heart. My head was still spinning. My lungs were filled with the smell of spices that seemed to sting my brain. My feet were all over the mud track and I was grasping the small branches that came in my way to keep my balance. I don't know how but I had reached the edge of the forest. The lights of the houses ahead added a comfort as I half ran and half walked my way home.

The Trade Off

My heart was still doing a manic beat. I lay on my bed and I had repeated the encounter with Thelda in my head a million times. How did she know about me? How did she know about Danny? How did she know about my dream to be an author? How did she know that Danny and I had problems? How did she....? The questions kept coming, but I had no answers..

I stared at the ceiling and a horrid thought infected my mind. Thelda had seen into my life. So her *stuff* was not all hogwash. She was right about Danny. It was best we parted ways. At least that way we both could be happy. She was right about my dreams. I had never shared them with anyone. I was too introverted even to tell myself. She had said that I would be led to my desired destiny. Maybe Thelda was not a hoax. Maybe she was real. Maybe she was really a sorceress, a real sorceress. I could see why she had a following and I could see how people became believers.

I sat up on the bed. My muddy shoes had soiled the bed sheet. In my perplexed state I had crashed onto the bed without removing my shoes. I absent-mindedly took them off and flung them on the floor. Thelda had said that she was expecting aliens. She had said that they were evolved souls from another world called Zedius. Could it be true? I tried to shake off that thought. What was I doing? I had enough problems already. Why was I making Thelda my problem?

But she had said that I would come back. Why would I go back? I never wanted to see her again. Heck, I had sworn I would never set foot in the forest again. My life and my mind were safer here, in my own little miserable world, where my pain and my despair were predictable. I shot a glance at the clock on my study table. It was quarter past eight. I still had four hours to deal with imaginary aliens in my head along with the sorceress who needed a break, before they landed and took her away.

A knock on the door brought my madness to an abrupt halt. Danny! My heart sank. This was not the time I wanted to see him. I had too much to deal with right now. Maybe I could tell him about Thelda. Maybe I could tell him what Thelda said about us, about my destiny and the aliens that she called evolved souls. And maybe then Danny would advise me to get mental help.

I walked towards the door, my heart skipping beats. I squinted through the peephole. It was the neighbor, Susan. False alarm. I tried to ease my heart.

I opened the door and there stood Susan, flustered as always. I loved her for her English accent.

"What is this smell that is coming from your house?" She asked shriveling up her nose and sniffing towards me, "this smell of spices. I was curious. Are you cooking something, or is something burning?" she spoke in her typical accent, peering inquisitively behind my back.

"Huh?" I staggered. "I ummm. I'm roasting some spices. I think

I overdid them," I stood at the door as I stumbled over my own words.

She deliberated a few seconds and smiled, "Oh!"

I stood still at the door. I had no intention of inviting her into my mental disaster. I was better off alone.

"Come by sometime," she said, "haven't seen you and Danny around for a while."

"I will," I put on a nervous smile and nodded goodbye.

That was rude! I chided myself as I shut the door behind my back. Had I carried the smell with me? I had it in my lungs and felt it had penetrated my very being, but now it was spreading to the neighborhood? This was crazy! I sat at the kitchen table staring out the window at Susan's house. Her cottage was at least thirty meters away. Not only had she smelt the spices, but she had also located the source of the smell to me! That was weird.

I went back to bed and tossed and turned for hours. Thelda's words and Thelda's face kept playing in my mind non-stop. The aliens were coming, she had said. They were evolved souls. I had always wanted to meet some evolved souls, the non-alien kind though. I would come back, she had said. My body began to ache with restlessness. I looked at the clock. It was half past ten.

I was exhausted. I knew that within minutes until the fatigue would knock me out. And then I could wake up to a new morning. Thelda would hopefully find a new home on another planet and we could all be free of her madness. I chuckled at that thought but my smile was wiped off the next second. How had she known about me?

I must have dozed off because I woke up with a start with one sentence echoing in my mind – 'you will come back'. I was breathing heavily and my heart was still skipping beats. I looked around to see where I was. I was in the safety of my room, far away from the Sorceress. My hand groped for the clock. It was quarter to twelve. I frantically leaped out of the bed. I slipped on my muddy shoes, grabbed my coat and headed for the door.

I was going back to the forest. Damn it! I was going back! I had to put Thelda and her madness to rest. If I didn't go now, that Sorceress would haunt me for the rest of my life.

I shut the door behind me and darted for the forest. The lights of all the cottages were out. There were no streetlights because no one ventured out at night, let alone go into the forest. I was lucky that the full moon shone above and so I could see clearly into the night ahead.

The sky was alive with stars. With only a few clouds speedily drifting away, the wind was a little stronger as compared to the evening. I reached the edge of the forest and hesitated for a second. Did I really want to do this? Did I really want to see what was happening with Thelda and her supposed alien nonsense? My feet didn't wait for an answer. They headed for the track and soon I was consumed by the darkness of the forest.

The moonlight dripped from the gaps between the trees. The track was familiar, spooky, but familiar. I didn't need to navigate my way around. The smell of the spices had filled the forest and it was much stronger now. I jogged my way up to the clearing. My mind was alive with all sorts of possibilities of what was going on at the clearing. I was breathless. It was only a few feet away. I could see the clearing from where I now stood. The moonlight had spread magically on the grass and the smoke had a silvery shimmer as it emerged from the tree stump like it had earlier in the evening.

I walked cautiously towards the clearing. I did not want to be seen or to disturb the, er, ceremony. I just wanted to see for myself what was happening. I jumped off the track into a thicket of trees and crept towards the clearing. Luckily the mud was wet and no dry leaves or twigs crackled under my feet. The smoke was steady and the clearing was empty. I hid behind the trunk of a large tree and had a direct view of the clearing.

My eyes searched the area and there was no sign of Thelda or her aliens. I twisted my wrist and looked at my watch, it was 11:59. Before I could drop my hand to my side, I heard Thelda's voice. There she was, by the tree stump. Where did she appear from? I had looked away for less than a second and there she was. The smoke crackled and silver sparks burst out from the base. I shivered and a chill ran through my whole body. Either the temperature had dropped below zero degrees or I was having a panic attack. My body shook and I held on tightly to the bark of the tree lest I would collapse to the ground.

The smoke streak cracked open at the centre and more silver sparks flew. Through the curtain of smoke a creature appeared. Half man-like, half god-like. He was facing in my direction and I had a clear view of him. An over-sized man-like humanoid, about six and a half feet tall, dressed in a black full-length cloak that hid his form. He had large black wings that shone greenish blue in the moonlight. His face was sharp, chiseled to perfection. His eyes were ocean blue green that twinkled in the dark, the kind of eyes that could cast a spell on your soul and trap you in them forever. His eyelashes were blackish green and rather long and swept his cheeks when he blinked. His hair was black, long and thick. His locks fell lazily on his shoulders reflecting the color of his wings. They danced around his neck in bouncing curls as though they were alive. His lips were a melting pink and he held his hands raised up. My mouth fell open with a little popping sound.

This alien was not a three-eyed, four-legged, fork-tongued, repulsive creature. It, er, he was one of the most desirable men I had ever seen. The only thing that made him alien were his wings, that lay neatly folded on his back and his hair that seemed to be alive with motion. Despite my exasperation and initial shock to see him, I could not shake off this aura of superiority and serenity that surrounded him.

The smoke shivered and sparkled with thrusts and cracked open again. Through the open centre another god-like creature walked out. He was very much like the first one, except that his frame was larger, his hair was shorter and his eyes were jet black. His face was brazen, expressionless. He moved swiftly and stood by the first alien's side.

The adrenaline jolted through my veins. I didn't know what to make of this. The first alien flapped his wings open with a thundering sound. I saw that the wings were at least four meters wide from tip to tip before he folded them neatly on his back.

So it was true. Thelda was for real and so were her aliens, the evolved souls from another world. It felt like there was something big sticking in my throat. I gulped in an attempt to clear the obstruction.

Thelda spoke to the creatures. I could not hear clearly what she was saying but the two creatures nodded in agreement. She was speaking English and they understood. They really must be highly evolved souls to understand our language without any training.

"You came back!" Thelda turned around and pointed in my direction. The two god-like aliens spun around together and the three pairs of eyes looked in my direction. My stomach churned and the blood drained from my face. I froze. My eyes were wide open, horror struck. My hands lay frozen on the bark of the tree

I was clutching onto. My feet fixed on to the wet mud as though I had existed there for years. My breathing had stopped and so had my heart.

The alien with the blue green eyes began to advance in my direction. He was not walking. He was gliding. His cloak flapped in the breeze. His hair moved in an uncanny way as though it was alive, every strand of it, bouncing and curling in delight.

Run, I screamed to myself. Run!!!! I screamed louder without uttering the words. But my body was frozen in shock. My cover was busted. My destiny was about to unfold, as Thelda had predicted it would.

The alien stopped about ten feet in front of me. Half my body was behind the tree clutching it tight with my head popping out sidewards. I stared at him without blinking, my eyes ready to pop out and land on the moist grass below.

He stood there still, as if to allow me the time to get over my shock. His black hair matched the color of his wings, radiating sparkles of greenish blue. His hair flowed dreamily, with life. He pursed his lips as though wanting to say something. He flapped his wings and they made a thundering sound that jolted me out of my trance, and then folded them on his back.

He stood stationary, with his hands folded in each other. I could see that his expression was torn between amusement and concern for the shock that I was apparently in. His face was so perfect. And then it came, his smile. And then it went further; he began to move towards me in calculated steps. I stumbled backwards in fright. I tried to speak but my voice was gone and all that came out was some tremulous gibber.

"W.. Wh..Who are you?" I choked and stammered not taking my

eyes off his even for one second.

"I'm Acrodorf!" he said staring at me with incredulous eyes. His voice was husky and musical.

I stared at him wordlessly. He still wore the angelic smile and was still gliding slowly towards me. His pale white skin radiated like the morning sun. He looked like a cross between an angel and a super model. He seemed too good to be bad. He seemed too pure to hold evil. He seemed too angelic to mean harm.

Though I was in a state of shock at seeing a creature appear out of thin smoke, something in my heart told me I had nothing to fear.

"I am Acrodorf," he repeated. He blinked and his eyelashes swept dreamily over his cheeks closing the world in his eyes for a momentary flash. "I come from Zedius, The Perfect World."

"I don't mean any harm." The angelic Acrodorf said. I stood still studying his expression, totally baffled with the encounter. The kindness and melody in his voice was altering my heartbeat.

"I come in peace!" His face stretched out into a wide smile that made him look even more enigmatic. My eyes were riveted on him as he spoke. I exhaled. How long had I been holding my breath?

He stood less than three feet in front of me radiating a kind of energy that was unmistakably magnetic. His essence that he came in peace and meant no harm was shining through for real.

I was overcome with a euphoric feeling. A state where you are so happy that you cry; when you meet with a long lost friend. What was happening? Why was I experiencing this emotional roller coaster? My body and my mind were no longer in my control. My body was retracting in fear and my mind was reveling in joy.

Thelda came up behind him. "Oh come on out. I knew you would come back. And you knew that too," she yanked at me and I stumbled out of my hiding. I collapsed on the ground, into the clearing.

My hands groped the ground; I kneeled forward and I hastily tried to stand up. I stumbled a couple of times before I stood up straight, shaking uncontrollably.

Acrodorf stretched out his hand to me, offering to take mine in his. I deliberated for a short second and then I stretched out my hand too. I didn't want to, but I was driven, my mind and body seemed on two different purposes. Thelda's presence was reassuring. If she trusted him, then maybe I could trust him too.

His hand felt soft and warm and melted around mine. I stared at his eyes, ocean blue green and unreadable. I could feel his eyes searching me, waiting for me to say something. I calmed down somewhat from my initial state of terror and gulped.

Still holding onto my hand Acrodorf led me towards his partner. Thelda bounced along by my side, like a guardian. Acrodorf was huge and had the same scent of spices emanating from him. My body brushed against his cloak as I walked alongside him and it sent chills up to my brain. He let go of my hand and introduced me to his partner.

"This is Bren, my brother."

Bren nodded, his face brazen and expressionless. His deep black eyes stored a mysterious world in them, one that I didn't intend on exploring. His hair was as alive as Acrodorf's, only less mischievous. He seemed like a no nonsense person and had a very rigid demeanor. He was a towering creature.

"Why is she here?" he turned to Thelda for an explanation of my alleged intrusion. Bren's voice was heavy like percussion drums. His words rolled out musically but with an edge that made me uncomfortable. I instantly didn't like his tone. He made me sound like an intruder.

"It is her destiny.... to be at the wrong place at the right time." Thelda cracked up. She circled around Bren who kept spinning to make eye contact with her. "She was destined to come, like I was, from my decision to die."

"She can't come. We don't have room for two," a worried Bren looked at Acrodorf signaling him to take over the conversation.

"I didn't bring her here," Thelda shrugged, "and so it must have been your calling," she roared with laughter. Her saliva spurt out from her quivering mouth. The two aliens watched the Sorceress crack up at her own joke, in utter silence.

"I... I..." I mumbled and no other words followed. Thelda became solemn and the two aliens turned to me. "I... I j..just came here out of curiosity. I ... I... d... didn't mean to intrude. I will .... h... head back," I stammered out to clear my status out of this gathering.

Bren didn't have the kindness that Acrodorf exuberated. If Bren had come alone, evolved soul or not, then he would be the alien I would have run away from.

Acrodorf raised his head and took a deep breath in my direction, "How did you get this smell?" he asked, sniffing closer into my face.

How did I get that smell? I asked myself too.

"She is a non-believer who must *see* to believe," Thelda quacked.

She came and stood at Acrodorf's side. It was a frame shot from the beauty and the beast,,,,,,, Thelda being the beast.

Thelda smacked my hand and smiled.

What the hell was she doing? What had I landed myself into?

"I.. I have no idea what you are talking about." I stuttered at Thelda. Maybe this was the time to go back home. Maybe I needed to sleep. I had gone through too much in the past few hours. Stress did this to people. Stress killed people. And I was about to be a victim of my own imagination.

"Let me explain," Acrodorf stepped in. He held my hand and led me further into the clearing, leaving Thelda and Bren in conversation. My hand melted in Acrodorf's like butter. He had a sense of well-being around him. If he held on to my hand forever, I would never let go. It felt like home. It felt like I had felt him before. It felt like I was meant to be here, by his side. It felt like my destiny. I was certainly in a trance.

"We come from Zedius, the Perfect World. We sent out a communication to Earth and we got a response. Thelda responded. And so we are here," Acrodorf explained.

I wanted to tell Acrodorf that Thelda had been preparing to die. I wanted to tell him that it was a Sorceress that had communicated with him but something kept me from opening my mouth.

"Zedius, the Perfect World is in trouble. To tell you in short, our world is so perfect that it sucks. Everything is so perfect on Zedius that it's almost impossible to live there. The creation is there, the choices are there, but something very big is missing. That missing piece is so significant that Zedius is suffering, and has been suffering for a long time. So, in an attempt to save our

Perfect World, we decided to ask other planets for help. We need some fresh perspective, some imperfections so that it can add some spice to our Perfect World, and make life fun. We got a response from Earth and we are here for the trade off." Acrodorf sang out his whole story to me. He could continue to talk the way he talked and I could continue to listen to him for my entire life without breaking his flow. Acrodorf's voice was hypnotic.

"S..So you are taking Thelda away," I concluded for him. It was more of a statement than a question.

"Yes," Acrodorf smiled.

"I will go to Zedius with Bren and Acrodorf," Thelda exclaimed excitedly walking towards us.

"I will help them with some of my magic to make their world more fun, and in return they will give me the powers of Zedius."

So it was true. I found a sudden surge of energy flowing through my veins.

"The power to be, the power to do and the power to have anything I want!" she exclaimed. She looked towards Bren and Acrodorf who nodded in acknowledgement.

"Whoa..." my words drifted off. First of all this was real. And secondly, this was huge.

"And you can come too," Thelda chirped with delight.

"But we have permission for only one," Bren growled and looked towards Thelda, bringing her back to his first concern before Acrodorf had pulled me away.

I didn't want Bren to pick up a fight with Thelda because of me. I was the least of their concerns because first, I had no mind to go anywhere with them, and second I should not have come here in the first place.

"She is a delightful package of imperfections. She has an incredulous knack of creating disaster in her life with every decision she makes. It's a very rare ability. I have never seen that before. Normally the intention of evil is to destroy others. She is a rare being that spends every living moment in self-destruction. You could use her power at Zedius. We could use her ability to limit herself to bring some fun on Zedius." I fumed at Thelda's description of me. Bren and Acrodorf were amusingly impressed as she spoke so highly of my ability to sabotage my own life.

"That's unbelievable," Acrodorf looked at me in amazement.

"And it's true," Thelda jumped in.

"I will take her if she is willing to come," Acrodorf's words hit me like a bolt of lightning. My heart stopped and then broke into a sprint.

"Are you crazy? I am not going anywhere," I yelled at Thelda to make sure that I made my point clear.

"This self-sabotage mechanism. It's extraordinary, isn't it?" Thelda motioned to Bren as I displayed my ability to limit myself, to hold myself back from the seemingly extraordinary opportunity the evolved beings from Zedius were offering me.

Acrodorf spoke with admiration and he looked into my eyes deeply. "Come with me to Zedius, we need you. And you need us, to save you from you."

"My life is fine," I spoke unconvincingly. "I will make it fine. I will find a way, and that does not lead to Zedius."

"With the mess you have made with your life, you would need divine intervention to straighten it up." Thelda interjected. What was her problem? She wanted to go to Zedius, so she should be off. Why was she dragging me into her scheme? I was not going anywhere. I was not crazy enough to leave my life here and set off to some other planet.

"Think about it. You will have the power to be, the power to do and the power to have anything you want!" she croaked out loud. "Think about the life you can create with that power. Think about the lives of others you can touch with that power. This is your chance. The one and only chance for the destiny you desire. You willed yourself here. You led yourself here. The way back, is the way back to your life you want an escape from. Freedom is not in retreat. Freedom is in the way forward."

My skin had broken into goose bumps as Thelda spoke. I shook my head. I was not ready for this.

Acrodorf stepped forward. He shouldn't have. This was not fair. Acrodorf made me melt. I felt an instinctive drawing towards him. He had a power. I could feel it. He had a power to persuade someone and then make it seem like his own decision. Though I knew it, I also knew I would be victim to it.

"We came here for Thelda. But, if you like, you can come with us too. Two is better than one. And with your classic imperfections and natural affinity for disaster, you could prove to be an asset," Acrodorf's eyes sparkled and his voice flowed straight through my ears into my soul.

"But what about trespassing? What about The Game?" Bren

interjected in his attempt to deter Acrodorf from speaking any further, "She won't make it through the magnetic field of Earth and she certainly won't survive The Game."

"Give me some credit Bren." Acrodorf glowered in his direction, "I am cleverer than The Game."

"But what about the magnetic field?" Bren protested, frustrated with the argument.

"I will get her through," Thelda chimed in.

I was appalled. Acrodorf should listen to Bren and withdraw from me for all the complications he was mentioning. If something could possibly go wrong, I would make it go wrong even if I didn't want to. Bren was right. I would not make it through the magnetic field, through The Game or through life.

"W..Why me? Danny would be a better candidate. Susan would be even better. Why me?" I mumbled.

"Because you are here, they are not," Acrodorf answered gently, almost whispering, "you will drive yourself crazy with this encounter if you turn back and left. Your life will never be the same again. Every waking moment and every sleeping hour, this encounter will haunt you and take over your life. You should not have been here. But since you are, coming with us is the only route to your sanity."

I stood motionless.

Acrodorf was right. I could turn back and go home. And then spend my whole life wondering about what happened? About what could have happened? About what did happen? And about what I could have done? I had lived many years in turmoil like this. I had lived many years in regret of all the things I didn't do and should have done and what would have happened if I had. Half my life was lived in all the possibilities that I did not take, wondering, wondering, what would have been, if it had been that way. Acrodorf was right. This encounter would never leave me. But that was not reason enough for me to leave my life and join Thelda in her madness of saving some Perfect World.

"Why did you come here?" Acrodorf's eyebrows narrowed. His gaze was laser sharp. His hair stopped flowing and stayed still in neat curls over his shoulder.

"Because I was curious. I could not sleep. I was restless to the point of hysteria. I had to come here and see what was going on. I was driving myself crazy with my own imagination. I had to see with my own eyes if what Thelda had said was true. I had to come back, for if I didn't, I would never rest in peace again," I rumbled out the words like a runaway train.

Acrodorf smiled. His eyebrows relaxed. His eyes began to sparkle again. His hair resumed the bounce. I was shocked at my own words. Until I said them out loud, I didn't know that Acrodorf was explaining the same thing to me.

Acrodorf raised his eyebrows, waiting for my answer.

I was stubborn to the point of disaster. I was not ready for this. I was not prepared for this. I shook my head.

"We don't have time to waste!" Bren frowned at Acrodorf disapprovingly, "And besides, taking her would only mean trouble."

Thelda shook her head and turned away. Bren and Acrodorf spun around together and they all moved towards the base of the smoke by the tree trunk. I stood there, still shaking my head, in an attempt to keep myself convinced of my decision.

"See you later," I heard Thelda mutter in my direction. I had never imagined in my wildest dreams that I would have such an encounter with Thelda, the crazy Sorceress. I guess whoever had said never say never, had found himself in my position at one time.

I moved backwards, still facing the trio. They seemed to be in conversation and then stood beside the smoke trail. It seemed to grow thicker and the silver sparks began to spurt again. My heart raced and pounded in my body in apparent mutiny of my decision to be left behind. My feet moved further back in total disagreement with my heart.

The smoke sputtered and began to part with more flashes of silver sparks. Bren gave me one solemn look that spelt 'you are better off where you are' and disappeared into the crack first and left behind a fireworks trail of silver glitter.

Thelda cast one look at me. Her hunch began to straighten up. Thelda stood upright and gave me a mocking smile. She turned her head away and faced the smoke trail that was shaking violently. The crack opened again and an upright Thelda stepped in and disappeared. The smoke trail shook violently, spitting out liquid sparks of silver and then began to calm down.

Acrodorf was next and then it would be over. I would walk back home into a world of self-inflicted misery. I would break-up with Danny and find another man to blame for my lot. I would quit my job and find another one that would pay my bills till I could become an author. As time would go by, I would move from one man to another, from one job to another, until I forgot about my dreams and I forgot about my destiny. Maybe then I would be happy.

The smoke grew thicker again. It shook and swayed. Acrodorf

would disappear in it, and it would all be over. I would be the sole witness to two aliens, evolved souls, who came to planet Earth on a mission to save their planet, the Perfect World, from its own perfection. I would be the sole witness to their offer of a trade-off. I would be the sole witness to Thelda who would return after one week with the power to be and to do and to have anything she wanted. I would be the sole witness to my own denial to all of that.

Was I out of my mind? This was a jackpot! This is exactly what I needed, a new chance to life. I could not bear to live one more day of my life that was not lived my way. I no longer had the strength to be instructed, to be told, to be counseled, to be fussed over, to be possessed, to be protected,,,,, anymore. I had no confidence left in myself. I had no courage to even believe I could amount to anything. I had never written a book, because honestly I didn't think I could. My lack of self-belief kept me pinned to the ground. I had prayed for a window of hope and the Lord had opened a whole door for me to run through. And here I stood shaking my head and retreating from the one real opportunity to greatness. Was I out of my mind?

The smoke split open and began to spatter out sparks furiously. Acrodorf turned towards me and the silver gleams reflected in his ocean blue green eyes. His eyes searched my soul and said something unsaid.

My heartbeat seemed to stop. *This* was my chance to be bigger than I was. *This* was the break I had been waiting for. Danny was gone. My job should have gone long before. Coming to think of it, I had nothing to lose, for I was already lost. My life was an incurable mess and I had no plan for greatness, let alone success. Even if I did not come back and died on Zedius, it was better than dying to a miserable life. Who knows, I could come back and build the life of my dreams. Maybe I could turn myself around and be the best selling author, a part of the powerful 1% that shapes the way the world thinks and feels and grows. Maybe I could have my share of power, glory and happiness. Thelda was back from the dead. She had predicted my destiny. I was here now. Acrodorf and his energy were real. Maybe this was that 'help' I had been begging the universe for.

The smoke trail shivered violently and threateningly. Acrodorf blinked his eyes and turned towards it.

"Wait!" I said excitedly with a sudden compelling urge.

Acrodorf's lips parted in a smile. He opened his arms wide and his wings flapped thunderously. The smoke trail trembled violently as the slit began to collapse. I ran as fast as my legs could carry me and dashed towards Acrodorf, the evolved soul. He grabbed me in his embrace and I got pulled into the crack with an electric jolt.

The Maya

Acrodorf's wings flapped violently and he held me tight. We were sucked into the crack of the smoke trail.

The feeling was like being swallowed into a jelly-like substance. The smoke trail was not a smoky airshaft. It was solid inside, like a passage. Though I was locked in Acrodorf's arms, we both were held still in the substance, immobile. I tried to move my body but the substance was so dense it didn't allow any struggle for freedom. My only solace was that I was stuck *with* and *to* Acrodorf in a death-defying glue-like substance.

My eyes were open, staring at Acrororf. His eyes were open, ocean blue green, still sparkling. I wanted to ask Acrodorf what was happening, but I could not move at all. I could not breathe. The jelly-like substance was pressing against my eyes and I could no longer close them. The smoke trail shuddered on the outside; the jelly became thicker on the inside and became tighter around my body. It started to seep into my nostrils. My lungs began to sting and my head began to throb, screaming for oxygen. If this was not bad enough, I felt the jelly harden further, its grip tightened on, me squeezing the life out of me. The pressure was increasing with every passing second and I felt my brain would explode, that it would simply pop out of my head, like seeds pop out of a ripe grape when pressed.

Acrodorf's face was next to mine, expressionless. His eyes were open too and they were alive and communicating with me.

Don't resist. Let go.

I could hear the words through Acrodorf's eyes. Don't resist what? I was stuck anyway. I couldn't resist the deathly grip of the substance even if I wanted to.

Let go.

Acrodorf began to blur in my vision. I thought I would faint. I could feel a pain that was inexplicable. I could feel my eyes widen and widen, till I was certain they would pop out just before my brains did. There was a sinister silence and then I heard the sounds of my bones grinding together as the jelly tightened and crushed them against each other. I was passing out. It turned dark and then, as though to play a wicked joke, the jelly lit up in a silver lightning. I saw Acrodorf shatter into silver sparkles.

The smoke lit up again, this time with powerful tremors. I felt a tug and I felt myself rise. If someone was to tie your feet to the ground and then pulled you up from a helicopter, you would have the experience of your body ripping apart, that's exactly how I felt. I felt a painful rip, and then a final torturous rip, and then it stopped. I felt afloat.

I could see the ground below me. I could see the entire forest range; I could see my house at the foothills, as I rose higher. I looked around but I really could not see myself. There were no hands, no legs, nothing. Imagine that you woke up one day and did not find your body. My body was missing !!!!! But I was alive.

I could feel the rise. I could feel myself moving upwards. I could feel the gravity and I could feel the pressure tugging from above. The gravitational and magnetic force was fighting 'me', a formless, bodiless, er.... person?

Giggles. I heard giggles from nowhere. Thelda! That was Thelda's voice. The giggles came closer.

"You did it kiddo. I told you so," Thelda screeched in a giggle. I could only hear her, like me, she was formless.

"Are you ok?" I heard a voice that sounded like wind chimes. Acrodorf.

"I...I don't know!" I muttered. I actually didn't mutter. There was no body around to create sound, there was no tongue that could roll out the words, but a communication had occurred, by my mere intention.

My communication was at a whole different level. And even though I did not exist, physically, I could still communicate. Without words or body or even making a sound, I could communicate.

I felt Acrodorf. I could feel his essence. He was no longer the dreamy god-like man. It was more like I could sense him, sense his awareness so strong, that I could virtually see him, engulfing me.

"Welcome aboard. I'm sorry about the inconvenience of letting go of your body. But you were good." Acrodorf's voice had a texture and a resonance that was musical. And it brought back the peace in my heart, er, there was no body and so no heart, er...

"Aboard what? Where am I? Am I dead? What am I?" I heard Thelda chuckle somewhere close. I didn't like that she was behaving like a 'know it all' smart alec.

"You are not dead and you can never be dead." Acrodorf comforted me and I heard Thelda snicker. She was an annoying witch.

"You are an immortal, indestructible and creative soul," Acrodorf continued talking to me, ignoring Thelda. "Your body cannot leave from the gravitational aura of your planet. Your body survives in this realm, the limits you created. You cannot get out of the planet with your body."

"So I'm dead?!!" I tried to keep my panic in control.

"A soul never dies," Acrodorf continued calmly, "You are an immortal soul choosing to have temporary pleasure experiences through your body. Your life is equal to the life of the universe, which is calculated to be infinity. I cannot kill you even if I wanted to and neither can you kill yourself if you so wanted. The only perishable matter in question here was your body, which you had to leave behind. However you can retrieve it on your way back, I will promise you that. Leaving from your body might sometimes be an unpleasant experience for you, if that is what you have built your identity around." Acrodorf spoke kindly, gently, patiently.

"Thelda had been briefed regarding the process and the journey, so it was easier for her," Acrodorf explained. There was no chuckle from Thelda this time. "But you were a last minute entry. I must say that you did very well." Acrodorf was appreciative.

Leaving anything is a difficult process. The thought of leaving my job felt similar to the thought of dying. What would happen to my income? Would I ever get another job? Would I ever be successful? And because the answer to these questions were negative in my current job, the fear of leaving it was even greater. The thought of leaving Danny felt similar to the thought of dying. I had personally never had the courage to leave anything. And so, I was always the one left behind. There is no greater horrible feeling than that. And that made leaving even more difficult because I knew the pain of being left behind firsthand.

But what Acrodorf was implying was another kind of leaving. He was talking about moving ahead. Just because I would leave my job would not mean that I would move ahead. Moving ahead is another game altogether. Acrodorf was making me understand that sometimes to move ahead, you have to leave the things and people that hold you back, behind. And since they stay back, you can always come back to them later. But you certainly can't go ahead with the whole herd that is uncertain about their own progress, let alone yours.

The ground below was disappearing fast and I could see the curve of the horizon. A booming sound suddenly emerged from close by and I saw an aircraft a few meters above us.

"The Channel will hold your body until you return." Acrodorf referred to the line of spicy smoke that we had jumped into. "The Channel tracks your movement into space and will also make your body available at points in our journey when you will need it. Our friends from another planet devised The Channel and thanks to their creation we are able to take beings from one planet to another without risking their lives on their parent planet," Acrodorf explained to my relief.

"So where are we? What's happening? So, we are going to travel to Zedius like this? Invisible?" I was a little disappointed. It would have been nice to *see* Acrodorf, Bren and Thelda the whole journey. Travelling formless was not an exciting way to travel.

"Travel in space is best experienced formless, in one's native nature, as an immortal, indestructible, creative soul," Acrodorf explained, "If one took a space craft it would not only add many years to the travel but it would also attract unnecessary attention."

"You are traveling with me, in the space of my soul. Thelda is traveling with Bren, in the space of his soul." Acrodorf's words gave me imaginary goose bumps. I had no body but the feelings were there intact.

"Watch out!" I shrieked, as we headed steadily towards the Boeing 777.

"Oh My God! We are going to crash into a plane!" I wanted to close my eyes in a situation like this but being formless was worse because there were no eyes to close. I was in a state of total awareness and I was about to witness the worst nightmare I had ever had as Niki Sanders, to die in a plane crash.

The aircraft was roaring in the sky and now only a few inches away. Before I could scream again, we were inside the plane. Nothing happened. *We were inside the freaking aircraft.* I think Acrodorf was having fun with me with the gate-crashing into an airplane bit.

I could see people, who obviously were oblivious to my presence, our presence. One old lady turned around and looked directly at me and smiled. Did she see me? How could she see me? I could not even see myself so there was no way she could see me. But she looked in my direction and smiled. The old lady had perceived me, I could see that, she had acknowledged my presence in a very uncanny way and went back to reading the magazine she had in her hands.

"Did she see us Acrodorf?" I asked but Acrodorf jerked us out of the aircraft.

"Only a person aware of his spiritual nature can perceive another." Acrodorf said, "very soon, we will break free…." Before Acrodorf could complete his sentence, Thelda jumped into the conversation.

"Kiddo, we are going to break away from the planet, from its magnetic force that keeps our bodies glued to matter, that keeps our spirits glued to 'things'. The purpose of our planet is to *materialize* the universal soul," she spoke frantically out of a newly acquired wisdom. I wanted her to shut up.

What in the world was Thelda blabbering? I was not particularly interested in the immortal spiritual enlightenment bit. I was only interested in the powers of Zedius. My realization of my immortality would not pay my bills and my spiritual status had no bearing on the realization of my dreams. I wanted my share of power and er, a share of Acrodorf. I wanted to be like him. There was something extremely enigmatic about him, and I would like to learn to be like that too. He had this connection that he had made with me from the instant that he had set foot on planet Earth. He had this way of making me feel comfortable, of bringing out of me that self that I was afraid to be. He had this sense of well-being that urged me to be a bigger me.

Acrodorf laughed. Why was he laughing? I wondered.

"Can we please move faster or slower, so Thelda need not hear what we speak?" I complained to Acrodorf. I didn't want to be interrupted by Thelda's wise and spiritual comments the entire journey. Acrodorf's answer had a smile in it.

"As souls, you can hear the thoughts of others you choose to connect with. And especially so when you are bound with the same purpose or in the same space as the other soul. So far or near, Thelda shares our purpose, and so she can hear you."

"And Acrodorf can hear your thoughts because you are in his space," Thelda yelled out laughing.They both seemed to be laughing at me.

It was only moments later I understood the joke. Acrodorf finally stopped his giggling but Thelda's teehee continued.

No more thoughts. I told myself sternly. I could feel Arcodorf suppressing his laughter.

"Why can't I hear you or Thelda or Bren?" I asked Acrodorf. It wasn't fair that only they were prying into my thoughts.

"You need to connect to the soul and its purpose," Acrodorf explained. I could imagine connecting to Thelda and Acrodorf, but Bren; I don't think I wanted to be connected to him. I had this feeling that he didn't like me and I thought I was better off not intruding on his opinion about me. I felt that he considered me a hindrance to their purpose, which I suspected could be true.

"Look, I don't understand this soul business. I cannot think beyond my miserable reality on planet Earth. I want nothing more except the power of Zedius so I can have a better life when I go back. I don't know how to be a soul," I poured out my heart. There was no point in pretending to be wise like Thelda was doing. There seemed no point in being someone I was not, or even more pretending to be someone else. I had done that enough in my life and I refused to be anyone but myself anymore... even if that would mean to be stupid, ignorant and having a natural affinity for disaster.

"The realization of your immortality and your spiritual status has everything to do with your achievements on planet Earth. You are a spiritual being. When you deny that, you subject yourself to the cruelty of your physical universe." Acrodorf's tone was serious as he said this.

What?? Acrodorf's words were news to me and I wanted to hear more.

"You have a dream, right? You want to be an author, right?" Acrodorf asked.

The Earth below us had become very small. At a distance, I saw a satellite. It was a majestic machine that connected us all electronically. That one machine alone had made our world smaller and faster.

"Yes, I have a dream. To be an author," I said, bringing my attention back to Acrodorf. Now Acrodorf was getting it. Now he was realizing that spirituality had no place in the life of an ordinary sales executive.

"And whose dream is it? Who has that desire? Is it the dream of your body? Does your body desire to be an author? Which part of the body does it generate from? Do you have a particular organ in your body that secretes a hormone, which when found in your blood stream, pumps into you the desire to be a writer, and write books that would change the way the world thinks and feels? Is achievement and success a physical urge?" Though Acrodorf was as formless as I was, I could imagine his eyes boring a hole into mine with the intensity with which he was speaking.

I was lost in a daze. Partly because of what Acrodorf said and partly because we were speeding upwards really fast.

"Yea..Y... Umm... N..No. I mean. I don't know." This conversation was causing a lot of strain on my mind. I guess opening one's mind and thinking differently does that to people, that's why they stick so obstinately to their limited ideologies and beliefs. Was Acrodorf implying that it was my soul that generated the desire, the dream, the calling for success? Was he suggesting that to dream and to desire is a spiritual state? I suspected he was hinting at that because one thing I was certain about was that my dream to be an author and my desire for success was not a physical need. That need, that calling was emerging from the depths of my soul, as though *that* is what I was meant to do, that is what I was *born* to do, that was my *life's purpose*.

"The spiritual state is the state of pure creation. When *creation* is the desire, you are operating out of your spiritual consciousness." Acrodorf's words had the tone of compassion, compassion for a soul who was en route to realize her spiritual state.

"You are so spiritually naïve. The beings of Zedius would be so delighted to meet you. I can't wait to get you there," he chuckled. I found myself focusing on the moon, which looked really close. It was not as romantic as it seemed from Earth. It looked barren and deserted and just hung in space like a light bulb, a cheap substitute for electricity if one may really assign it a purpose.

Acrodorf zoomed us quickly away from the moon.

"I had always wondered what my life's purpose was. Isn't doing a job enough?" I asked curiously. I was working, and that seemed to be everyone's purpose; to go to work, to make some money, to spend the money and go to work again to make some more.

"A job cannot be mistaken for one's life purpose. A purpose is something you would do even if you didn't get paid for it. A job is a necessity. A purpose is your own drive for contribution. A job is something you do, even if you don't want to do it. A purpose is something you do because you *want* to do it." Acrodorf was silent, allowing me my time and space to understand what he was saying.

Acrodorf was so wise. I wished I could take him back with me after our journey to Zedius. With him, my life would be safe and fun.

Acrodorf chuckled, Thelda followed. Damn this intrusion. I had no privacy, even for my personal thoughts. Traveling so transparently made me feel vulnerable.

"The universe has only one purpose and so do all beings residing within: Creation. When you are creating, you are in essence an immortal spirit. When you stop creating, you collapse and introvert into the matter that you surround yourself with. When you stop creating over long spells of time, there reaches a point, when you become as mortal as the matter that you have around you." Acrodorf spoke and left me in an even deeper spell of silence.

Creation! Was I creating at work? I was a rote machine at work. I didn't even need to think. I was doing as told. I was working as instructed. I was worrying about the results that I couldn't create, because essentially I was not creating in the first place. I was only doing as told. I was apprehensive about the future. I was unhappy about my life. I was stuck in my own trap of 'non creation'. With Danny, I didn't even dare think. Like in my job, if I began to think, I would have left him long ago. So I was doing as told. I was working as instructed. I was worrying about the consequences. I was apprehensive about our future. I was unhappy about my life. I was stuck in my own trap of 'non creation'.

I had become a mortal dead spirit, in everything; at work and in life.

I had never thought like this before. Why?

"Because you had made yourself believe that you are the same matter that you created. The body is a creation. How can *creation* cause any creation? Only a *creator* can cause creation. Does your hand write the stories? Your hand only makes movements in sync with the thoughts your soul creates. The stories are created in your soul, your hand only puts those out on paper," Acrodorf answered my question even before I completed thinking about it.

I was silent. Acrodorf's words pierced my soul and I wanted to slow down. I think it was too late now to emphasize again that I was not ready for this.

"Did you tell her about the rules yet?" Bren's voice echoed, implying that Acrodorf should cut the small talk and get down to business. His voice still had the percussion bass. Until now Bren had been awfully quiet. And I couldn't shake off the gnawing feeling that he did not like my addition in their purpose.

"So here are the rules." Acrodorf complied quickly. "I will be in command of your journey to and fro. Since you are a traveler in time, you will be guided and led two light years from here. I hate to tell you this, but take it in good spirit. When in the journey you have no choice except compliance. If you were out on a journey of your own determinism, no one can come in the way of your choices, but since you are a partner in my purpose, your power of choice will be suspended, only for the duration of the journey," Acrodorf sang out the deal and then paused apologetically.

Actually, Acrodorf didn't know that the rules were not a menace, they were a relief. I would have been too overwhelmed if I had to span the journey into the universe on my own determinism. I was happy to lay the burden of my choices on Acrodorf. With him, all my choices would be safe. I was a threat to myself and I was grateful that Acrodorf was in charge.

I heard a mocking chuckle. It was Thelda. She was a mean witch.

"Since you are on my purpose, it is my responsibility to take you to Zedius and to bring you back," Acrodorf said, ignoring my thoughts and Thelda's response to them.

"You mean I could choose not to come back?" I was unsettled that Acrodorf would even consider that as a possibility.

"As per the laws of the Universe, he will bring you back even if you don't want to return," Thelda chimed in.

I fell silent, for a long time.

"I'm sorry to interrupt your silence but we have now come to the most crucial part of our journey to Zedius, the Perfect World." Acrodorf's announcement shook me out of my daze. The earth looked rather small, like the little globe on my study desk. It was a stunning piece of creation, with majestic colors and shades of blue, green and white that did a moving dance as the earth spun, very cleverly yet noticeably on its axis. The moon looked dark and cold like a solid stone suspended in the sky. We had obviously tracked behind it.

"What's the crucial part, Acrodorf?" I asked with my attention still on earth. Something strange had taken over me. It was a strong feeling that I had to return, almost instinctive. I began to tremble, a formless tremble. I could feel it. I was consumed by this overpowering feeling that I must not leave and that I must return.

"We are about to break away from the magnetic field of Earth, and that is the most difficult part. The rules in your original purpose of Earth do not easily allow departure from the planet. It's like the mafia. You can enter the planet at your own will, but you cannot leave after that. I know of beings that have been stuck here for lifetimes, never been able to break free. I would someday like to meet the creatures who built this planet," Acrodorf spoke with a suggestive irritation. "When I move across the magnetic field….. there….. can you see it?" Acrodorf suddenly exclaimed.

I could see it! I could see it. It was a strong force like a net, like the ones that surround the world's worst prisons. It was very visible. Just as you can see heat rising from a hot street on a scorching summer day, the magnetic field curved around the horizon. I looked at the magnetic field and I looked down on Earth, and I wanted to go back. A cloud of fear began to take over. Add some self-doubt and confusion to that, and in a few moments, the only thing I knew was that I wanted to go back – home.

"The nearer we get to the magnetic field, the stronger your urge will be to go back. You will have to fight that urge. You will have to fight for the opportunity to venture out into the universe, your real home. The urge will draw you back, it will tug at you, it will even threaten to destroy you, which by the way is impossible, but you must be determined, determined to break free. Many of your earthlings have attempted to break free, unsuccessfully. They came up to the magnetic field and then went right back to the life they had prepared to say goodbye to. Only a very determined few have broken free. But you have to stay focused and bring together the universe to support your determinism because that is what you will need to break away from, with me." Acrodorf spoke and I caught in his voice an unmistakable hint of worry.

"What if I don't break free? What if I *want* to go back? It's not what *if* I want to go back, I *want* to go back. There is no life outside of Earth. It's a dead universe. I have a life down here. This has been my home since time eternity. I want to go back." I spoke, lost in a trance. The words rolled out like the well-rehearsed lines of an actor in a very diabolical plot. I felt possessed. Something was taking over my spirit. I could feel it but I could do nothing but allow it to act through me.

This was a strange phenomenon. I had experienced this before; an urge to quit just as I was within reach of my goal. I have had this same urge to quit when things were finally working out. I guess I was so used to my misery that the thought of a new and better life was unthinkable. I was miserable because I had never thought about happiness. I was unhappy because I had never imagined what it would be like to be happy. Misery has a magnetic pull, a pull so strong that it won't ever let you reach towards a better life.

"Well, if you quit now and go back, which, by the way, you can, you will start your life on planet Earth all over again. Half way into the purpose you cannot obtain the body you left behind. The Channel will only appear at the end of your journey. You will have to start your life from scratch and build a new one. There is a price of quitting on your purpose, on your promise, the price is to start all over again!" Acrodorf spoke intently with a trace of urgency as the magnetic field came closer and closer, increasing my determinism to go back to Earth.

"You can't do that. You can't send me back to be born again! Where will I be born? What about my career? What about my dreams? My job? You can't do this Acrodorf!!!" I screamed from the bottom of my soul.

"You are right. I can't do that. I don't have the ability or the inclination to be a part of this crazy purpose you have created your planet by, but *you* can do that. And only if you so will. That's your rule. That's your game. Doesn't it sound crazy if you just hear yourself say it? Hear yourself? Don't you want to break free for a few moments in time and at least come back with powers that will set you and your fellow beings free forever? Don't you want to be a universal being or do you want a job and a family and then die and then start over again to create all of it, one lifetime after another? That's not even creation. That's repetition. You put a being in a magnetic trap, a powerful universal being and ask him to repeatedly do one project over and over, and there, you have created a rote creature out of a spiritual being. A deteriorated, shriveled, introverted spiritual being. And that's your calling? Is this what you want? You can experience the universe and then choose to create a new life on Earth. But for that you need all the determinism a free spirit has, to break free from the magnetic field. If you are not able to do it, you will be thrown back to the planet and I will move on to Zedius. You will be born again, have another lifetime on planet Earth thrust upon you. The body of Niki Sanders will be led to her funeral." Acrodorf raged, as the words flowed out in an electrifying speech of independence, to wake up sleeping souls like me.

"I can't do it, Acrodorf," I pleaded to go back.

I understood what Acrodorf said but didn't know how to lead myself to my own freedom. I couldn't do it.

"I am with you Niki." Thelda reassured me from the distance.

"I will bring her across," she seemed to say to Acrodorf or maybe to Bren.

"We are approaching the magnetic field and you have to prepare NOW! The magnetic field will create illusions. You can have illusions of your body. The Channel does not work in The Maya and so your body will be an illusion. You will see things that are not real. In the magnetic field, everything is an illusion to drag you back to planet Earth. Stay focused on your purpose." Acrodorf and Bren barked together and their voice echoed in my soul.

My being stayed glued to every word that Acrodorf communicated and I was sandwiched between my need and urge to go back and my instinctive desire to break free.

The magnetic field was about a hundred meters above us and I could see its electrical force creating a boiling effect on the edges. The urge to withdraw, and the urge to go back to Earth had taken over my soul and it was making me heavy. If it weren't for Acrodorf's insistence for me to see the truth that I was obstinately denying, I would have long past been pulled back to Earth.

"Stop Acrodorf, take me back, I cannot go ahead. I need to turn back, Acrodorf. I cannot break from the magnetic force, it will destroy me. Please Acrodorf." I pleaded but Acrodorf continued his way upwards totally ignoring my call.

"Acrodorf will go without you. Bren and I will go without you. If you continue this chatter, you WILL go back. The magnetic force is playing with you. It's playing with an immortal soul. Can you not see it?" Thelda's voice rang fiercely.

"You have made yourself an effect of your own bloody creation. You make the car to drive and what's ludicrous is that the car begins to drive you. You make a computer for computation and then you allow the computer to decide for you. You make machines to make your life easier, and guess what, the machines live your life for you. Wake up from the hypnotic state you have put yourself in, Niki." Thelda the dead Sorceress was waking me up from the ignorance she herself had recently woken up from.

I shuddered. The urge to go back was only getting stronger.

"You can create planets, you can create galaxies, you can re-create the entire universe if you so will. You are an immortal soul who has accidently chosen mortality on planet Earth. Stay determined." Acrodorf took over from Thelda. His voice was musical with a pleading edge. I could hear him pleading but in this moment I was possessed with the force that was leading me to believe that I had to go back.

Bren growled and I could feel his voice rumble in my soul. This was the last thing I wanted, Bren's wrath.

"Your departure has no effect on our purpose." Bren bellowed. His words were only aggravating my urge to go back. "Your magnetic field has no effect on us. We are free. We are free on Zedius and we are free to journey the universe. I am free to entertain myself on your planet and I am free to leave. And you can have that, but first you must free yourself from the trap that you have built for yourself. How can any being, whose size is as big as the universe, be trapped in a stupid magnetic field? This is your chance, maybe your only one in the next million years to come." Bren spoke in heavy spurts, whipping my soul to wake up and take heed of the universe that lay beyond the magnetic field, ready to be claimed!

I wanted to go back, I was very certain of that. There was no denying the control the magnetic field had on me, but what created a conflict was the process to start life all over again. I didn't want to start all over again. Who knows where I would be born next? Who knows if I ever would have any talent? Who knows what kind of fate would loom over my existence for another lifetime? Going back was a gamble. It was not really even a gamble, I knew I would be lost to death even if I won. The outcome was already known. Going back would mean a never-ending battle, between the good and the bad, the ignorant and the not-so-ignorant, the rich and the poor, the powerful and the powerless. It was a battle that had no end because, as long as the duality existed, the battle continued to be fought. I didn't want to go back to that. There was certainly more. More about life and living that I had missed seeing. I needed to look beyond the obvious to find the picture in the hazy dots. My life on earth had been only about the hazy dots and I had missed seeing the picture that I was a powerful, indestructible, immortal soul.

"It is HERE. I'm going through it. The magnetic field has no power over me. Everything in the magnetic field is an illusion, remember that. Make it to the other side.!!!!!" Acrodorf screamed with a potency that was certain to send shock waves to the clouds and make them rain on the entire planet.

"Thelda! Bring her to the other side!" I heard Bren's voice rage before it fell silent.

I caught a glimpse of a whole pool of boiling electrical and magnetic particles as I crashed into it, bewildered. I heard a roaring sizzle as we entered it. It was the same sizzle and snap that you hear when a fly gets caught in the electrical net; only this one was audibly magnified.

I fell headlong into the magnetic field. My body hurled in and I tried to get a hold on my fall, grasping onto the shaky ground. I stood up and walked to the edge of the tunnel-like structure that seemed to span towards infinity. My muddy shoes left mud tracks as I walked around. Something was certainly not right. From the instant that I had entered this transparent and solid tube-like place I felt listlessly confused. I strained to think but just couldn't conjure up one darned rational thought. This was an eerie feeling. I was usually the person with a head full of thoughts. This was a feeling worse than death; the feeling of in-between life and death.

The transparent floor shook violently. An unpleasant woman tumbled in. She wore an orange robe tattered at the edges. Her silver hair was tussled in all directions. Her form was hunched and old. Her face was set in wrinkles and yet she looked pretty. Her grey eyes shot in my direction, confused. She nodded her head and smiled. She looked like an old witch of some sort.

"Who are you?" We both asked together as she stumbled her way up trying to balance her weight and her hunch on the ever-wavering floor.

"I don't know," We both answered together.

This was madness. I had no idea whatsoever who I was. This was strange.

I looked around. I was inside a very large ring. It was a solid bubble that seemed to be steaming on the outside. I looked below and let out a yelp. Holy Cow! The bubble ran around the whole planet, engulfing it within. Where in the name of God was I? I seemed to be caged in, stuck in this evil band of 'powerlessness' of 'lifelessness' that clutched the planet, like some sort of a curse. A giant tremor swelled in my soul and stayed stuck there.

I scrambled around to the other side of the tunnel and saw the most magical sight ever. Half a mile beyond this boiling field into infinity, I could see a darkness, alive with a motion of lights, lights that symbolized the existence of a living and intelligent universe. It seemed like I was at the edge, at the brink of freedom. It felt like I was at the last step towards infinity.

What was I supposed to do? How did I come here? No thoughts supported that question. It was as though the raging transparent bubble that had surrounded me swallowed the question itself.

I darted to and fro searching for a clue but found none. The strange old woman darted to and fro with me in the same fit of confusion. We looked like houseflies caught in a glass jar banging into glass walls on all sides not realizing that they were in a trap laid by some idle and demeaning mind. I could perceive that there existed a world and freedom outside in the magically enticing darkness. I could also see clearly that there existed a very alluring planet below. I could only see them but not access any. I was here, hung, for reasons I could not remember, waiting, for a verdict.

I wondered if I were dead. What else could I be doing here? Suspended in space, in a state of exile? Maybe this was the place between heaven and hell. Did I die in a plane crash? The questions tumbled out through my confusion. There was no one here but me who held the answers. I had no clue what I was doing here and the only obvious thing to do was to get back home.

"Are we dead?" the strange old lady asked.

She sure should be, I thought. She was old, really old.

"I have no idea," I shrugged.

I looked below again. The Earth was partially dark and partially lit, both at the same time. I instinctively knew that it was my planet and I belonged there and that I had to get back. That was the only thing that I seemed to know. A heavy weight was building around me. Nothing made sense to me except this urge that I must go back.

"We need to go....," and before the scary old lady could complete her intention, there was a loud snap above. A loud cracking sound of a whip lashed out and interrupted our conversation. I sped towards the other side of the magnetic bubble that seemed to shield the planet from the rest of the universe. The old lady stumbled speedily behind me. In the distance of half a mile above this magnetic field ring I saw him; a creature, a god-like man-like creature with large greenish black wings.

"In the name of hell! What is a creature like that doing there?" The old woman spat out in disbelief.

I didn't hear her. I was riveted. Something stirred in my soul; a knowingness. It was a feeling that I knew him; a feeling that he meant 'home'; a feeling so huge, a drawing so intense, that I could not help but just stand still and stare.

The creature grew bigger and bigger and I was spell bound.

"Let's go on the other side," The nasty old woman caught hold of my hand and I jerked it free.

I was spell bound. My heart was spell bound. My soul was spell bound. I didn't remember who I was. I didn't remember my name. I didn't remember my purpose. But I knew him. As though I had never forgotten his essence, as though he was that part of me that I could never lose. As though he was that part of me, that made me complete.

The old lady was pulling at my arm but my eyes were glued on him. She began to pull at my arm and we both tumbled down.

"We have to go on the other side," she spoke, spitting her saliva on me like raindrops.

Alarmed, I searched for him again. He was there. His wings in full span, he grew larger and larger and larger till the point that his eyes were staring right at me at the edge of the magnetic field. They were ocean blue green and they sparkled and my heart leapt in my body.

He closed his eyes and his long eyelashes swept them shut. I read his lips as he opened his mouth and emitted the inaudible words, "BREAK FREE".

My soul jolted out of my body instantly.

The crazy old woman was dragging my lifeless body to the other side with all her might but my soul was rooted at that moment.

The creature opened his blue eyes and I lip-read him as he spoke the words that only my soul had the capacity to hear.

"Break Free. You are an immortal, powerful, indestructible soul. Reclaim your identity as the spirit of the universe. Reclaim your ability to create and be free. Move it. Now". His eyes began to sparkle like fireworks and his wings began to flap violently.

"ACRODORF!!!!!" I screamed.

The strange old woman stopped in her tracks with my limp body in tow.

"THELDA!" I screamed in total awareness. I darted towards her.

The body of Niki, the illusion of my body cleverly created by The Maya, lay lifeless in her hands and I yelled at her soul. Her hair was blown back with the force that I was emitting.

"We need to break free. We are going to Zedius. You are Thelda. You are on a mission. This is all an illusion!" I could see the light in Thelda's eyes.

"Y...Y ...es," she said in cognition as her eyes turned wide. "I am on the way to Zedius. This is an illusion!"

Her body dropped next to mine as her soul became cognizant to the delusion.

"Break Free!" we rumbled in unison.

The minute our intention was made, the magnetic field began to erupt out like a very angry volcano and I started to experience the spell of 'blankness' again.

I saw the delight in Acrodorf's eyes and his lips opened as he said "NOW" and with one mighty plunge Thelda and I heaved ourselves through the very intense and gravitating hold of the magnetic field and literally popped ourselves up on the other side right between the eyes of the gigantic god-like man, Acrodorf.

The Game

I was suspended in what I suspected was an ever-expansive space. I stayed motionless between the eyes of a very pleased Acrodorf. He was huger than huge and I felt like a tiny housefly buzzing near his eyes. Thelda popped out next behind me shoving me into Acrodorf's eyelashes.

We both looked at each other. I could not read Thelda's expression but it was somewhere between relief and embarrassment. Thelda saw me searching her soul and turned to look at Acrodorf who was now speedily shrinking to his regular size.

"We made it!" She danced around in glee.

I could see Bren next to Acrodorf shaking his head solemnly. He did not seem pleased with Thelda's behaviour, or maybe it was just my presence that was putting him off. I felt that he was counting on me to be stuck in the magnetic field so I could return back to planet Earth. Bren didn't like me. I cringed at that thought.

"We made it kiddo," Thelda held my shoulders and shook me with force, bringing my attention to her madness. I smiled feebly.

I was delighted to see Acrodorf. More than being happy about having broken the magnetic field of my planet, I was happy to see Acrodorf. His energy of well-being attracted me towards him. I had never felt energy like this before; an energy that disentangles confusion and brings serenity. But before I could say anything or express my delight, my body faded away, it just disappeared in a flash and so did Thelda's. Acrodorf's form was next to collapse and he engulfed me in the same way that he had in the entire journey here.

I could hear Thelda's chatter with Bren. We were formless spirits and for the first time in the whole journey I could hear Thelda's communication with Bren. In urging her out of the magnetic field, I guess I had connected with her. I smiled to myself.

"I thought you were smarter than The Maya," Bren scolded Thelda.

"I can hear Bren!!!!" I squealed in delight to no one in particular.

"I don't know what happened Bren," Thelda stammered. "I forgot everything. I forgot who I am. I forgot my purpose."

Thelda was right. I had felt the same way. It was a very sinister plot, the magnetic field. It was an evil trap.

"We had prepared you for this, Thelda. I had been very thorough in my preparation with you. The Maya is the only place where your body is an illusion to take your attention away from your spiritual purpose. You should have known that." Bren continued, clearly disappointed. He did not leave anything unexpressed.

"I...I..." Thelda stammered. I could not believe Thelda the Sorceress was being reprimanded. She would kill herself if she found out that I was witness to her loss of face.

"Niki's presence makes sense now. Her being with us is not an accident. If it were not for her, we would have lost you forever. Heck, if it were not for the spiritual force of Niki Sanders, you would have lost yourself forever on planet Earth." Bren grumbled.

I could feel Thelda's soul retract. I did not have a high regard for Thelda but my heart reached out to her. She was an unbelievably strong person. She was not an ordinary soul. It was not at all ordinary to have your life's purpose to heal and uplift others. That's what Thelda had done for her self-acclaimed two hundred and fifty years on planet Earth. What was more, she had the ability to communicate with spiritual beings from outer space. And she had the courage to leave her planet and help them heal theirs. Thelda was a nice soul.

I had this ridiculous ability, an ability to resist people. I would keep people at an arms length. But when crisis struck, I was the first one to jump in and help those same people that I kept away from. I was beginning to understand Thelda, but I was nowhere close to understanding myself.

"Thank you," I heard Thelda say to me.

Oh no no no. Thelda had got it all wrong. I had nothing to do with breaking the magnetic field. It was Acrodorf!! It was his spiritual force that got us both across. I was terrified with all this acclaim of breaking the greatest force on planet Earth, The Maya.

My greatest fear was not of being put down by people, I was very used to that. My greatest fear was being recognized by people. Anytime someone gave me credit for something, I had to quickly disown the credit and keep myself small. That way, I could justify my mediocre life and my misery.

"No, no, Thelda," I spoke with mortal dread of any credit that was thrown my way, "I forgot everything too. Remember we both were totally blank. But it was Acrodorf. Remember he was on the other side and he got us across." I tripped over my words to set the record straight that I had no spiritual force and that none of this should be expected from me in the future. I was happy to be led and I was happy to be in the shadow of Acrodorf.

"You are right," Bren came to my rescue and I heaved an imaginary sigh of relief. Bren didn't like me and it was in his interest to keep Thelda's image as the hero.

"There are two forms of connections; one with matter and one with the spirit. When you connect with matter, with things, you attract more mortality. You drift towards it; you seek it, that's the only thing you hear, that's the only thing you see, heck, that's the only reality that exists for you. Maya is matter personified. It keeps you in the illusion of mortality, of possession, of pain. When you connect with matter, it keeps you bound to it..." Bren paused.

"The other connection is a spiritual connection. When you connect with yourself, your spiritual state, you also connect with other spirits and souls. You connect and you communicate with them. You develop a natural tendency towards immortality, you drift towards freedom, and your natural state is creation. What's more, you are guided, towards your own state of bliss." Bren had started to send shivers in my soul.

"You connected with Acrodorf, an evolved soul, Thelda connected with The Maya." Bren concluded his talk and left me in regret of my own defense that triggered this whole conversation.

I dared not speak again.

What was this Maya? I wondered, taking my mind off Bren.

"The Maya is symbolic of illusion ." Acrodorf answered my thoughts.

I was happy to hear him.

"This phenomena exists nowhere else in the universe. The Maya, the magnetic force of your magnetic field is meant to have a neutralizing effect on a spirit's intention to break free. It cannot destroy your powers; it can only suspend them from your reach. It cannot destroy your soul; all it can do is neutralize your intention and confuse your purpose. The Maya keeps your attention on things. And so your purpose becomes a desire to acquire more material commodities. When your purpose becomes the acquisition of objects, you lead yourself to a spiritual suicide. When acquisition replaces creation, you know The Maya is fiercely at work to keep you away from spiritual realization."

"That's The Maya, the Illusion, the whole universe disapproves of," Acrodorf spoke, with no respect whatsoever of the rules in my world.

"And some of your species have an inkling of the universe and an inkling of their immortality. Every so often we see a spacecraft from planet Earth on its investigation of the truth that the rest of your like are in denial of. And even though the clever beings venture out of the magnetic field, their soul is still entangled in The Maya. So they leave, only to return back to mortality.

"You have broken one of the biggest barriers to your spiritual redemption. You have broken free from The Maya that holds the purpose of your planet in a state of constant doubt!" Acrodorf was delighted.

I stayed silent.

"Where did I go wrong?" Thelda moaned. I suspected that she was perturbed more by my sudden glory than by her inability to break free from the magnetic field on her own account.

"You are an evolved spirit," Bren said to Thelda's relief and mine. "But the mistake you are making is that you are carrying your mortal rules into a universe that does not recognize them. On planet Earth, you were Thelda, the magician, the Sorceress. But here you are as ordinary and as extra ordinary as the rest of us. Life in the universe is not about giving advice to others or cleaning up other's mess. Life in the universe is about creation, about responsibility, about self-discovery."

I had begun to like Bren. He was not like Acrodorf but that didn't mean that he was bad. Bren was Bren. He was objective. He called a spade a spade. He focused on ability and purpose. Acrodorf was full of affinity. He had the ability to see a heart in a spade and was willing to explore it. He focused on potential and had the patience to see it through. And because Acrodorf was different, that didn't make him better. Bren was as important in my journey as Acrodorf was. I had disliked so many people back home because they were, er, different. I had at least a dozen Bren-like associates and co-workers, and just because they were not as nice and easy to please as the Acrodorfs in my life, I didn't like them. What was worse, I thought that they didn't like me either. The truth was that I didn't like them. So if I didn't like them then assuming their lack of affinity for me was quite natural. What struck me really hard was that I interpreted every action of their to be directed against my work and me. Could it be true that I was wrong about people? Could it be true that in my naiveté of expecting everyone to be like Acrodorf I had failed with people? I twitched with discomfort.

Being in space was a very light feeling . As long as we were in the magnetic field of Earth, there was a weighty pull from the bottom and a weighty push from above. We had literally been fighting our way up. Being in space however was a weightless experience, so light and free that I felt I could dart to that twinkling star in an instant.

There was around me a gigantic expanse of space, dark but full of life. Though I could not see any living creatures I could sense the life force that it held. I could sense a party happening here and I was here to gate crash.

A few gigantic planets were suspended around us and the sun was in the centre, much bigger than it had originally looked while on Earth. I looked around from within the solar system. It was a million times more magical than being in a planetarium, which I had visited while on my term on planet Earth. There was sunlight everywhere. I had a three hundred and sixty degree vision. I could see everything, everywhere, all at once.

"When the spirit regains some of its original powers, it becomes bigger. The reach of your vision symbolizes the size of your soul." Acrodorf said, delighted.

"I can see the galaxies and the milky way," Thelda was doing her best to reclaim her superiority.

"We have time and distance to cover." Bren interrupted Thelda's sashay. He was really a no-nonsense person, er, soul.

"Zedius is in wait for our arrival. So brace yourself, we need to speed up," Acrodorf added and I felt the space around me literally go 'whoosh'.

I sensed lightning speed. The entire solar system contracted, signifying that we had moved ahead in time and in distance. What was odd was that we were not moving through a track. It felt like we were standing still while planets, stars and meteorites were growing smaller around us and new ones were emerging. We were sort of hovering over everything in space. As we moved along, the universe seemed to expand. So we were no longer passing anything by. Stars, planets, galaxies and solar systems began to emerge in our space. It felt as if I was growing in size and getting a better and better view of the entire universe.

"Do you feel what I feel Acrodorf?" I asked him curiously to see if he felt as big as I suddenly did.

"What do you feel?" Acrodorf asked, as the Universe seemed to grow even bigger around us.

"I feel very big. Like very very big; nearly as big as the entire universe. If you wanted to know my size, it would be from that end of the universe to the other end," I grinned to myself at that thought.

"Notice that even as you feel this, the ends of the universe are expanding," Acrodorf chuckled in amusement. He was thoroughly entertained by me, a new entrant to the game of the universe.

"Ye..Yes, that's exactly how I feel, so big, and growing at the rate of the expanding universe!" I exclaimed.

"You are not even at Zedius and yet you seem to have re-claimed some of your abilities," Acrodorf sounded quite impressed with me. "Considering where you come from – thousands of years of bondage, you have made some massive headway."

"Me too!!!" Thelda added in. She did not seem to be having any fascinating conversations with Bren and that explained her interest in ours. I guess when you don't have your own business to mind, you begin to mind others.

"Acrodorf! We don't seem to be going anywhere. What kind of travel is this? All I can see is the universe expanding. So are we really traveling?" I asked. I could not feel any movement. I could not feel the rush of traveling at the speed of light or the dash of moving two light years into time. Actually I would have liked that; to go whizzing past heavenly bodies; dodge some meteorites speeding my way; or try my hand at some alien attack encounter. But this…. this kind of travel seemed very boring to say the least.

"The spirit does not travel by the same principles of the body that you left behind. To travel on earth you need to physically carry your body from one place to another. However when the spirit travels, it bends time and distance and reaches the destination. It is similar to how your mind works, so when you think about being in New York while in India, you get there in an instant. You didn't first think of standing in the queue to buy a ticket, then boarding a plane, and then waiting for the aircraft to take off to land your thoughts in New York after several hours. You just reached there in a flash in your thoughts. The soul quite travels in the same way. But because you are really going to get to Zedius and take form there and participate in the experience, you won't reach there in a flash. You have to travel *through* distance and time though much faster than you think." Acrodorf explained.

"Oh, I understand," I said very thoughtfully, not sure if I fully did understand what he meant.

"You do?" Bren interjected quite surprised that I did, but I didn't mind being underestimated. If Bren underestimated me, then *he* underestimated *me*. And because it was his doing purely, it had no effect on me. Boy, this kind of attitude would have saved me a lot of heartaches and sleepless nights back on Earth. Somehow being here in my spiritual existence seemed to restore my intellect and my understanding of life, and I liked it.

"And The Channel is a powerful creation. It will make your body available to you wherever its use is necessary in the universe. In time you will get the hang of it. When you stop in your journey, The Channel will make your body available to you and you will snap into your form. When you start your journey again, you will be formless. This transition is the mechanics of The Channel." He added.

I wondered how The Channel would do that. I wondered how The Channel would keep track of where we were headed.

I stayed silent.

"Look Acrodorf, what is that?" I said spotting at a whole array of bright planets that had emerged on the far end. There were three planets that had shown up suddenly. My gaze was everywhere and I could swear that they were not there just a moment ago.

"The Game!" Bren gasped.

"Wh..What can you see?" I heard the hesitation and suspicion in Thelda's voice and that surprised me. She obviously had not or could not see what I saw.

"There, look there. Can't you see?" Darn, there was no way I could point to the planets because there was nothing to point with.

"The Game!!!" Now Thelda, Bren and Acrodorf exclaimed together.

"Look..." I started and then stopped at the sight that lay before me. The three planets shone like floodlights in a football stadium and then the two planets on the sides imploded in a fraction of a moment and disappeared. What stayed was the middle planet with a light so fierce that it could light up the whole universe.

"Acrodorf!!!" Bren screamed and like a speeding car is brought to an abrupt halt, everything stopped with a jerk.

The universe stopped growing. The light emitting from the planet shone static. It seemed like somebody had hit the pause button while watching a movie.

I saw Bren first, his expression worried me. Acrodorf appeared next and then Thelda and finally a totally confused Niki Sanders made the last appearance.

"The Channel!" I gasped as I groped my arms. I had my body back. The Channel was a very clever creation that brought you your body when the journey was halted.

"What is happening?" I asked looking at Acrodorf. Everyone else seemed to know, except me.

"Look, you are not supposed to be here. The universe does not support illegal immigrants." Bren took over the conversation to my dismay.

"Which means, you are not here by invitation. You were more than happy serving your term on planet Earth. You are a last minute entry." Thelda hastily took over from Bren.

"In simple words, it means you are trespassing. Traveling without a ticket. You are out into the universe while your term, responsibility and karmic debt is still pending on planet Earth." Acrodorf said gently softening the despair that I could sense in Bren and Thelda's voice.

"Huh?" was my only response. Just when my excitement about the universe and my spiritual consciousness was building up, this trespassing business had put a rude and sudden brake to it.

But Thelda had insisted I come! She was the one who had instigated Acrodorf to bring me here. Why didn't she think of this trespassing stuff then? I was a bit mad at Thelda.

"Acrodorf!!" Bren growled again.

Acrodorf looked into Bren's direction calmly.

"Give me some credit Bren," he said with no irritation towards Bren's heated temperament.

"You are important in our journey, and we are now understanding why. If it weren't for you, Thelda would have been sent back to planet Earth." Acrodorf stood in front of me, blocking Thelda and Bren out of my view. I thought that was a smart move, for if I could not see them, then their doubt and worry would not affect me.

I heard Thelda groan over the mention of the fiasco in the magnetic field again.

"We are now at the .... patrol... immigration check whatever reference that you understand.... of the universe." Acrodorf tried his best to explain to me in a manner that I would understand.

"The Game is a planet that moves around the universe. It's like the police of the universe. It keeps a check on runaway souls, souls that immorally escape their responsibilities or even souls that create trouble," Thelda bobbed her way around Acrodorf and stood beside me.

Acrodorf placed his arm on Thelda in a manner to imply that she need not interfere in the conversation.

"You are important. And you *will* come with us. The only hitch is that we have not taken prior permission for your departure." Acrodorf continued, his hand still on Thelda's arm.

"We have two options now. One, you stay silent and inert with me, so we can take you along without bringing notice to you," Acrodorf paused to estimate whether I understood.

"Silent and inert?" I asked.

"Just be yourself," Thelda jumped in again despite Acrodorf's attempt to keep her enthusiasm under control. "That is your greatest strength!" Thelda pointed out.

I looked confused.

"Don't think anything. Exactly like in the magnetic field. Don't think. Don't hear. Don't see. Don't talk. Be inert! Exactly like you were living your life!" Thelda continued before Acrodorf brushed her behind him.

"Be still. Contract your awareness towards nothing. Introvert. Be still. Take your attention and focus it inward till you are lost in nothingness. And we will escape The Game," Acrodorf took my hand in his and gazed into my soul. I caught his eyelashes sweep his cheeks as he blinked patiently. I could see the depth of his soul in his eyes.

If Acrodorf had asked me to do this just a few moments ago when we had met, I would have done it naturally. I could be so still that you would wonder if I was even alive. I could sit for hours and think deeply about nothing. I could be so introverted that even if I died I would not notice. But now, I was as big as the ever-expansive universe. My soul was alive with thoughts I should have thought all my life. My awareness was so sharp I could see more than the wise and magical Thelda. I was alive. I was awake. Just the thought of being inert and dead to escape some deadly police of the universe was repulsive.

"Or?" I asked desperately. Acrodorf had said that there were two options and I was hoping that the first one was the bad one.

"Or, you will have to pass through The Game," Acrodorf said, as his eyes filled with sadness. He was obviously banking on my ability to be the introverted dead spirit when he had told Bren confidently, 'give me some credit'.

"What is The Game?" My voice trembled. I had no idea what The Game was but with the fuss that everyone was making of it, I figured it was terrible. I guess you don't need to be told in so many words that disaster is around the corner. When Danny said, 'Niki we need to talk,' I knew that disaster was on its way. When my boss sent for me through someone else, 'Boss wants to see you,' I knew that disaster was on its way.

"We don't know." Bren hurried around. "That's why it's called The Game. It changes every time."

"The creators of the Planet, The Game, put the 'illegal immigrants' through a test. That test is a karmic trade-off of their past debts which gives them permission to traverse the universe, without infecting it with their unethical presence. The test varies from soul to soul. It depends upon who they are and what they are escaping from. From what we hear, the test for you Earthlings is the most severe. That's why your co-operation for the first option is very crucial," Bren spoke pleadingly.

I was totally taken aback..

"Ok," I whispered. Why was the thought of being inert and thoughtless suddenly so abhorrent to me? No one would believe me if I said that I could no longer relate with my old self. I remember as a child I was afraid of falling and so I would never ride a bike. Finally, my father intervened and taught me. Once I had learned how to ride it, I could not understand what the fear had been all about. And now imagine if you told me, here is a bike, sit on it and pretend you can't ride it. That would be crazy? Knowing is instinctive. Once you know something, you cannot act as if you do not know what you know. The pretense itself is evidence of knowing.

"Ok," I whispered feebly.

"We will pass through the zone, be inert and be silent. Once we make it across, we will tell you and then you can relax," Bren concluded.

I could not believe that I had led myself here. Back on planet Earth my weakness was killing me. Here in the expanse of space my strength was going to kill me. I just could not believe my luck.

Bren disappeared first and I was too pre-occupied to be startled that I was formless again, engulfed tightly in Acrodorf's space as we started on our journey again.

"Shhhh," Acrodorf whispered and the whole universe came alive the next instant.

I tried to focus inwards on nothing - but I saw the ever - expansive universe.

"Shhhh," Acrodorf begged.

I tried to be inert. I tried not to see. I tried not to hear. I tried to introvert. I tried so hard that I could implode with the resistance.

"Please," Acrodorf begged.

For Acrodorf's sake I tried to be dead and the more I tried the more suffocated I felt. And then it happened. With a silent burst I came alive with the whole universe. I radiated out in the universe so big that the police or whoever they were would have to give me a run across the universe with their chase and I could beat them to infinity.

"OHHH NOOOO!!" I heard Bren's shriek and then I saw.

The planet, The Game exploded again with a bang, with a bright light. Then its light contracted and shone in my direction like a spot light. It shone on me as though it had caught me in my escape to the universe.

Acrodorf was silent. And I could feel him squeeze me further into his space.

"I'm sorry Acrodorf," I apologized for being me, the new me.

"Look...." I said bewildered. The spot light dropped and the overly large planet revealed a mesmerizing and inviting pathway that seemed to stretch in my direction.

I knew that Bren and Acrodorf were disappointed with my sudden explosion to come alive. I knew that I had let them down by not being small. And strangely, I did not regret it. Strangely, I was not afraid. I was curious and excited.

Bren and Acrodorf would never know about all the people back home who could stay big because I chose to stay small. They would never know how people would do their best to make me believe that it was my destiny to suffer so that I would never rise and compete with them. Maybe greatness and introversion was a choice for souls like Acrodorf and Bren but after lifetimes of deadness, greatness was the only option for me now.

It was a magical moment. A large milky white planet emerged frightfully close. I could not take my eyes off it. A pathway of light rolled itself out to be treaded upon, which led to that mesmerizingly beautiful planet.

The silence around me was deafening. No one spoke anything. Not even Thelda.

I stared at the pathway. It was like a silken sheet inviting to be walked on.

"U..." I had not even started the word and there, on the edge of the silken pathway appeared two creatures. They had similar forms like Bren and Acrodorf but they were more like shadows. They had long flowing robes and would have looked like identical shadows of Bren and Acrodorf except that they did not have any wings. The head was covered in a hood that seemed to extend from the robe. I tried to look but there was nothing except darkness in their form. This was a rare sight; darkness standing in the middle of light.

"Acrodorf. Bren. Thelda. Stop!" The voice rang from the shadow creature on the left.

The minute he addressed them, a jerk brought us all to a halt and we all snapped into our forms. Now, this is the point that The Channel should not have intervened. The Channel should have kept us formless so we could run away. But alas, The Channel was not only connected to our purpose, it was also connected to the laws of the universe.

My eyes were riveted on the two creatures.

"And a trespasser," The second shadow stretched out his arms, thrilled with my presence.

"So we get into The Game after a long time ha," The first shadow spoke to the other.

"Yeah. Things were beginning to get a little slack. The universe is too orderly and the souls are too well-behaved." The second shadow creature snickered.

"This is Black," Acrodorf introduced me to the shadow creature on the left, "And this is White," he motioned to the shadow on the right. I admired Acrodorf's grace. Though we all were clearly in a pickle, it was evident that the pickle was my fault, but Acrodorf was gracious. He introduced me to trouble - respectfully.

I guess the test of a person's character is, how they face challenges and trouble. If I were in Acrodorf's place I would be screaming down on my face for being clumsy, inattentive and distracted. I would have beaten the person down with accusations for putting us in trouble. However, when the volume of accusations went up, the problems did not go away but the solutions sure did. At some point or the other we all make mistakes. At some point or the other we all fall short of others' expectations from us. But that does not give us the right to treat people disgracefully.

"This is Niki Sanders, from planet Earth. She was a last minute entry," Bren took over the explanation, bringing my focus back to the shadowy creatures. I didn't understand the logic in their names because they both were pitch dark.

"You know Zedius is in trouble. And we believe that Niki Sanders would assist us in setting things right," Acrodorf continued.

"But you have permission only for Thelda. Isn't she enough? We have her credentials and she would be valuable for many projects across the universe. The purpose to heal and the purpose to set things right is a very evolved purpose." Black spoke to Thelda's delight.

"Yes, but Niki has a natural affinity for disaster. Her ability would bring a fresh perspective towards perfection," Bren continued.

I felt the energy of Black and White in my direction. I felt a sizzle up my spine as though they were scanning my soul.

"No she doesn't," White frowned. "Her call for disaster is a cover up. She is here, isn't that hint enough for you?" White read my soul.

There was silence. I wanted to deny what White said but something told me that it was not my turn to speak yet. Sometimes it's best to leave trouble alone, and sometimes trouble leaves for your lack of interest in it.

"Can we ask for an exception and take her with us?" Bren tried to sound assertive in seeking for permission. "She won't make any trouble. And besides, she will certainly not survive The Game."

"Aha!!" Black clapped his hands together and the sound echoed in the space around us. "You are asking us to break the rules of the universe! That's impossible."

"That's impossible!" White chimed in quite thrilled at the prospect of me being a player in The Game.

"She won't make it," Bren said solemnly. His tone was more pleading than assertive now.

I felt bad. I didn't want Bren to plead for me. It was unlike Bren. I had half expected him to hand me over to Black and White and leave me to my destiny. I guess we don't give people a chance to be themselves. Sometimes we taint people's character with our opinions of them and block any goodness that is coming our way from them.

"Everyone makes it from The Game," White reminded Bren.

"Yes, they do. But this one won't make it in time to save Zedius," Bren tried to reason.

"If Zedius is to be saved then Zedius will be saved." Black thundered, "but rules are rules."

The silken path began to shake and small waves of white light began to flow through it.

"Let The Game begin!" Black and White spoke together in sheer delight.

Acrodorf turned to me, shielding me from the reach of the path that was growing and undulating in my direction.

"Whatever happens, remember that you are an immortal, indestructible, powerful soul. No matter what The Game is or what happens during The Game, remember that there is always a way out. No matter how futile your efforts may seem, know that the answer is right in front of your eyes. No matter what happens, know that I have immense respect for who you were, who you are, and who you will be. And above all else, remember that I will never give up on you!" Acrodorf stood towering ahead of me and my eyes moistened. I could see the pathway just a few feet behind him.

I wanted to say something. I wanted to tell Acrodorf that even if this was the end of my journey, it was worth it. I wanted to tell him that no matter what consequence awaited me on the other side of The Game, I was grateful that I had come this far.

Bren rushed forward and heaved Acrodorf away from the path that now was seeping in just three feet away from me.

"Wait!!" Thelda shrieked. "I will go with her!"

"Nooooo" Bren bellowed towards Thelda.

Black and White stood in the pathway totally amused by all the drama at our end.

"This one will be fun," White chuckled.

The light path touched my feet and its radiance blinded me. I was consumed by the light and found myself on the path with Black and White shaking each other's hands in the distance. I was totally cut off from the universe. There was a black wall that shielded me from the world outside. The path began to shake violently and Black and White disappeared.

"I will go with her. I will bring her back!" I could hear Thelda and a fiercely audible communication behind the black wall. My body began to feel faint and before I collapsed, I saw a frantic Thelda break through the black wall, staring horrified in my direction.

The Game Begins

I collapsed on the silken path of light, which felt as solid as concrete. Thelda was peering over me. She had managed to fight through a raging Bren and obstinately made it into The Game to help me through. I guess old habits die hard. Thelda, the immortal spirit, could not help but be Thelda the Sorceress. It was not in her nature to see another suffer. It was her purpose to help. Even though she knew very well that her purpose on planet Earth had no place in the universe at large, she was adamant to bring me back from my own destiny. She had taken a break from being a Sorceress only to return to being a Sorceress with a vengeance.

Like Thelda, I had taken many breaks but taking a break is not the same as breaking free. After taking a 'break' from an unhappy job, I had just walked into another unhappy job. Taking a 'break' from a disastrous relationship just landed me into another such relationship.

I was happy to see Thelda. I was happy that I was not alone. Thelda was certainly superior and if she was certain she would get me out, that was good enough for me.

My spell of dizziness was worsening. Thelda's face was fading away from my sight and I felt the milky white planet reeling around me, spinning at neck-breaking speed, and then darkness fell.

"Thelda….." I attempted to say something.

"You will make it Niki, I am here," She spat over my face as she spoke, the drops of her saliva breaking my dizziness.

Black emerged next to Thelda and bent over me so his face was directly between my eyes.

"The Game has two levels. You need to cross one to get to the other. Our toughest game is inspired from planet Earth. So we are assuming *that* will be fun for you." Black chuckled in sadistic delight.

"It's good you brought Thelda along to complicate it. The Game is best played alone. This is really going to be fun!!" White said, who, by the way, was black as Black.

"What is The Game?" I asked feebly.

"It would cease to be a game if you knew. That's The Game. It's a game because you don't know it. It's a game because it controls you. It's a game because you play it." Thelda said, desperately trying to educate me about how to escape from The Game. Little did she know that her words of wisdom sounded good but had no bearing on what lay ahead of us .

"Thelda…." I fought the blackout that was raging over me but before I could speak any further it was all gone. The light was gone, the pathway was gone, Thelda was gone and I was gone.

A loud explosion erupted around me. I frantically opened my eyes and the light blinded me. I covered my eyes with my hand. I sat up and looked around. I was lying on the same solid path of light. Thelda was sitting right beside me looking as confused as I was. She was also in The Game.

"What is going to happen now?" I asked her. I wanted to tell Thelda that she would have to take the lead in The Game because I was clueless. I didn't play any games back home, though I had been victim to many.

"Look!," she said, pointing to a solid door that had appeared further up on the light path.

Thelda and I jumped to our feet. She and I shared the same unsaid urgency of winning The Game and being on our way to Zedius.

We ran towards the door. As we got closer, we saw that the 'door' was actually a block of darkness surrounded by light. It was made of the same element that Black and White were made of, a void. Thelda gave me a look as if to imply that it was inevitable that we would have to go through the void.

"What is that?" a flickering motion caught my eye behind Thelda.

"That's the key!" Thelda jumped in glee.

It didn't look like a key to me. It was more like a scroll that had instructions on it. Thelda picked up the cylindrical object that shone with a golden light. There was a little piece of thread hanging from one end.

"Pull the thread," I told Thelda, quite annoyed that she was just holding the object. She was so slow. She was so all knowing. It irritated me. I didn't know what she knew; I just wanted her to pull the thread.

"This is the key to The Game," she said, inspecting the object from all angles. She tried to peer through the opening of the red thread and I had to do my best to control my impatience.

"Should we pull the thread?" Thelda asked cautiously, as if she were holding a hand grenade and pulling the pin would spell disaster.

"If you want to," I muttered, gritting my teeth and raising my hands impatiently.

Thelda pulled the red thread and to my shock it exploded and the cylindrical object rolled out like a glowing red scroll. On it rolled out the following words:

"Welcome to Level One of the Game. The players are Thelda the Sorceress and Niki Sanders - residents of planet Earth."

The words rolled out and disappeared. Thelda looked excited.

"In the Game, survival is crucial. You must not die. If any of you die, both of you lose."

Thelda looked at me, horrified. This meant that if Thelda died in The Game or I died in it, we both would lose. Helping others does have personal implications. Thelda should have known better.

"Level One is the land of the Cannibals. May the best player win."

With those words, the red scroll collapsed into a dot of light, leaving Thelda's hand empty and her mouth open.

"Let's stick together. I won't let any harm come to you." Thelda put her hand on my shoulder and I was surprised that I was not reassured.

"We need to get going," she said, raising her robe with her right hand lest she tripped over it and tumbled out through the dark door leading into a frightening void.

I grabbed Thelda's hand. She turned around and gave me a smile. We both stood in front of the door that seemed to lead to more darkness.

"Cannibals, here we come!" Thelda screamed, to my dismay.

She was a crazy Sorceress. Why did she have to announce our arrival? Maybe if we were quiet, we could lie low and escape. I disagreed with Thelda's method of helping me survive. This was suicide.

Avoidance and ignorance were my greatest weapons of survival back home. If I didn't know about it or if I pretended I didn't know about it, then I was safe. That's how I justified my poor performance at work. 'Oh I didn't know about that,' and that's how I justified my lot in life. If I knew something then I would be accountable for the results. That is exactly what I was afraid of, my own capability to deliver results. I was afraid to deal with my shortcomings head on. I was prepared to cry in hiding, but I was not prepared to speak out in public. Thelda was the extreme opposite. If the Cannibals were the threat, she wanted to bring them out of the closet and deal with them head on.

Before I could protest her ways, Thelda pulled me into the black door and we both were wheezed into a slithering tunnel and crash landed on wet ground.

I sprang up to my feet urgently. I was hoping the Cannibals had not heard Thelda's war cry.

We were in some sort of tropical forest. There were large slimy trees and a slimy undergrowth. I took a step ahead and slipped and fell on my back with a thud. Thelda cracked up laughing. I lay on my back hoping I had not broken it and Thelda stood there laughing, pointing her finger at me.

We were in a crisis situation. We were in The Game, which Black had declared was the toughest for earthlings. Our task was to escape the Cannibals and stay alive. But that did not deter Thelda's ability to have fun and indulge in a good laugh. She was a strange Sorceress.

"The Cannibals are not here now. And that was a hilarious fall," Thelda read my thoughts. "Why should I not indulge in the humor of the moment?"

I smiled at Thelda's logic. The Cannibals were not here now. Trouble was not here 'now'. Her rationale was, why be stressed about what hasn't happened yet? I loved Thelda. In all the stress that I had built my life by, I had forgotten to laugh; I had forgotten to be cheerful. I was so stressed about the Cannibals that hadn't shown up as yet, that I had forgotten that I could still find happiness in the moment.

"This looks so much like planet Earth. Look," I said, turning around. I had quite expected other planets to be different than mine.

"Well, I was told that matter and the basics of life, like vegetation, birds, animals and even other life forms follow similar prototypes on many planets. Especially when the planets have a supporting star providing light energy." Thelda, the all-knowing explained.

"But we need to find the Cannibals first. Cannibals - here we come!" Thelda shouted in all directions.

I sprang up on my feet, spreading my arms out to grasp a branch in case I slipped on the slimy mud again.

"Thelda don't!" I protested, "What if they hear you?"

My question was answered by a sharp sound that whizzed past my left ear and boomed into a loud thud a few feet behind me. I turned around petrified. On the tree behind me was etched an arrow that was still vibrating with the impact.

"Behind the tree!" Thelda whispered loudly.

We both stumbled and bumped into each other behind the same tree that held the arrow in place.

"I doubt that the arrow is poisonous. They wouldn't want to kill us without making themselves known. They wouldn't kill us without torture. Just shooting an arrow in your heart would not be a fun game," Thelda spoke as though she knew the mind of the cannibal.

Her words were not a solace. In fact, if I really had to die I would prefer an arrow in the heart and that way I would be saved from the torture.

"It's important to know your enemy. Running away only multiplies their forces. And when you have been running away for a long time, you don't even know who the enemy is anymore. And so you treat everyone suspiciously because you don't know the enemy, and so he could be anyone. It is important to discover the enemy and know him. Then you will know who to fight and not make other people victims of your cowardice." Thelda warned.

Oh my god. I remember at work I heard rumors about me. Someone had said that I was sucking up to my boss and the only reason I had a job was because I had an immoral relationship with him. That had hurt me a lot. But I never bothered to dig out the enemy. I never made an attempt to find out who said it. And because I didn't know who said it, it became possible that anyone could have said it. And so I treated everyone at work with the same contempt that I would have treated that one person who deserved it. One of the prime reasons that I hated my job was that I hated everyone there. The reason I felt that way was because I did not find out who the enemy was.

"They are close," Thelda estimated, breaking into my thoughts.

"How do you know?" I whispered. I could not believe that I was going to be witness to the supernatural powers of Thelda.

"It's common sense," she spat in my direction in a whisper. I could swear that her hair had grown denser and messier and she looked like a silver mop mounted on a bent over orange robe.

"Look at the dense formation of the trees. It would be impossible to shoot a target from far," Thelda pointed out. Actually it was common sense, and I wondered if all magic was too.

I saw a movement in the distance and I panicked. I looked at Thelda for instructions and she seemed to be looking in another direction.

"I saw something," I trembled. "Should we run?!" It was more of a command than a question.

"Your seeing something is not reason enough for you to run. Did it see you?" She asked.

Thelda's wisdom was a little uncalled for at this moment. This moment was about survival, about staying alive, about escaping the Cannibals. We could talk about all this wisdom later, if we were still alive.

"How will you be alive if you don't use your head now?" Thelda barged into my thoughts.

"The right time to think is now! It is pointless to think after you are dead or after you have lost. If you think now, chances are you will be alive later." Thelda scowled at me for not co-operating, with, er, my thinking.

Maybe she was right. I had let the urgency of the situation always get the better of me. When angry, I would spit out words that I would later think about and regret. At work, I would only be handling crisis and urgent matters and later think about what I was really doing? If only I had thought first and then acted, I would have saved myself a lot of personal and professional disasters.

"So how long do you intend to hide here?" I whispered to Thelda.

"Not long," she smiled as three medium-sized men armed with bows and arrows emerged from behind the trees in front of us. They wore short skirts made of animal hide. Their chest and legs were bare and well-oiled.

"Run Thelda," I screamed, and I darted into the trees behind, without waiting for Thelda to follow.

I ran as fast as my feet could carry me. I did not even stop to turn around and see whether Thelda was following me. I guess when it comes down to survival, only your life counts.

I ran in a frenzy without stopping for miles. I was out of breath and I felt that my heart would go into a convulsion and I would die. I slowed my pace. The trees were more spaced out now and I could see the sky above. The only sound I could hear was of my own feet running and my own heart pounding. I slowed down further till I could run no more. I stopped and leaned against a tree, my glance darting in all directions. The forest was clearing out and I could scan the area around me for meters. It was not possible for anyone to be moving in from far without being noticed.

Where was Thelda? I felt really bad for leaving her behind. She had risked her purpose and had come into The Game to help me out and with the first hint of danger I had abandoned her. I had abandoned my only window of hope to make it through.

I looked around and I was lost. I was lost in a forest that was infested with Cannibals and to top it I was alone now.

Why did I run? I cursed myself. The madness was that I was running away from a potential threat towards nowhere in particular. Sometimes we are so focused on running away, that we pay no attention to what we are running toward. In running away from Danny, I really hadn't really gotten anywhere. In running away from work I really hadn't gotten anywhere. The mistake was running away. The answer was in running *toward* a purpose, which I failed to have.

Something silver in the grass caught my eye near a tree by my left. I went towards it curiously. It was a small metal container. I picked it up and was shocked to see the words engraved on it. "Poison". Two broken arrows were scattered close to it. I gasped. This was the poison that the arrows were dipped in. I shook the metal container and it was half full. I put the container in my pocket. If there seemed no escape, I would drink the poison and kill myself. It was better to commit suicide than die a torturous death at the hands of the Cannibals. But before I made any decisions about my life to end The Game, I needed to find Thelda.

"Thelda!" I shouted hesitatingly, hoping that she would magically appear. She was a Sorceress and so it should be easy for her to find me. There was a long silence. I had left Thelda miles behind.

"Cannibals!" I shouted doubtfully. If the Cannibals had her, then they would lead me to her. To my alarm, two dozen cannibals dressed for war stepped out of their hiding from the trees ahead. I was horror struck. They were always there. With the looks of it, they were everywhere. That made my entire run into nowhere look even more absurd.

I stood there frozen. 'They would kill with torture,' I remembered Thelda's words and I shrank from them.

There were about two dozen men. They all looked similar. Their faces were painted in stripes with black paint circles around their eyes. They were scantily clad around their waist and wore armbands and necklaces made of bones and stones. They all had a quiver strung on their back that hosted dozens of arrows similar to the one that I was attacked with. They all held a bow in their hands. They all looked in my direction. It was difficult to read their faces with all the paint but I had my doubts if they looked at me with any other intention except what I would taste like at evening supper. I clutched my pocket with half a mind to gulp down the poison. But I had to find Thelda first.

"Thelda," I shouted and turned around and ran madly forward. The entire army ran behind me. I dashed through the trees. Images of extreme torture only added more power to my legs.

As I darted around a large bush, to my dismay, I realized that the forest had come to an abrupt end. My eyes opened in disbelief as I saw the sight that lay before me. There was a large gathering of the Cannibals. I gasped. I was trapped between a dozen cannibals and a hundred Cannibals. This was it. I was going to die.

I turned around and the army of the dozen men had also stopped behind me. I looked ahead and there was a large fire burning in the centre of the gathering. There were about twenty drummers that stood still at the edge of the clearing awaiting a command. On the far side of the fire stood an extravagant tent. Another twenty or so scantily clad men sat around the fire. A few feet away from them was a raised platform which had a tall pole with a very large skull on top of it. The platform was painted red. I guessed it was the sacrificial place. I shuddered.

Seeing a few women carrying large skewers sent chills down my spine, but a commotion distracted me. The source of the chaos was a large orange bundle on a horizontal pole. The bundle seemed to be alive and it was only when I caught the shine of the silver hair that I gasped, "Thelda."

I had not spoken above a whisper, but a hundred cannibals turned to look at me. I was an easy catch. Imagine the food walking into the lion's den. They left Thelda and started moving toward me, the mood was euphoric.

My heart sank. Strangely the troupe behind me stood still like watchdogs. I think they knew that I was trapped. They seemed aware of my helplessness. After all, I had nowhere to run.

Someone must have signaled them to start, because the drummers started to passionately beat the drums and a few of the men started to do a manic dance around the fire, throwing some strange things in it that burst into sparkles.

What had they done to Thelda? I saw the skewers. I saw the fire. I saw the ceremony. I had to save Thelda.

"Thelda," I screamed in her direction.

Thelda looked my way. She looked pitiful. She was hung on that pole like a wild boar about to be roasted. Her arms and legs were tied to the pole, her head hanging loose. Thelda smiled and I stopped dead in tracks totally oblivious to the mob of women who had now surrounded me.

Thelda smiled !!!!!! How can she smile? Is she retarded? She is going to be cooked alive and she smiled??? I was speechless.

One woman caught my hand in hers. Her gentle soft hands made me jump. I was raided by a dozen hands on my body touching me, feeling me, even squeezing me. They were estimating their prey, I shrieked at that thought.

"Thelda. I'm sorry." I looked over my predators towards Thelda.

"Don't worry. I'm working my magic," she smiled back.

I shook my head and swallowed hard. One woman tugged at my hand, leading me towards the fire. I was finished. The Game would soon be over.

The drums changed beat as I approached the fire. The men stopped throwing the explosives in it. The crowd parted as I was led towards the sacrificial platform. I didn't know what to do. I was going to be killed; there was no doubt about that. I wondered if I would get some points if I killed some of the cannibals too? It would be easy at least to dunk one of them in the fire and injure another with the metal skewers that lay close by. I eyed my options.

One large Cannibal lady came my way and bowed towards me. She was as skimpily dressed as the rest, except that she had a small band made of fur that covered her breasts. She had beautiful long hair and was overly voluptuous. She parted her lips and bared her canine teeth in a smile. She bent over and removed my shoes and placed some flowers at my feet. My gaze darted from her towards Thelda. Two large men had picked up the pole that Thelda was tied to and were carrying her towards me.

I felt choked. I was overcome with a grief so huge that I felt like I was burdened with all the grief in the universe. The sensuous lady who seemed important continued her task of playing with me. She rolled up my sleeves and caressed my bare arms. She held an armlet in her hand and it sparkled in the dancing light of the fire. It looked like it was made of precious stones. She tied the armlet on my right arm. She then raised my jeans and tied a similar anklet on my feet. And then she took off the large skull necklace from around her neck and placed it around mine.

I think the one thing worse than torturing your prey is playing with your prey before torturing it. Kill me. Damn it, just kill me. I prayed that they would kill me before Thelda. It would be a nightmare to watch her die first.

I sat there as the cannibal woman smiled her canine smile. She bowed again and turned to walk away. Her job was done and now the butcher would take over.

Two men came running toward me. One held long skewers in his hands and the other had a large axe. I hastily pulled out the metal container from my pocket and closed my hands around it. I would pull the plug on my life if they as much as touched me. The men didn't touch me. They placed the metal skewers and the large blade by my side and turned around and left. Maybe someone else was to do the killing.

I turned to Thelda and looked at her with moist eyes.

"Make the fire bigger, you fool," she barked at one man who stood next to her. He bolted towards the fire.

The Sorceress was crazy. I felt sorry for her. She had embraced her own death so gracefully that she was helping her assassins with her own murder. There was no greater misery than being witness to your own helplessness. Crisis and trouble had surrounded us from all sides and all we could do was watch all our nightmares unfold before our eyes. I had been here before, back in my life on planet Earth. And each crisis had hurt my soul to the extent that I stayed still. I quit on my dreams. I became bitter and a magnet for more trouble.

I sat there clutching the poison tin in my hand, staring at the anklets on my legs. Under other circumstances, I would have been delighted about the jewels but today I felt like the sacrificial goat decorated with ornaments before the sacrifice. The dance in the distance had reached an ecstatic height to the beats of the drums. What could I do? There must be something I could do? There must be a way. I looked at the axe and skewers. I could pick them up and go on a mass massacre frenzy. But there was no way I would stay alive. I sure would kill a few but my death would still be certain. Acrodorf had said that there was always a way. I sat upright startled. What would Acrodorf do if he were here? I closed my eyes and saw Acrodorf in front of me.

"Whatever happens, remember that you are an immortal, indestructible, powerful soul. No matter what happens, no matter what The Game is, remember that there is always a way out. No matter what happens, no matter how futile your efforts may seem, know that the answer is right in front of your eyes. No matter what happens, know that I have immense respect for who you were, who you are, and who you will be. And no matter what happens, know that I will never give up on you!" I could hear Acrodorf say the words when The Game had consumed me.

An electric current ran through my body.

"Yeah baby!" Thelda screamed with delight whether at the raging flames of the fire or at my spiritual cognition, I could not tell.

"Excuse me," I spoke for the first time in my whole encounter with the Cannibals. I put the poison tin back in my pocket. Thelda's head turned in my direction and she had the foreboding look that spelt trouble. It read 'surprised horror' that told me that I should not have spoken.

One woman turned around and hurried towards me. My words were merely a whisper but the sound was somehow amplified to echo through the whole clearing. The entire activity including the drumming, the dancing, everything came to an abrupt halt.

"Yes," the woman looked at me eagerly. She had the same set of canines that the other woman had, only hers looked sharper.

"Are you hungry?" she asked apologetically, which made Thelda burst out into laughter that roared through the whole forest .

"Feed her!!" She mused.

"I... I..." I stammered, trying to ignore Thelda and her supposed magical madness.

"KEEP THE FIRE RAGING, YOU FOOL," she yelled at deafening decibels at the man who had also stopped pouring the liquid into the fire during our conversation.

I could see the fire tower behind the woman.

"I, er, need to speak to someone. Is there a chief, or someone who is the leader here? Someone I can speak to?" I asked her, looking in the direction of the lavishly adorned tent on the side. Acrodorf would have done that. Acrodorf would have treated the enemy with grace. He treated Black and White with immense respect even though they were an obstacle in his purpose. Black and White were opponents but that did not stop Acrodorf from giving them respect.

"Ah, yes, yes. The Chief, Ababa, is getting ready for you!" She said excitedly, sending a chill down my body.

Two men scurried towards the tent, as did the voluptuous lady.

"Chief Ababa!" I heard someone yell and the drums started a percussion beat, like a marching tune.

The flap of the tent shifted and two large men smothered with greyish black ash walked out first. They held the flap open and out walked a gigantic, majestic Chief Ababa. His body was tight and muscular. His walk was stiff with every muscle movement intentionally exaggerated. His arms curved outwards and swayed by his side.

He had the same paint on his face and the same black-circled eyes, only bigger. He wore the same cloth around his waist except that he was loaded with jewels similar to the ones that the lady had adorned me with. He gazed in my direction and smiled with glee exposing shark-like double-layered set of canine teeth.

He walked towards me hastily. He carried a large saw-like blade in his hand. That man could just bite my head off with the set of teeth he had, he really didn't need the saw.

"It is time!" Thelda barked. The fireman poured some flammable liquid and the flames extended towards the sky.

I stood there trembling. The Chief Ababa came towards me hastily and I had lost all control over my legs. I clenched my jaw and grit my teeth to stop them from chattering. I hated to admit it, but

I was petrified. He stood in front of me with the plump lady by his side. He stretched out the blade and touched it to my head. I closed my eyes resisting the urge to shrink and to run. It was better I go first.

I felt the cold metal blade on my forehead. And I cringed ready for the impact.

"Are you alright?" Ababa asked seeing the disturbed look on my face.

I opened my eyes to see Ababa peering down at me. The sight startled me. His face was huge. My head could fit neatly in his mouth, it was so large.

"Is something the matter?" he pressed on.

"I have a request," I muttered, cautiously not wanting to excite or disturb him. You never know how cannibals respond to requests. I didn't want to lose my self-respect in pleading or begging. Acrodorf would have kept his posture in dealing with Ababa. So what if he was a cannibal? I was somebody too, er, in this moment, his meal.

"Gladly. Consider your wish my command," Ababa smiled and then nodded to the lady next to him. His teeth clanked maliciously as he spoke. At least he was open to grant me my dying wish.

"Can you let Thelda go? She is on a purpose. I am the trespasser in The Game; a last minute entry on the journey to Zedius. You can kill me and torture me. I can bear that. But I can't bear that a soul like Thelda be denied her purpose," I found my tongue and could feel Acrodorf speak through me.

Ababa looked horrified. He looked over his shoulder at the cannibal lady who matched his dismay.

"Pray why would I kill you and torture you? You are our guest!" Ababa complained, looking around at others for some explanation to my behavior.

Thelda was silent and still. Was she dead? I pushed Ababa aside and ran towards Thelda. Immediately three men leapt out and defended her.

"Is she dead?" I screamed at them.

Ababa grabbed my arm. I spun around expecting the blow of death.

"Thelda is not dead," he narrowed his brow and the sound rolled in his mouth before it was released out as words. "And we are not going to kill anyone." He said looking sadly at the lady to his left.

"Wh... What? You are not going to kill us? You are not going to eat me?" I asked in confusion,wriggling my arm in his hand in an attempt to free myself from his grip. I had spent my entire time here in mortal dread of death and losing The Game and Ababa the Cannibal Chief was telling me that I was crazy?

"But... But you are Cannibals right?" I was horribly confused. I stared into Ababa's parted mouth and his double set of canine teeth confirmed that he was. He released his grip on my arm.

The lady on Ababa's right, the lady who had adorned me with the sacrificial jewels held my hand.

"I am Lima, the Chief's wife," she said, her eyes filled with sorrow. She had almond shaped eyes, almost as pretty as Acrodorf's. She tugged at my hand and led me by the fire which by the way seemed like a path-way to heaven with its flames so tall, they seemed to touch the sky. I could see her face golden with the hue of the flames. Surprisingly, the fire did not feel hot or maybe I was losing my mind.

"We were Cannibals. During our term on planet Earth, we were Cannibals. We found satisfaction in eating our own. Food was not just food for us; it was entertainment. Something we could play with, and then eat. Something we could even fall in love with, and then consume it," she said.

The entire troupe around the fire had cleared up and I hadn't noticed that within seconds, a sitting area had been arranged. Ababa and a few others joined in. Lima seated me on the low-lying wooden stool in the middle and the others quickly squatted on the others around.

"It was a sadistic way of living, almost evil. We were spiritually dead. Our life was only about food and cold-blooded pleasure." Ababa spoke solemnly.

I squinted towards Thelda. The three men stood in front of her blocking my sight.

"And there reached a point in our lives that no humans would tread our way. We had banished ourselves from our own kind." Lima took over, as I glanced towards Ababa, cautiously.

"And then with no food and no game, we started to eat our own," she continued. I could see her eyes moisten. "One had to be alert at all times because no one could be trusted." she paused, "not even your own husband," she let out an abrupt sob.

Ababa placed his hand on Lima's shoulder and bit his lip.

"It is then we sent a plea to our neighbors, men, humans that lived in fear of us. But no one trusted us. When you live in betrayal for centuries, trust is no longer possible. We then sent a plea for redemption, and we were willing to do anything to change our lot. It was then that we got a call. Black and White invited us to be The Game bearers and await our redemption." Ababa said earnestly.

"And what is that?" I mumbled. This was too much for me. I was sitting in the middle of a Cannibal tribe that was claiming to be good and spiritually ignited people. This was not a game, this was madness.

"We are Cannibals. And the meaning of the word is so powerful that it makes us inhuman. When spirits enter The Game, they play by the rules. They know they must fight us to live. They know they must kill us to live. And what is worse, they kill themselves before they find out that we won't." Ababa said pausing to make sure that I was following him.

"Huh?" was my blank response.

"When one enters The Game, the instructions say that you are entering the land of the Cannibals and that you must survive. Cannibals are people who eat the flesh of other people. So their understanding is that we are the opponents in The Game; opposing their survival. Little do they know that a game exists only as long as the opponents exist. But we don't eat human flesh, and haven't done so in centuries. So we are actually on their side. But people fight us, they threaten to kill us and kill themselves for the fear of who we were, without stopping to find out who we are." Ababa's words blew the living daylight out of me.

"They enter The Game with fear and they fail the game with the destruction and devastation they cause. Rules don't lead to victory, rules are there to keep the game fair. It is one's own courage and ability that leads to victory." Ababa continued.

"So how does one win? How does one pass to the next level?" I asked, curiously. Maybe I could trick him into giving me the answer and I could set Thelda and myself free.

"Exactly what you did!" He exclaimed in delight.

Now Ababa was playing with me, his prey. What did I do to pass? I didn't feel like a winner. I was still in The Game. I had not yet come to any conclusion about the cannibals. Thelda was still in their captivity. He was certainly playing with me.

"People pass the Level One of The Game when they are no longer afraid of meanings. People move higher when they are no longer afraid to challenge the obsolete, when they dare to move beyond their fear of death and the fear that others will harm them. In doing that they earn their freedom. People move on to the next level when they don't need to kill their desires, their purpose and their lives on fictitious threats." Ababa said and his face showed a sign of relief.

"And we owe that to you and Thelda," Lima took my hand and held it tight. She bent down and kissed it.

"What did you do to Thelda?" I wanted to tell them that I was afraid of them and that I still had my doubts about them, but I wanted to free Thelda first. If they were playing games with me like Cannibals do, then I wanted to first set Thelda free.

"Thelda offered to help us," Ababa stood up. "She is helping us make a pathway of our release," he smiled and he pointed towards the fire. "We have been in The Game for centuries, I guess. Though our term seems like eternity. Now that we have earned our freedom, Thelda is working her magic for our liberation." He continued.

I could not believe what I was hearing. Thelda had tackled the Cannibals headlong. They were man-eating Cannibals, but that had not deterred her from knowing them. And in getting to know them she understood them. And in understanding them, she set them free. I shuddered. I on the other hand wanted nothing to do with the Cannibals and yet no matter where and how far I ran from them, I ran into them.

"But I was afraid of you," I tried to clarify to Ababa that maybe his freedom was still another game away.

"You couldn't be," Lima said caressing my hair.

"I was afraid when I was attacked by the arrow. I was afraid when your army confronted me. I was petrified with the whole adorning ritual you did. I was afraid in every single moment that I stepped into The Game. In fact I still feel that you are playing with my mind." I defended.

"Then why did you call for me?" Ababa stood up. Either he was very ticked off with me or by his towering presence, he was threatening me to admit to my own courage.

"Because I wanted you to release Thelda. I didn't want her to pay the price on my account," I reasoned.

"When you dare to reason with fear. When you dare to confront it. When you dare to face it. When you dare to even believe you have a chance, then you are no longer afraid. Fear makes you shrink. Fear makes you introvert. Fear makes you believe you have no chance, it makes you helpless. If you were afraid of me, I don't think you would have had the courage to send for me to reason with me." Ababa said, leaning onto my face.

What? I thought to myself. Was it really true that I was not afraid of him? Is fear a self-invented belief? Ababa was telling me that I was not afraid of him whereas I believed with all my might that I was.

"Fear becomes evident in your action. The fear in your mind shows up in the reserved and trivial actions you take. Any spirit of the universe would testify that asking a meeting with the Cannibal Chief is no act of fear, it is an act of extreme courage." Ababa said seriously.

Holy Cow. This was news to me. I had courage. I thought I was meek, scared and lonely, not to mention reserved. I was so hiding behind my own cowardice that I missed seeing the glimpses of courage in my daily actions. I was my own enemy. By virtue of my misplaced thoughts about myself, my innate nature towards courage and greatness, I was eating myself up. I was eating up my dreams, because I believed I was too small to even dream. I was eating up my chance to glory, because I believed I was unworthy of any virtuous attention. I was eating up any opportunity for progress and abundance that came my way, because I was too negatively involved in self-defeat. I was the cannibal eating up my own life!!!

My body broke into a shiver.

"The Game is in two parts. One part is where you perceive a threat. Someone is threatening you. Someone is standing between you and your purpose. The trouble starts when you abandon your purpose for the fear of losing to the threat. In doing that, you lose even before you start."

Ababa's words stung my brains. Thelda has entered The Game to aid my survival. But with the first hint of threat, I abandoned her, and in doing that I destroyed her purpose of being there.

"The second part is," Ababa said hurriedly before I got lost in another mental chatter, "where the opponent is perceived to be so powerful that you destroy yourself. The poison, the metal skewers, the axe, all hint to the second part. Many times, the people in The Game kill themselves before finding out that we would not," Ababa explained.

I had had the same idea. I had wanted to kill myself. The opponent was too big. I had almost convinced myself that I would not make it. If it were not for Thelda I would have drunk the poison, when the army in the forest confronted me. I was alive because of Thelda.

The urge to destroy myself had tugged at me very too often. Because it seemed too difficult to survive without a job and steady income, I had killed my dream to write. If I perceived a situation or person or task to be difficult, I killed my approach to it. I had never bothered to find out if it was really difficult to survive without a job. Maybe, I could have written part-time for my own publication where I worked. Maybe, I could have gotten an advance from a publisher. But I had made things so difficult in my mind that a solution never even occurred to me.

I stood up and ran towards Thelda. Lima caught my hand. I struggled to set it free.

"I need to speak to Thelda. This is too much for me to handle." I begged.

"Thelda is connected with the path. If you shake her out, we will all lose our salvation from our karma," Lima begged in return. "You have set us free," she let go of my hand and grabbed my feet. "I beg of you," she pleaded.

I stopped dead in my tracks. These were cannibals that didn't eat human beings and hadn't done so in centuries. These were Cannibals that were ready to pay the price for their misdeeds. These were Cannibals that were begging me to let them go towards their long-awaited freedom. A hundred pair of eyes looked my way. The drummers had stopped beating the drums. The fire dancers had stopped their dance. The fire tender had stopped tending the fire.

"KEEP THE FIRE BURNING, YOU WRETCHED RASCAL," I heard an infuriated Thelda. I heard a thunder and the next minute an angry Thelda was hopping on her tied feet with her tied fist raised in fury. She hopped towards the fire. Lima and a few other women let out an ear splitting shriek. Thelda snatched the large wooden spoon from the fire tender's hand despite her tied hands and shook her head violently. Her feet were a few inches above the ground and she furiously began to add the liquid into the fire with the motion of both her arms.

"It's time!" She barked. "The Chief goes first!"

Thelda was half into the flames and half outside. I stood frozen.

The Chief Ababa looked towards me. His face lit up with a smile of relief. He ran towards the flames and hauled himself into them and a loud sizzle echoed into the forest. A cloud of dust rose and then settled.

"Do I need to personally invite everyone? Move it, you rascals!!!" Thelda bellowed hysterically.

Lima let go of my hand and ran towards the flames and disappeared into them. One by one, all the man-eating cannibals hauled themselves into the flames turning to gray dust. With each entrant, the flame grew smaller and smaller till the last few of them had doubts if the flame would even last before their turn came. Two or three of them began to jump into the flames together and in the end, the last two had to wriggle into the flame that was fast receding into a pile of grayish black dust.

I looked around. The drums lay abandoned. The tent shook in a sudden breeze. The bows, the quivers, the knives lay scattered. The pole with the large skull shook and I barely skipped out of the way of the skull that crash-landed next to me.

"Haul it in!!" Thelda barked.

There was no one around, so I assumed the nasty instruction was for me. I grabbed the human skull and cautiously hauled it into the ash. Without as much as a hiss, it turned to dust.

Thelda stood by the fire area still in a trance. I didn't know whether I should tap her and get her out of it, so I decided to wait for her arrival back to my reality. This whole episode with the Cannibals had put a strain on my soul. I sat down at the, er, sacrificial platform and I could not help but smile.

I was not afraid? I had discovered courage in me. I always had it in me but I had failed to accept it. I smiled.

Ababa was right. There were many man-eating people I knew. People who had hurt me in the past, people who had wronged me, people who had cheated me; the Cannibals I had vowed to stay away from. We all hurt others, wrong them, cheat them knowingly or unknowingly. And we do so out of fear of others and fear of ourselves. And then there comes a day when we realize our blunder and we gather in ourselves the courage to make amends. We desperately try to put our past behind us and want to be accepted again for the goodness we had in us but failed to show. And that day, nothing hurts more than the disbelief that people throw our way. And that day it hurts our soul for the ill treatment people give us for our past and for having no trust in our remorse. It is soul shattering on how when bad people become good, we keep them bad; when misled people come home, we mistreat them. Goodness deserves a chance. No matter how bad anyone may have been, when they seek redemption, it must be granted. I could not wait to go back home and liberate others from my judgment of their misdeeds, even though they had long stopped doing them. I could not wait to go back and free others of my meanings and opinions that I had formed of them and was not willing to change, even though they had.

Thelda moved. She fell to the ground and I shot up and ran towards her.

"Stay away you crazy creature," she spat out, smiling wide. She wriggled her feet out of the ropes and then untied them with her hands. She flung the ropes into the ash and sat on the ground cross-legged.

"That was some task!" She said, rolling up her sleeves. I could see a glow in Thelda's grey eyes. She was a good soul in an alarming package. Her silver brows had specks of the gray dust, but she didn't seem to mind it.

I could swear that Thelda was growing more and more youthful with every passing moment. Her hunch had straightened up to a great extent, though I felt she hunched more out of habit than physical pain. Her skin was tighter around her face and her smile much more divine.

"You freed them, Thelda," I must say that Thelda the Sorceress was working her magic and healing even in the universe.

"You did too," she winked.

"Yeah. I was not afraid of them," I burst out into laughter at my own declaration of courage and Thelda joined in.

"Why did they tie you to the pole, Thelda?" I questioned. "You were helping them to set them free, then why did they treat you like that?"

"That's my position to create alternate pathways," Thelda scowled. She was annoyed that I would think that she was held captive. "I told you I was working my magic." She tapped her head to imply I was a crazy creature.

Thelda got up, dusted the ash from her orange robe and walked towards the abandoned drums.

"These are magical. I can make them beat without touching them," she grinned and the whole forest came alive with heart throbbing percussion beats. And abruptly there was silence.

"I am going to take one with me, would you like one too?" She said looking in my direction.

"No, I'm good," I nodded my head. I had no intention to carry anything with me. I had the precious jewels and I was happy with that. Though I took out the skull necklace and placed it on the ground next to the drums.

"We better get moving," she said.

"To where?" I asked looking around where Thelda wanted to go.

"To Level Two, you crazy creature," she trumpeted and started to walk back to the forest.

Level Two

Thelda and I walked towards the forest.

"Why are we going towards the forest?" I asked Thelda. I wondered if she had already been briefed about the next level. I wondered if she had worked up her magic to decode the next step too.

"Where else do you want to go?" She stopped and raised her eyebrow. The clearing was surrounded by the forest on all sides and I could see the naiveté of my question. Her face was certainly younger and fuller. The bags around her eyes were barely visible and her grey eyes were shinier and brighter. Her nose had become rigid too. It was more loosely hanging when I had encountered her first. I wondered if I were growing younger too.

"Any way that we head leads to the forest. Unless you can see something else here," she chuckled.

We were about to leave the clearing and enter into a rather dense forest.

"Are you sure you want to carry this drum along?" I asked Thelda, alarmed at the sight. First of all she was so hyper. And second, the drum was rather large and she had pulled a line in the ground by dragging it along.

"You should carry one too." She giggled.

"So, how do we get to the next level?" I asked Thelda. She was the wise one and I was curious to know what she thought about that.

"The next level will come when we get to it," she said compassionately, "What is important is that you carry with you what you learnt from level one into level two. I am sure that level two will be a whole new challenge and a whole new learning, but it is only a level up on what you learn from a level down. Remember that. It is when people forget where they came from, when they forget what they needed to remember, life's beautiful lessons, life plays to remind them that again. That would be a foolish game; to come back to square one, because you didn't care about what you learnt. Learning should serve you life long."

"Yeah sure," I agreed, trying to speed memorize all the lessons I had learnt with my encounters with Ababa and his tribe.

"You never know when what comes in handy," Thelda continued, as she dragged the drum along and stopped to part a low-lying branch of a tree.

I wondered how far Thelda wanted to carry the drum along. It sure was a beautiful instrument, but it was large and cumbersome.

"Why must my decisions annoy you?" Thelda asked from the corner of her eye. "I like the drum. I am carrying it. You refused to carry one for yourself, but you are carrying mine in your disgruntled thoughts. Get your own drum and stop carrying the weight of mine." Thelda scolded me.

Though we were not formless souls anymore, Thelda still held her ability to connect with me. I wondered what it would take for me to acquire that.

Thelda was right. Just because I didn't want to carry the drum, I also didn't want her to carry it either. Just because I found it annoying to carry, her carrying it was annoying me. Why couldn't I let her be? Why did I have to be irritated and judgmental about a drum? Danny would often be mad at me for that. Just because I loved dogs and he didn't, I reprimanded him for being heartless. Just because I loved my space and time out, I reprimanded him for not wanting that too. Why did I have this need to expect him to do what I liked? Why couldn't I let people be, do and have what they wanted to be and do and have?

Thelda tapped her drum and I leapt out of my skin with the abrupt sound. She roared with laughter. She pointed ahead to a gap between two trees. As I looked carefully, what looked like a gap between two trees turned out to be the same black void door.

"The door," I inhaled sharply. Thelda and her drum dragging came to a halt.

"You are right." She was delighted. "Can you see a scroll?" And before she even completed the sentence, we could see a similar shining object. Only this was a leaf hanging next to the door.

We both hastened towards the leaf. On it read the following:

"Welcome to Level Two. In this level, Thelda and Niki Sanders will play as individuals. You will be playing the same game, but individually. Which means that the identical situation and the identical challenges await you. You will be able to see each other, but you will not be able to communicate with each other. What one does will have no impact upon the other. At any point, there is no turning back. The purpose is the same, to survive. If any of you die, both of you lose. You have to reach the castle. Black and White will meet you there."

"Let's go" Thelda said excitedly.

The leaf did not disintegrate like the last scroll had.

"Wait," I said, still looking at the leaf.

"And Thelda will no longer have her magical powers. You both will be playing on equal ground." With these words, the leaf shrunk on its light and shone green like the other leaves on the tree.

"Darn!!" Thelda muttered. "Did you have to stay to read that?" She scowled as though the rule would not have applied if we had not read it.

Actually, the last rule had me worried now. If Thelda did not have her powers and if we were playing as individual players, then survival would certainly be a challenge. My challenge. With my natural affinity for disaster, this level was lost from the start. Thelda had come into The Game to help me out and now that effort seemed to be a waste, if she could no longer help me.

"So you learnt nothing from level one," Thelda slapped her head and sat on the drum, making herself comfortable in the middle of the forest.

I looked up to her nodding my head.

"You made it through level one on your own," She rolled her eyes up to the sky expressing her exasperation.

"No, Thelda. I made it because you were there," I tried to explain to her.

"I am still there then," she reasoned. "We actually didn't play together in level one because you,,,,,, er,,,,,, ran away." She added raising her eyebrow sarcastically, "So what difference does it make in level two? When will you stop being a sissy and own up responsibility for your life? At least we can see each other. We are playing the same game. So if you can see me, then do what I do."

Now she was talking. This witch was really clever if you made her talk. If we were playing the same game and if I could see her then do what she did, then I would make it. I smiled. Cheating brought pleasure. It brought a thrill. It brought glory in challenge. When things got tough and if I couldn't find a way to cheat, then there could be a way. Little did I know that if I could find a way to cheat, then I could have certainly found a legitimate way out also. For if evil is one way, then goodness is only another way around.

"I like that," I rubbed my hands together.

"Let's go then," Thelda said, hopping off the drum with a popping sound that seemed to dance around in the trees.

I held Thelda's hand and she looked at me and shook her head. I needed her. And she found that ridiculous. She smiled and dragged the drum along with her and we both stepped into the black void door together into Level Two of The Game.

"Oh shoot!!" I exclaimed out loud as we were once again spiraling down the same slithering tunnel as before. I should have let Thelda go in first so she could be ahead in The Game for me to follow.

We both crash-landed in to an open space. It was stunningly beautiful. The ground seemed to radiate outward. The grass was lush below my feet and I caressed it with my hands before I stood up. Thelda was a few meters away. It was an identical scene on her side. We were in two identical and parallel realities separated by an imaginary partition. There were trees around in the distance and the sky was sprinkled with stars that shone in the blue sky. I stared upwards in delight. It was beautiful to see stars twinkling in the daytime. I looked around, trying to orient myself to this new level. There was a little hill in the distance towards the right and I was standing at the foothills. I stared at the little hill on top of which stood a beautiful castle. I could see the steeple jutting out. It looked straight out of a fairy tale. Even if the instructions would not say so, I would have instinctively known that I had to get there. The space to my right was pretty plain, interspersed with a few trees and a few rock formations that led to what seemed like the edge of a cliff, because the vision broke into the clear blue sky just beyond the trees. I squinted and there were a few large white boulders arranged on top of each other with a little vegetation around it. It was a picturesque sight. So what was the game? What was the challenge? This place seemed too beautiful for any sort of vicious games. I turned to look towards Thelda to see what she had figured of The Game and when I turned to see into her reality my heart sank and my soul almost left my body.

Thelda was walking ahead in her game, a few steps ahead from where I stood in mine. A hungry saber-toothed lion was running towards her from the valley. Its canine teeth were like the gigantic tusks of an elephant except that they were sharp enough to pierce through a body in one blow. Its mane was pulled backwards with the wind as it arched forward in gigantic leaps towards Thelda. I froze where I stood. That was my fate in the next few steps. We were in the same game.

"Thelda!!!" I screamed with full force though I knew she could not hear me.

She could see the saber-toothed lion running towards her but that did not deter her from moving forward. The witch was crazy. Maybe she forgot that she had no magical powers with her anymore. All she had was that over-sized drum that she had been trudging along with, all through into Level Two. Drum?? I gasped. The man-eater was only a few meters away when Thelda hauled the drum in front of her and began to beat it like a concert artist. The lion screeched to a halt a few feet away with the manic banging that Thelda was creating with her drum. The loud drum beats startled the lion. I could see the fear in his eyes. I could see the fear in the lion's eyes!!!! Thelda's eyes were closed. She was moving forward, beating the drum with wild excitement. Her hand movements were exaggerated with her orange robe flaring up, making her look bigger than she actually was.

I saw a sight that left me stunned. The hungry man-eating saber-toothed lion began to retreat slowly and slowly as the loud drumming continued. Thelda tilted the drum with one hand in the direction of the lion and banged it with all her might. Her hair was blown back with the wind and her robe was dancing in rhythm of her movements. She looked like a very ferocious lioness establishing her superiority over the retreating male.

With another blow on the drum, I could see the lion scowl and run towards the boulders and then it disappeared behind the rock formation.

I was dumbstruck. A victorious Thelda looked my way and waved excitedly. I needed that drum. I knew if I took any step forward, the lion would come leaping from the hills.

"I need the drum," I yelled at Thelda. I knew she couldn't hear me but I couldn't bear to face the hungry lion that would soon be heading my way.

Thelda turned towards me and smiled. She couldn't hear me.

"I need the drum," I yelled again and again, louder and louder. Thelda could not hear me. She sure could lip-read me. She smiled again. I could have murdered the witch. She knew that the drum was needed in the next level. She knew it. Why else would she trudge along with it? It seemed ridiculous. But she knew. She should have told me. She should have told me to take the drum too. I was so mad at Thelda. I felt cheated. She knew she had come to save me. She knew I needed her. And she didn't tell me that the drum would save my life. She didn't tell me!!! She cheated.

I had driven myself hysterical with my rage and large tears welled up in my eyes and I began to sob deliriously. Thelda looked at me unperturbed by my state. She smiled at me and tapped her head as though to imply again that I was a crazy creature. But she should have told me…. I half-stumbled over my own sob. Thelda *had* told me to carry the drum. In fact, she had told me to carry the drum more than one time. I had refused every time she told me to carry the darned drum!!!! She had told me, but I didn't want to carry it.

But why didn't she tell me it would save my life?!! My soul screamed out loud. It's funny how I believed that Thelda's presence would save my life and help me through The Game, but what is sarcastically funnier is that I did not do what she told me to do. Because she had volunteered to save my life, I had left everything on her shoulders. So because she was there, I didn't have to do anything. I could ride on her shoulders.

What a disgraceful attitude! I scolded myself as I angrily wiped hot tears from my cheeks. She told me to take the drum; but no; I didn't listen. I didn't treat Thelda with the respect she deserved as someone who was there on a purpose to help me. I took her for granted. I didn't listen to her whereas her only purpose of communicating with me was to help me. I took her words and instructions for granted. You can't spell out in so many words what will help another. One step leads to another. When someone has your best interest as their purpose, listen to them, damn it!! I screamed at myself angrily. But it was a lesson learnt too late. Right now, I was stuck to be potentially eaten by a wild lion.

Thelda was trudging uphill. The castle looked even more beautiful as Thelda got closer to it. It seemed to be made up of greyish white marble and was shining brightly, signaling its presence into the universe. She reached the foot of the castle. There was a long tower on one side that had a sharp pointed roof. The sharp cone-like roof was made of gold. Thelda placed her drum at the step of the castle and proceeded her way up. The large door opened and Black and White emerged from it. Thelda leapt with joy to see them and they instantly immersed in deep conversation, Thelda's end of the conversation being very animated. Then, the three of them turned and looked towards me. I had not moved an inch from where I stood. Thelda looked at me and slapped her head. I shook my head. I was not going anywhere. There was no way I could move past the lion without being killed. I had nothing with me. I had no drum, I had nothing. It was a futile attempt. Thelda, Black and White folded their arms and looked in my direction gravely. I decided to ignore them and remain where I was.

I didn't know for how long I stood there. Every now and then, I stole a glance in Thelda's direction and she and the shadow twins stood there amused, in wait. Thelda just kept tapping her head every time I looked at her and I found that annoying. I know I had goofed up, but instead of rubbing it in, she could help me. She could signal some ideas to me.

My legs were becoming stiff. I dared not even move a millimeter lest that would trigger the lion. I had no plan on what I would do.

I had no plan on how to overcome the lion. I had no weapons, I had nothing. What could I do to get there? Acrodorf had said that there was always a way. What would he do if he were here? What would Acrodorf do? I wondered. I looked at Thelda and she smiled. She smiled! She was no longer slapping her head. I smiled back for the first time. Maybe she could sense me. The instructions had said that we could not communicate with each other but I was certain that Thelda was still connected with me. That look on her face added to that certainty. She could sense that now my thinking had changed and was getting somewhere. I felt a relief.

The one thing Acrodorf would not do was stand still and accept defeat. Acrodorf would march up to the lion and somehow find a way to overcome it. Maybe it was not a man-eating lion like the cannibals were not man-eating people. Maybe it was a vegetarian lion. If this is a game then there is a way out. Acrodorf would move ahead to find that way, or heck, he would move ahead and make a way.

I lifted my foot and stepped forward and Thelda jumped with delight. So I could not be wrong. She had condemned my inertia and she applauded my action. Nothing happened. No lion emerged. Nothing. I hesitatingly took another step forward. Nothing. One more step. Nothing. Nothing was happening. Oh no! This was The Game. It was a trick to keep me in fear and rot away to my own death. There was no lion for me. It was only for Thelda and yet I feared her reality.

I squealed with delight and darted forward towards the castle to embrace Thelda and meet Black and White. I ran and waved to Thelda, "Here I come, you crazy creature," and the look on her face left me horror struck. I turned my glance forward and saw the same man-eating saber-toothed lion running down the hill at lightning speed towards me. I stopped dead in my tracks and so did the lion.

This was crazy. We *were* in the same game. I *had to* confront the lion. I don't know what stroke of brilliant intellect made me think that we were not. I guess we are all in the same game of life. We are all in the same boat. It's the same story for everyone. It's the same struggle, the same challenges and the same worries. Only some of us make it to the castle and the others think they are too smart and fail. I didn't want to fail.

What would Acrodorf do? What would Thelda do? She would look for the obvious in the situation and Acrodorf would handle everything with grace without shrinking in panic. What was obvious here? What would Thelda see? The lion moves when I move. My every step sets his every step in motion. If I stop the lion stops. So, if that were true that I can cover the distance safely till I am one foot away from the lion, it's the next step that would bring my head in his mouth. What would Acrodorf do? He would move till the last step.

I took a deep breath, looked at Thelda for reassurance and began to walk forward hastily. I did not turn to see what Thelda's reaction was, whether she would approve of it or not. I was doing out of my own knowingness and my certainty was so absolute that I did not have to verify it. With every step I took, the lion covered ten times the distance. And in a few seconds, the lion was just a few meters ahead. I stopped, not taking my eyes off the lion and the lion stopped too. It roared loudly with its mouth wide open. His white fangs arched as he did.

What now? I dared not look towards Thelda. No matter what she would signal to me, I had reached the last threshold, the last step towards my fate. And no matter what, I had to take the step forward. There was no turning back, here and in life.

I looked at the lion. It was majestic. On a different context, like on TV, I would have said that the lion was beautiful, but when your life is at stake, beauty turns to ugliness. The lion was golden brown, a young male. Its mane was long and fanned around its face and caught the starlight as it did. His eyes were dark brown and I quickly averted my glance from them. I could feel it's leonine stare in my direction. His large fangs were bared, as his mouth was slightly open with a little froth on the sides. It was an extinct species- the saber-toothed lion. As though to entertain me, he opened his mouth wide and let out a lazy yawn. It was huge and with one leap would crush me to death. My heart did a manic beat and I had to take deep breaths to calm myself down.

What could I do? What could I do now that would get me past this creature that was purpose-bound to kill me?

What would Thelda do? Well, she would start giving instructions to the lion and maybe put it to work like she was doing at the Cannibal Camp. She would join its mission and liberate it. Thelda was a crazy witch but her ways seemed to work.

What would Acrodorf do? Well, he would give the lion the respect it deserved for his purpose and then he would try and persuade him towards his. Acrodorf always had his way. At least with me.

I took a deep breath and looked towards Thelda for reassurance. She was beaming from ear to ear. I was on the right track.

I had to take another step in faith. I had to do something. Acrodorf said that no matter how challenging things may seem, the answer is always in front of my eyes. And the only thing in front of my eyes was the man-eating lion I had to find my way around. I had reached the threshold of The Game. I stood face to face, a foot away from a hungry man-eating lion. The only way out was the way forward and the way forward threatened to end my life.

The lion twitched and sat down with a plop on the grass, not letting me out of its sight. I could feel the heat from his body. I could feel his lazy vibe. If only it could fall asleep, I could tip toe my way up. The lion stared right at me adamantly.

Danny had told me this story one night.

It was the story about this rat that lived a rat's life. He woke up one day and decided that he no longer wanted to live like a rat, i.e., he no longer wanted to be a rat. So he decided to find a new life for himself at the top of the mountain where liberation was found. So he decided to go to the top of the mountain. But there was a challenge. He had to cross the river to get to the side of the mountain. He went to the banks of the river and asked for help. An alligator came to his aid and said that he could get him across, if he offered to let him have his tail. The rat thought a little. He looked back at his rat life and then looked at the mountain of liberation. His cousin had gotten into a brawl with another rat that had chewed off his tail in the fight. Losing his tail was a threat on both sides of the river. He agreed to give the alligator his tail. The alligator got the rat safely to the other side and in exchange chewed his tail off. The rat rested a little and overcame his pain and his wound healed. He was off towards the mountain in no time. But there was a challenge. The valley was infested with rat eating snakes. He stopped at the foothills and asked for help. A mongoose came to the rescue. The mongoose agreed to help the rat cross the valley of snakes if he could have one of his legs. The rat thought a little. He looked at his rat life behind across the river and he looked at the majestic mountain of liberation above. He agreed to give one of his legs to the mongoose who would keep him in his mouth and take him safely across the valley. The mongoose kept his word and dropped the mouse to safety mid-way into the mountains and the rat allowed the mongoose to bite off one hind leg. The rat rested a little. He overcame the pain and the wound healed. He looked up at the mountain with only half-way to go and was delighted. But there was a challenge. The mountain was filled with wolves that love to feed on rats. With one leg gone, he would be an easy prey. The rat asked for help. a Llama came to help. The Llama agreed to hide the rat in his coat and take him safely to the mountaintop in exchange for his eye. It broke the rat's heart. He looked back at his rat life and he looked at the mountain of liberation. He was almost there. Turning back was not even an option. He had lost a leg. He had lost his tail. How would he go back anyway? What would he go back to? How would he live his life again knowing he was so close and didn't take the last step? How would he make peace with his sacrifices that brought him to his last step and then quit? He agreed to give the Llama his eye and the Llama hid the rat in his coat and brought him safely to the top of the mountain. The Llama set the rat down and the rat gave the Llama his eye. With no tail and three legs and one eye, the rat was at the top of the mountain of liberation. He could see with one eye and it was divine. Sore with pain but soaring with delight, he began to walk towards his liberation from his rat life. He wobbled a few steps ahead and he felt a large shadow cast on his back. His hair stood up. Even without looking up or ahead he had felt the shadow. It was the shadow of the mountain eagle. He could feel its intent and he could feel its purpose; to consume him. The rat ran as fast as his legs could carry him uphill to the peak of the mountain to at least touch it once before he was consumed by the eagle. He could feel the eagle close in on him and then it happened. The eagle clutched the rat in its claws and flew off with him. The rat felt dizzy with the height at first. The ground spun below him. And then he could see clearly. The open sky, the majestic mountaintop, the Llama, the wolves, the snakes, the alligator. He could see the river that he had crossed and he could see his fellow rats and the life he left behind. He soared the skies in sheer delight and squealed, "I AM FREE".

The eagle circled the mountain with the rat clutched tightly in its claws. This was not an ordinary catch, for the prey was delighted with the predator and rejoiced in its company. The eagle swooped low and perched on the highest point on the peak of the mountain of liberation. It placed the rat on the rock and looked straight into its eye and said, "You are free! I feed on rats, but you are not one. Rats are not found here, they live at the bottom of the hill. You are in my territory, my home. This is the peak where only eagles dare. You have a mighty soul like mine. You.... little one.... are an eagle."

Soon the word spread in the mountain of liberation. The rat had been liberated and inhabited in the land where only the eagles dared. The alligator, the mongoose, the wolf, the llama all started towards the mountain peak to meet the rat whom they had taken advantage of and to ask his forgiveness.

The word spread high and low of the courage of the rat. Animals from faraway places began their journey to meet the rat who became an eagle, and in setting off towards the mountain of liberation to be in the company of an evolved soul, they unknowingly set upon their own journey of evolution.

Little did the rat know that in his quest to free himself, he had unwittingly freed a thousand others.

I had not slept that night. The rat had a purpose that could never be fulfilled by living a rat's life. In saving his life, he was letting go of his purpose. And in fulfilling his purpose, he was putting his life at stake. It was only now in retrospect that I understand that purpose is bigger than life. Without a purpose to follow, there is no life, then that's a rat's life. Life will throw challenges at you, irrespective. Your life will be at stake irrespective. In the end, either your purpose will consume you or your compromise will consume you. There are no guarantees of comfort on either side of the equation. But when you have a fulfilled purpose, the arm and leg that you lost is nothing compared to the inner joy and strength you gained in getting there.

Every story of greatness that I had heard about was similar to the story of the rat who wanted to break free. In real life, one does not pay the price of physical deformation but one sure is challenged to let go of his home, live alone in a strange city away from his family, shell out money that puts his future at stake, work at lengths that brings pain to his body and upsets his emotional state. There are instances of people who got tricked in the name of help by the alligator who didn't take them across. And some had to give more than that was agreed in the start. Some were lucky enough to make it to the mountain of liberation with no trouble at all. But every person who did make it to the top of the mountain had to go through every step of personal challenges that transformed them. In reaching one's purpose, one regained their spiritual self.

Only the naïve would believe that the challenges were only on the mountain. Only the naïve would believe that a rat's life was a life of safety.

I had held on to my rat life so firmly that I had never dared to venture to the mountain of liberation. Sure there are challenges and sure there are risks, but the rat would lose its tail on a petty rat fight and the threat of predators was there on any side of the river. In fearing to embrace the challenge and in fearing to take the risk, I had sentenced myself to the rat life forever. I never dared to be an author because then I would lose the steady income from my job. But because I did not dare to become an author, was there a guarantee that I would not lose my job?

I wanted to be greater than I was. But how could I do that without becoming greater than I am? How could I move beyond the lion?

I looked into the lion's eyes, like Acrodorf had looked in mine. And as much as this may sound crazy, I could see his soul. I shivered. The lion had a soul? If he had a soul then he must also have a purpose. What was his purpose? He is here in The Game. Is he serving a term for his redemption too like the Cannibals? What binds him in The Game? If I am being tested, then so is he. I froze as the realization dawned on me. My heart threatened to explode through my chest, as the answer dawned upon my soul; the only way to communicate with the lion was to be in the same space with the it, soul to soul. I shivered and my teeth chattered.

I stared intensely into the lion's eyes. And surprisingly, he straightened up and gazed into mine. I connected the intent of my soul onto his. I wanted to go within and understand him. Like Acrodorf had held me in the space of his soul, why could I not share my space with the lion? I held my gaze locked in the lion's eyes and expanded my awareness and my energy and brought the lion into my space. The lion flinched, confused with the intrusion. I could see the lion closer than it actually was. I could also see myself standing a few meters away from him. In connecting with the lion I could feel his every intention as though I was the lion.

"Why isn't she moving?" I could hear the lion mutter impatiently.

"It's all about the food. I have waited for so long for one meal and here she is and she makes me wait. She teases me. Why doesn't she get it? There is no other way?" The lion growled and roared.

"I am hungry," I felt it grunt and I felt a pang of hunger run through its stomach.

"And then what about the next meal?" I questioned the lion, keeping our eyes locked. The invasion of it's space made the lion sit up.

"You will rip me apart and I won't even make a complete meal. Then what? How long must your next wait be? Am I your game? Is this even *your* game? A game you can't play at will!!! A game you must wait for? Who is the game? You or me?" I questioned. The Lion stood up staring at me, Niki Sanders.

"But if I don't eat, then I will starve," I heard him reason.

"If you don't eat, then there will be no game. If there is no game, then you are free," I reasoned back.

"What???" The lion's eyes narrowed in confusion.

I stood silent, allowing him to digest my words.

"Yes," the lion pranced up!

"Yes," it roared out loud for the forest to hear.

"You are right!" It purred softly this time.

"I have spent hundreds of years in The Game waiting for my meal to arrive. I came here with a few others that had been left to die on planet Earth. Life became tough on planet Earth and so we left. But we had to go through The Game because we were illegal immigrants."

"Until now I thought life on The Game was better than the life on planet Earth. At least we had food. At least we were not hunted for reasons other than hunger. But in being here in The Game, it never occurred to me that I had become it."

"I left planet Earth because I didn't want to be a lion anymore. I wanted to be a free spirit. I had lived a lion's life long enough to not want to live it anymore. I wanted to roam the universe to find another creative purpose. But The Game kept me in it, because I just could not stop being a lion. The Game kept me in because I could not let go of my lion ways. How can I stop being a lion if in the same breath I behave like one?"

"I don't want to be in The Game. I want to be free. This is not why I had left planet Earth, to live a lion's life in the ever-expanding universe all over again. I want to be free." The saber-toothed lion roared with all its might, the roar of freedom.

I was delighted. I looked at Thelda and her expression made me smile. Her mouth was open and her eyes were wide. I didn't care whether that spelt worry or wonder. I opened my arms and lifted my foot forward towards freedom.

The lion looked at me intensely and roared so loud my hair was pushed back with his breath. He crouched back and leapt at me. I did not flinch. I took another step. The lion soared above my head and ran majestically towards the edge of the cliff. I ran with freedom towards the castle. Panting, I reached the step of the beautiful white marble castle with the golden steeple. I turned around just in time to catch the lion leap off the cliff, to his liberation.

The door opened and an excited Thelda and Black and White walked out. Thelda did not wait to climb down the stairs. She threw herself at me. We both rolled on the ground as the two shadows stood witness to the overjoyed madness of the witch and her ardent follower.

"You made it kiddo! And how!!!" She squawked as she sat on my stomach.

"You should have made sure I carried the drum," I complained and Thelda pinched my face till I kicked my legs in the air.

I stood up with Thelda holding me by the waist.

"Congratulations!" Black stepped down from the castle steps with

White following suit. The shadow twins were a magical sight. A black void in the middle of a living illuminated world.

"You have passed The Game!" White said to us and though I could see nothing of him except darkness, his body language spelt delight.

"You didn't just pass The Game, you freed your opponents as you freed yourself," he continued and Thelda clapped her hands together.

"Though I must add that the Cannibals added a lot of drama on Level one. In serving their redemption, they liberated others of their obsolete fears." Black shook his head.

"Now we will have to find new players!" White turned to him.

"And these had potential when I first saw them." Black motioned towards Thelda and me. "But they turned out to be too clever. I can see what Bren sees in them and why he risked taking the trespasser." Black was conversing with White about us.

"And the saber-toothed lion, Couga, has been with us for over six hundred years. Never once had the lion questioned his purpose or his evolution." White spoke about Couga, the lion with a soul.

"It's a great joy to see the predator free himself of being a game for his prey. The prey binds the predator to kill, as much as the predator binds the prey to die. But it will be tough to replace Couga." Black added.

"Er, excuse me," Thelda interjected. She was a Sorceress and she didn't generally like to be left out of any conversation.

"What would happen if we did not make it past the levels?" She asked Black and White. I wanted to know that too. Knowing what consequence we overcame would add more thrill to our victory.

"Then, you would be The Game for the next entrant." Black said hesitatingly.

This was big, man. If we didn't make it past the levels, then like the Cannibals and the lion we could be the game for the next trespassers, challenging them to be bigger than themselves and set us free. A chill ran down my body.

When any one participant grows towards greatness or evolves spiritually, he not only frees himself from the clutches of misery, but also frees many others from theirs. What we do and who we are impacts others, it impacts what they do and who they become. And all that puts the responsibility of the state of the world on our daily decisions and actions.

If we had failed The Game, if we would have become prey to the predators, then by default we would become predators for others. When I felt prey to the angst of my seniors, I made Danny the victim of my unexpressed resentment at work. When I fell prey to Danny's need to always control my life, I made my work the victim of my frustration. We all take over the guise of what we lose to. When you lose to confusion, you become the confusion for others. When you lose to betrayal, you become the betrayal for others, when you lose to sorrow and grief, you become the sorrow and grief for others. Winning is not in making another lose, winning is in liberating yourself and another from the need to win or lose.

"Can I keep the drum?" Thelda asked Black and White breaking my thoughts.

"Can I keep the jewels?" I added in my request along with hers.

"They are yours to keep," White said and we both smiled joyfully. "Let's get going," Black said, "Bren and Acrodorf will be delighted to see you."

A black void appeared in place of the castle door and Black and White darted towards it, creating a long shadow in their trail and they disappeared. Thelda dragged the drum up on the stairs, making annoying drumming sounds. We cast one last look over the breathtaking scenery below, a world that was lit up in the light of a starry blue sky and then rushed into the dark slithering tunnel.

The Planet of Truth

The slithering tunnel spat us out on the light path that had brought us into The Game. The black wall blocking the rest of the universe from our sight had dissolved. Black and White had already taken position at the same place on the path that we had first seen them. I popped out before Thelda who came out rolling down the path with her drum clanking and vibrating behind her.

"She looks younger, doesn't she?" Black said to White pointing towards Thelda. My observation had been correct. She *was* looking younger. They made no comment about my appearance so I guessed it was only her.

"We are handing you back your lovely ladies," White said to Bren. "They did well and made it through The Game."

"I will tell you all about it," Thelda chuckled at a dumbfounded Bren whose expression stated that he needed an urgent explanation about the drum.

"Ladies, immortal, indestructible spirits of the universe," White said clapping his hands, bringing Thelda's enthusiasm to order.

"Niki Sanders and Thelda, beings of planet Earth, you have been granted permission to travel the universe in the custody and guidance of Bren and Acrodorf, beings of Zedius, the Perfect World." Black announced, taking over from White.

"You have successfully passed The Game which is designed to test whether you are ready for the ways of universe. The rules of mortality that you have played by so far, have no place in the universe. The universe is inhabited and traveled into with awareness of your spiritual nature, which was necessary to test," Black continued.

"The Game brings you back the awareness of your power, your immortality and your creative ability. For, if that is lacking, then you will latch onto the freedom and power of others like parasites do and suck the life force out of them. We keep the universe safe and we keep the universe fair. You have been granted permission to taste your share of freedom. And you may roam free in the universe. Go!" Black said.

"Er, one thing!" I turned to Black.

"Why aren't you made of flesh or bones or for that any matter at all? Why are you this darkness?" I questioned, "What are you?"

I saw Acrodorf smile in the distance and I saw Bren frown at Thelda. With the look of it, he would trade Thelda with me for the hideously large drum that she was carrying.

Black and White turned to each other first before they turned to me.

"We are the Game Bearers. We absorb resistance and evil intent from beings that trespass. That's why the void." Black explained first.

"And because we are made of nothing, you have nothing to fight with even if you chose to do so," White chuckled.

"Wow!" I exclaimed. Though it looked like I was the player in The Game, there were so many people who had helped me through, people I liked and also people that I disliked. I liked Thelda and Acrodorf and their essence had helped me through. I was grateful to them. Though I was growing to dislike Danny, but he had helped me through too. I was grateful to him. His presence in my life was not a waste of time after all. His presence in my life had helped me grow; it had helped save my life. No one is a waste and no one deserves to be treated like one. I had begun to believe that I had wasted two years of my life with Danny and there could be no greater lie than that. I had learnt that now. Danny had come into my life and touched it in a way that no other person could. His goodness had stayed with me and I needed to acknowledge his contribution in the person I had become today.

"We should be on the way now," Bren stepped in lest I take the conversation in some other direction with my questions.

"Yes, we should be," Thelda dragged her drum along.

I walked towards Acrodorf and his eyes searched my soul, just as I had searched the lion, Couga's soul. I knew he could see, I knew he was proud. Acrodorf stretched out his hand. I turned around and said, "Thank you," to Black and White.

The path behind us was thinning out and the bright radiating planet, The Game was dimming. The path dissolved and so did Black and White. With a sudden tug I was pulled into Acrodorf's space, formless. He held me in his space like he had the entire journey here.

The Channel was a weird creation. Without warning it would snap me into my body and without warning it would snap me out of it.

"So where do I start?" Thelda asked Bren excitedly, eager to share the experience we'd just had. I chuckled at Bren's solemn silence.

"We will break our journey soon," Bren said, the moment Thelda paused in her narration of what happened with the Cannibals.

"We have a meeting with other beings of Zedius at the Planet of Truth. A lot of us had left to bring back other beings to help us save Zedius, and we are meeting here to see which one will get there to assist us," Acrodorf explained.

"What???" Thelda complained. "You mean you bring me this far and tell me that I may not make it to Zedius?" She glared at Bren, accusing him of having cheated her with the trade-off.

"No, that's not what he means," Bren defended Acrodorf.

"We will be meeting other beings of Zedius here. We all had departed to bring back help and we have to be absolutely sure of the being's ability to help us. When help is offered by the wrong hands, disaster follows. You both will be left on the Planet of Truth and that will unfold for us who will be the one to help us on Zedius," Bren continued to explain.

"So if I am not the one.....?" Thelda scowled. She did not like competition or comparisons.

"Then you will be invited to Zedius nevertheless and you will experience life there. You will also get the powers that you were promised, it's only that you will not be assisting in helping us save Zedius," Bren tried to pacify her.

Thelda was not happy with this new turn of events. However, my emotion about this was quite neutral. I had no aspiration to be the savior of Zedius and I was more than happy to sight-see there and come back with the powers to change my life back on planet Earth.

I agreed with Bren that it is important to know that the person who is helping you or assisting you does have the ability to make things better. Ever so often I have tried to help others because I couldn't see them suffer. But, because I myself had no experience or ability to set things right, I only added to the confusion. It's an everyday life scenario on Earth, where we jump into other people's lives and business with a good heart to help, only to see our intention back fire on us.

"What is the Planet of Truth?" I was curious to know about this planet.

Acrodorf was happy that I had diverted the topic. Thelda's fluster was growing dense. How could she be denied of her purpose to heal and help others? She was nothing without her purpose.

"The Planet of Truth is a great experience. You discover the ultimate truth about your life and your purpose." Acrodorf said, and I could feel Thelda's energy shift from agitation to interest.

"Wow. I would love that," I exclaimed.

"If your paths cross, you may encounter other beings from across the universe, who have been invited by our other fellow friends from Zedius," Acrodorf matched my excitement.

"That would be really nice. To meet some more beings from other planets..."

"Or even other universes!" Bren added. I was speechless. And for a change, Thelda was speechless too.

"What planet is that?" Thelda asked, taking my attention towards a large green planet that had suddenly emerged in front of us.

"That is the Planet of Truth. You have a sharp awareness," Bren complimented Thelda, who had thankfully grown out of her foul mood.

"And we will break our journey there now," Acrodorf said.

No sooner than Acrodorf had made his intent about stopping at the Planet of Truth, we started to go closer and closer to the seemingly serene planet and the vision of the universe began to narrow.

The Planet of Truth was bright green. I could feel a release from Acrodorf's space as we grew closer and closer to it. We were so close to the planet that I could feel it pulling us towards it. Like a coin when tossed in the air comes flipping down, I felt the somersault as we all landed with a thud on the moist green ground of the Planet of Truth.

The minute we touched the ground we snapped into our forms. Thelda was struggling out of Bren's arms with her drum and Bren looked relieved to let her go. I could feel Acrodorf's hands grip my waist and he held me forward, so that I could free his space. I sheepishly stepped forward.

I looked at the scenic view around and the only word that would fit to describe it was paradise. There was lush greenery everywhere. I could hear the musical sound of a waterfall somewhere. Overhead were cotton-white low-lying clouds that were drifting away in different directions. In the distance, adorning the horizon, was a glossy green mountain range. The sun shone lazily above, with just the right amount of warmth.

"Feels like home," Thelda opened her arms and spun around.

Thelda quickly hopped up and sat on her drum. Her drum was a multi-purpose instrument. It made music, served her comfort and not to mention it also kept man-eating lions at bay.

"We are at the meeting point," Acrodorf said. "That mountain in the distance is called the Great Realization."

"But you will find your way around," Bren continued, "or best, the way will find you." He chuckled, suppressing his laughter. I frowned because I really didn't get the joke.

"We leave you here and we will meet you in time," Bren said hastily and he opened up his wings and flapped them with a thunderous sound. Acrodorf followed suit and the two majestic creatures stretched their wings behind them and then shot into the sky above like bullets and disappeared behind the clouds.

I looked above and gasped. Normally, I would have been mortified with the thought of adventuring on a planet alone, but with Thelda next to me, I was safe from my imaginary troubles.

I stared at Thelda. She looked really comfortable on the drum, dangling her legs and staring at the sky. I sat down on the grass. It was so green and so lush that it was inviting. I ran my hands over it and to my astonishment, the grass grasped my hand.

"Yikes!" I shrieked and stood up.

Thelda came down with a thud.

"What in the name of Satan happened?" She asked inspecting the ground I sat upon.

Before I could explain what had happened, the blades of grass grew around my foot and webbed my feet into a heart-shaped knot.

"Look" I gasped, not daring to move my feet lest the grass would sting me or bite me or rip my foot off.

Thelda stared at my feet and then at hers. The same web had formed on her feet. And then it unraveled. I tugged at my foot and stepped forward and to my surprise the grass parted before I set foot on it. It could sense my intention and got out of the way of my feet before I could trample on it. The same thing happened with Thelda, who broke out into a wild dance playing with the grass.

"Isn't this amazing!" She squealed. The witch was crazy. It was a crazy sight to see Thelda dancing on the grass and the grass was dancing its way out of her step. The grass was as alive and as aware as her. It was as though the grass was as participating in intentional action as she was.

"Stop, Thelda," I shouted at her. Sometimes the Sorceress could get out of control with her enthusiasm. "Don't you get it? This is not just grass, it is as alive and as aware as we are!"

"Look, Thelda," I said, pointing towards the pathway that the grass had parted to form. "It's guiding us forward."

"Yes it is. The path is leading us," Thelda beamed.

Thelda picked up her drum and we began to move forward on the freshly formed path.

"I wonder if we are supposed to get to the Mountain of Realization," I muttered.

"I wonder who will be selected to help assist at Zedius," Thelda muttered.

"Holy cow!" She yelped and I could see why. In front of us, the path had parted in a fork leading into two different directions.

"Which way?" I asked Thelda for an answer.

"Always the right way," she giggled and we both turned to the fork on the right. Though we both turned to the right, the grass under my foot quickly parted towards the left, threatening to throw me off balance. I tried to step right and the grass parted towards the left. This was crazy. Thelda was already walking a few steps ahead to the right and I stood there struggling with my foothold.

"What the...." I stopped short because the blades of grass in front of me shot up half a meter and bent towards the left.

"The path is forcing me to go to the left," I gulped.

Thelda was walking on, oblivious to my absence.

"Thelda, wait!" I shouted at her. Thelda turned around and began to giggle at the sight she saw. Some blades of grass had overpowered me.

"Come back this way. Come with me," I stood there with the grass obstructing my way. I tried to push the grass away with my foot and was shocked that it pushed me back.

"But I always go right," Thelda protested. "And besides, the grass is quite supportive of my direction," she reasoned, "maybe it's your path to go left and mine to go right."

This is exactly the idea that I was trying to persuade her away from.

"But come this way. We will go together. We will be together. It will be fun, Thelda," I was not giving up. I stood there obstinately and the grass thickened between Thelda and me in protest. The message was loud and clear; Thelda and my paths did not lead in the same direction.

"Why must you always have this compulsive need to cling onto my energy? Why do you have this need to constantly drag people into *your* world? Why do you expect me to abandon the path that awaits me and join yours; one that I have no intention to follow? Why can't you be happy with your way and let me be happy with mine?" Thelda scolded me from the distance. The grass swayed in amusement, signaling its agreement.

"We started our journey together and we must part ways temporarily. We will meet again at the end of the journey like always. And when we do we will share what we experienced. My growth lies this way and yours that way. When we meet towards the end in sharing our experiences, we both will doubly grow. Grow up Niki Sanders!!" Thelda tapped her head, banged her drum and then started off again leaving me alone to be led to my truth.

The truth in Thelda's words shook me up. I half-heartedly turned left and the grass shot back to where it was and rolled out a long neat path ahead. This was no ordinary planet. Every blade of grass had a purpose, to lead me to mine.

I walked a few steps ahead with Thelda's words reeling in my head. She was right. I not only wanted my way, I wanted others to live my way too. That was the beginning of the end of my relationship with Danny. I wanted him to live my way and he wanted me to live his. When I wanted to stay home over the weekend, he wanted me to accompany him to go drinking and partying with his friends. And we fought. So I would stay home and sulk and he would go out and sulk and get drunk. And when he returned home, we resumed the fight. Sometimes, I dragged Danny into my world and he would stay home and sulk. And we would fight again. And sometimes, he dragged me into his world and I would sit with his friends and sulk and we would fight again.

We both wanted to be together. We both loved each other. But what we forgot was that we were two different people. I liked Thelda and I wanted to be with her. But Thelda and I were two different people. How could she continue to be a Sorceress or how could she grow into an even more powerful Sorceress if I always dragged her in my world and my path? For her to grow and explore her own greatness, she had to follow her path and her purpose. And if I had any respect for Thelda, I had to grant her that. We were going to meet at the end of the journey anyway.

Danny and I had never granted each other the space to be and explore our own purpose and greatness. If he would have let me be at home and write over the weekend and if I had let him go out with his friends, then he would come back home with the latest about his world and I could read him the pages I wrote. When we allow each other the space, we appreciate one another more easily. When we grant people the freedom to be themselves, then our interest in them does not diminish, for the person is always growing and renewing. I had really made a mess out of my relationship with Danny.

I turned around and looked towards Thelda. She had walked far towards a thicket of trees. A stream came springing up behind her. A whole gush of water started flowing out from the right. Thelda stepped into the thicket and turned around. A stream had formed between her and me and the water was dancing towards her. I saw Thelda bend over and drink some water and sprinkle it around in delight. She didn't even as much as look in my direction. She was totally involved in her world. I smiled.

The stream was making a divide between Thelda and I, lest for some reason I decided to fight the grass and cross over to her side. I kept looking in her direction, so touched by her carefree abandon. Thelda was special.

The thicket of trees parted from the centre, exposing a dark sky with a full moon on the other side. I gasped. It was broad sunlight here and Thelda stepped into a totally different world and the trees shut behind her as she did.

Where was Thelda being led? Maybe to the truth about her and her life's purpose. I wondered what lay ahead for me.

I walked on with peace. I had made peace with the fact that my path was different and just because Thelda and I were on different paths didn't mean anyone's was less important.

Little shrubs of daisies sprang up on the side, as though to cheer me up and make amends for the earlier aggression. They danced and even shed some petals now and then in my way as I walked on. I loved flowers and more and more colorful ones sprang up on the sides of the path. I loved this. This was so beautiful. Butterflies with magical colors fluttered around my hair. The birds flew along singing. This was so beautiful. I looked up at the sky and I was startled to see a few clouds drifting so low, they were almost overhead. I stretched out my hand and one cloud swooped down and its mist covered me. I was walking in the cloud. I loved it. This was so beautiful. I stopped and couldn't believe my luck. Everything that I found beautiful had surrounded me. I didn't have to go to it, it came to me. This was a wonderful planet.

Outer space had earth-like prototypes for life. This was in no way even similar to the unfriendly planets that most of our science fiction movies showed. I guess the fact that I was here on this planet, meant that it supported life similar to that on planet Earth. I was happy with the familiarity of home, even though I was light years away from it.

I looked into the distance through the mist at the mountain, The Great Realization. It appeared to be getting closer. This was a strange land. Nothing was inert here. Even the gigantic mountain could move, towards its purpose, which er, seemed to be me.

It was breathtaking. I was at the foothills of the Mountain of Realization. It was completely covered with a growth of dense trees. I could see nothing but green on it. I stepped onto the mossy ground of the mountain and it began to rumble. With a creaking sound, the mountain began to part at the centre. I saw the crack first. I saw the ground and the trees part. I could see a few startled birds confused on which side of the partition to fly.

The divide was a few meters apart. There was a world inside the mountain. It was as though the mountain was the gateway to this world. I tried to crane my neck to see what lay ahead of me and the ground behind me began to rise and fold. I felt a rise beneath my feet. I spun around and to my horror, I saw the entire field behind me was folding in over me. I had only one option; to run into the opening. I ran forward, but the rising ground below my feet threw me off balance and I staggered through the opening and fell onto the grass on the other side. With a screeching sound, the divide closed shut behind me.

I got up and saw the same mountain ahead of me again. It was identical to the one that I had stepped off.

I caught my breath. There was the same bubbly stream that had formed between Thelda and me. It was flowing parallel from where I stood. Its water was dancing with life. Every few seconds it squirted towards me a fountain that sprayed the water around and then subsided.
There were strange trees everywhere. I saw a cluster of willows

on the side, but its drooping branches seemed at work. They were lifting things off the ground. Some of them were touching the clouds and withdrawing as they did. They seemed to be playing, not just hanging there.

"Hey!" I heard a voice from behind me. I turned around and a beautiful young woman was walking towards me. She was too beautiful to be human. Her hair was thick like solid bars. It was neatly combed back. Her forehead was brighter and the eyebrow was one thick strand of hair that ended in a lose curve. Her lips were full and her teeth were thin and sharp and sparkling white. Her body was a large frame and very sensuous. She wore a robe that clung to her skin and she walked towards me.

"You must have come for Zedius too," she smiled.

"Y,,Yes," I smiled back. It's good that Acrodorf had mentioned that I would meet other beings too, or else I would be freaking out right now.

She was such a pretty sight, almost mesmerizing. Her eyes had a kindness that could hypnotize any evil person and transform him into a saint.

"I'm Jini," she said.

"I'm Niki," I tried being friendly.

"So what do you bring to Zedius?" she queried, trying to evaluate her competition.

"I, er, don't really know. I was a last minute entry and so I really don't know," I know it all sounded stupid, but I really didn't know what ability exactly had brought me so far.

"Then that makes you extremely dangerous," Jini bit her lip.

Well, I was trying to sound harmless by being dumb and stupid, but in doing that I had made myself sound dangerous. When people play dumb and people play small, I guess that by itself makes them dangerous for their own purpose and in the purpose of others.

"No, no. I'm quite harmless," I defended.

"How can you be? How do you even know the extent of your ignorance, if you are ignorant to begin with? How can you even know the magnitude of the evil within you, if you don't even know that you are?" She said, with her eyes flickering with different colors as she spoke.

I was upset. I made myself look small, because I didn't want to be perceived as a threat. And now that I was perceived as actually small, I was upset. Damn it!!! When would I ever stop this manic self-sabotage drive?

"What do you bring to Zedius?" I asked her, trying to take the negative attention off me.

To answer my question, Jini stretched her hand forward to shake mine and the instant that my hand touched hers, I felt an electric shock that threw me twenty feet off and I fell towards a sleeping willow. The branches caught me as I flung towards them and held on to me to recover from my shock. The branches were clutching me from head to foot, neutralizing the current from my body. Once I caught my breath, they rocked me gently to calm me.

Jini walked closer and the branches swooped me upwards out of her reach. I was grateful that the tree was a participant and not an inert audience. Jini had perceived me as a threat to her purpose to get to Zedius and if it were not for the willow, she would have burnt me to ashes.

"I bring deception," she snickered. "I first reduce and then I destroy. I will love you for that would only make killing you easier. I will make you love me so that you help me in killing you."

"Why... Why would you do that?" I was shocked. More than shocked, I was disturbed as to why any being of Zedius would ever want to bring Jini there. She was evil. Her looks totally covered up for it, but she was pure evil.

"There is only one purpose for all evil. There is only one purpose for destruction," she said, as she grew bigger in size in an attempt to reach me, "to persist. And how can evil persist when goodness survives!" She scoffed and stretched her hand towards me.

The branch very cleverly swooped me out of her way. One branch quickly wrapped itself around her arm and held her there, while Jini groaned and cursed. I was out of her reach.

"But why would anyone bring you here? Zedius needs a perspective, it needs assistance, it does not need evil," I questioned as to why any rational being of Zedius would invite trouble.

"Deception my love. When goodness is built on ignorance of evil, it is easy to deceive." She grinned despite the fact that she was over-powered by the willow.

I felt a heave and I was in full flight as the branches heaved me forward and I was caught mid-air by the branches of another willow a few meters away. They caught me gently and put me on the ground. I staggered and stepped onto the ground and saw that the willow had totally obscured Jini out of view.

I hastily walked away from Jini. I think deception hurts more than direct attack. When someone attacks you directly, at least you can prepare for it. But when people stab you in the back, you stand no chance even at self-defense. I was happy that the trees were aware and participating. I was happy that the trees had intervened and saved me. Having aware and active people in your vicinity is very important for your own well-being. Evil persists not because it kills goodness. Evil persists because goodness remains unaware and inactive.

"Hey!" I heard two delighted voices from either side. I turned to my right first and from the large trees in the distance was walking a very lean young man-like, er, humanoid.

Thelda was right. The planets in general seemed to have similar forms like us, flowers, birds, grass, trees, but these were exceptionally beautiful. The humanoid seemed to be the most preferred prototype on other planets. I wondered if planet Earth had the original creation of the humanoid prototype or did we get inspired from other planets. I feel the human body is the greatest of all creations. It is the perfect vehicle of the spirit, to create, to express and to experience pleasure.

The creature, er, man came closer. He was breathtakingly gorgeous. The branches of the willows extended towards him and touched and caressed his arms and hair and he giggled and swiped them away. I saw that with his every step, the grass was also extending out to his feet and he was struggling to keep it away without uprooting it.

"Hey!" He smiled sheepishly.

The alien-man was so beautiful that I could marry him instantly and be his slave forever. His hair was dark brown that shone golden in the sunlight. His face was sturdy that broke into an array of expressions. His eyes were blackish grey and so deep that like the mountain, the Great Realization, they seemed to be a gateway, into another world, of love and passion maybe.

He wore a long brown robe like Acrodorf had, but his was not tied around his neck. The robe parted from his neck down making a V until his navel and baring his muscular chest as it did.

"I am Ray," he said, stretching out his hand.

I hesitated. My experience with Jini had taught me caution. I stammered, not sure if I should shake his hand. Jini was so beautiful too and she held deception. I guess if all the trouble mongers from the universe were rounded up here, then it was best I stayed away from Ray. Sensing my discomfort, he stepped forward and placed his hand on my shoulder.

I could feel an imaginary electric current flow through my body and I swear I could hear Jini laugh through the branches behind me. But Ray's hand was warm and I immediately felt a calm flow through my body.

"Are you alright?" Ray asked, sucking me deeper into the depths of that other world that his eyes held.

"Yes," I mumbled. I felt an intense drawing to Ray. It was an over powering attraction that was making me lose control. I averted my eyes from his.

"What do you bring to Zedius?" I asked, deliberately looking away from him. I looked towards the trees, wondering if any other beings were here.

Ray started to laugh and his hair ruffled up as he did. The expression on his face was so delightful that I could stare at him forever.

"I bring control," he said, "I draw other beings into my space and then I control them," he winked.

I immediately understood what I felt. I understood the attraction and the drawing and the compulsive impulse to be owned by him. He was doing that too me. I closed my eyes and took a deep breath.

"Don't do that," Ray nudged me, "don't break my control."

I opened my eyes. Ray stood ahead of me with his arms folded, frowning at me.

"Awareness is the enemy of external control. When you know it, it loses its hold on you." He said. "You are mean!" He frowned first and then smiled.

"What do you bring to Zedius?" Ray asked, putting his attention towards the stream. "That is the mountain, The Great Realization. We are supposed to head there," he continued without waiting for my answer and then paused. He brought his gaze back to mine.

"I..I... have the ability to make things go wrong," I muttered out loud quite confident of my shortcoming. Surprisingly I was not ashamed of it, and what was even more surprising was that I didn't feel small about it. Everyone has shortcomings. These were people from other planets from across the universe. Who knows, some of them were even superior to me, but they all had shortcomings. Acrodorf and Bren had shortcomings else they would not have traveled two light years to planet Earth seeking help. So why was I living in shame and despise of my own self because I was not perfect? Why was I pulling myself back from any share of goodness and greatness, because I was not perfect or good enough? I had goodness and greatness in me, and that like my shortcomings can never be an absolute. But, because I was so ashamed of my imperfections, I had never dared to step up and be a part of any greatness.

"That is an amazing ability!!" he expressed his delight animatedly.

"How do you do that? Can you teach me?" Ray said and his expression was dead serious.

"Hey!" A voice yelled from the back and I was thankful for the interjection. How could I possibly teach Ray how to make things go wrong?

I turned around and a very short man-like alien was walking rather hurriedly towards us. He was barely three feet tall.

"Did you hear that the mountain, The Great Realization, will be moving away shortly," he said, puffing out of breath.

"I'm Ona," he spoke in spurts.

"I'm Ray and this is Niki," Ray introduced us both.

I looked towards the mountain and it looked quite still to me, though I could believe Ona that it could move away.

Ona had a dark face, almost black. He looked a little repulsive on first sight and then once acceptance set in, you could communicate with him.

Two more very fancy creatures came in behind him. One was exactly like him, but his skin was a bright yellow. The other's skin was totally green. They all wore black robes and I was the only odd one out in blue jeans and a green sweater.

The green fellow spoke hastily, "We should be off now. Across the stream!"

"How do you know?" I jumped in their conversation. Who knows what these little creatures were here for? Maybe they brought distraction? Maybe they brought fraud? Who knows what else?

"Because we have been here before!" they all spoke together and lined up straight to look at me directly, the person that had dared to question their knowing.

"The water is deep and too fast to swim through," the yellow man spoke so fast, I had to literally open my eyes wide to lip-read him. He had not bothered for any introduction and continued, "The only way through to the other side is to walk on it!"

With that, the black weirdo turned around, lifted his robe above his ankle, exposing a set of black pixie-like feet and stepped onto the flowing water and began to walk on it.

The black creature turned around and looked at us, shrugging at his non-comprehension on why we were not following them.

The yellow creature stepped onto the water and began to walk on it. The water sprang up to him every now and then, mischievously spraying water on him and the creature's laughter echoed.

Ray lifted his robe and stepped on the water. He spread his hands and ran across onto the other side. The last green creature also ran across the water. All of them were headed towards the mountain, The Great Realization. No one even turned around to check if I needed help with the walking on water bit. It was in their interest that I stayed behind. One less person to compete with, I guess.

I folded my jeans and I stepped onto the water and to my dismay, my foot sank in on the pebbles below and the water covered my foot. I was puzzled. I looked ahead and the creatures ahead of me were fast disappearing. I held my foot steady in the water and put my next foot on it. It was liquid. It was not solid. My second foot also went through the water and landed on the stones below. Just with two steps into it, I was knee-deep in the water. I was exasperated by the sudden turn of events. The yellow creature was right. The stream was deep and it was too fast. I was swaying with its force. I could no longer keep my balance and I stepped back.

I looked behind, searching for Jini. She was struggling in the willow. To my relief, I saw half a dozen creatures clad in long robes running towards the stream. I could sense their hurry. They all ran over the stream to the other side without any consideration of falling in the water. They all walked on water. They all were doing it. What was wrong with me?

I retreated a few steps and hesitatingly ran onto the stream and fell into it with a splash. The force of the stream was so strong that I lost my foothold and began to be swept away. A tuft of grass stretched out and I grabbed it in time to be pulled out of the aggressive currents.

I coughed the water out of my lungs and sat up. Why was this stream not co-operating? Why was I not getting it?

The mountain, The Great Realization, began to rumble. I could sense what that rumble meant, it would move away. I could sense a racket break loose behind me. I could hear a raging Jini bellow. Curious, I turned around and saw smoke emerge from the branches. The branches parted and a steaming Jini fell on the ground. Now this was a nightmare. I was stuck between a non-cooperating stream, a mountain that was about to move and an evil woman who would electrocute me before she ran across the stream.

I shrunk behind, as Jini came running towards me. She would destroy me with one touch. I froze. I could see the evil in her eyes. The beauty in her had vanished. I could see pure destruction ooze from every part of her body. She was only a few feet away from me and I closed my eyes. I felt a gush of wind blow past me. I opened my eyes, shocked to see Jini hurriedly running on the water towards the rumbling mountain. She didn't even as much as touch me. She was speedily shooting towards the mountain, her purpose.

I stood by the banks of the stream with my mouth open. I was not Jini's concern. As long as she had the time and energy, she had the time and energy to play with me and trouble me. But the minute the time ran out and her purpose of being there was endangered, she channelized her energy and moved towards it. Purpose is a powerful thing. It brings in us the focus and the energy that drives us towards it. And when that purpose begins to rumble and threatens to move away, it increases our urgency towards it. It took Jini across. What was I waiting for?

I took a deep breath and stepped on the water, and my feet hit the bottom!! Holy Cow! Damn it!!!!!!! Why wasn't I making it??? Could someone tell me what I was doing wrong?? I screamed in my head.

The ground had begun to shake now. And I knew that soon, the mountain would move.

A black cat pranced out of the trees and threw me off guard. I was startled to see that it had four bright green eyes arranged in a neat line on its face. It was a huge cat. It approached me cautiously. Four green eyes pierced my soul. It purred and shook its tail aggressively to match the rumble of the mountains.

"Do what I do!" It purred and my heart skipped a beat.

The cat looked at me intensely to see if I understood. I nodded. I was glued. I looked at its feet. The cat's tail slapped my face throwing me off balance. That stung.

"Do what I do!" It purred aggressively.

I nodded, crouching, and looked at its feet again. The tail hit my face again this time harder and my jaw hurt.

"Look into my eyes!" It shrieked.

The water in the stream was spurting with the rumble. I looked into the cat's eyes. Its gaze was fixed into mine and it bared its teeth and let out a cry. And then it slowly lifted its gaze from mine, fixed it on the mountain and with a leap galloped on the water.

I gasped.

When standing at the edge of the stream, every single being had kept the mountain in its gaze. The focus was the mountain and the challenge was the stream. The mountain was the purpose; the stream was the obstacle towards it. Every single being including Jini had kept their focus on the mountain and they had crossed the stream and gotten there. I had the mountain as my purpose, but the stream was my focus. How could I ever cross it?

Focus and attention are powerful forces. They create realities. The focus and attention must always be on the purpose, not on the obstacles. Ask anyone who has overcome any challenge and they will tell you that when they focused on the purpose, it gave them the energy and the wisdom to overcome the hurdles. If you make obstacles your focus, it will not only depress you in a pit of confusion and conflict, but you will also lose sight of your purpose.

I stood on the edge of the stream. It was spurting up like an angry volcano. I focused my eyes on the mountain, The Great Realization. I did not shift my gaze or energy or focus. I ran across the stream, and continued to run with all my might towards the foothills of the mountain that held the truth about my life and my purpose.

The ground behind me was rising. I could feel the water from the stream raining down on my head in very large drops that drenched me as they did. The entire stream was folding towards me and I could feel the ground ahead of me creak. I had to make it before the mountain parted away, leaving me behind to be drowned. I was leaping towards the crack and it was growing wider. The ground below me was rising at such speed, that I lost my balance and fell stumbling towards the crack. As I inched towards it, I saw a chasm so deep that I could lay buried there for eternity. I saw at the edge of the crack, a man-like creature with curly golden hair that was blown back by the gushing wind. He bent forward and stretched out his sturdy arm. I heaved myself in his direction and clasped his hand tight.

He held my hand firmly as the mountain uprooted from the ground and began to twist around like the cap of a bottle, and then it was afloat. I hung onto ther, er, man's hand desperately, trying to gain a foothold.

"Pull up!" He shouted above the rumble with the wind pulling the hair on his face and blinding his vision.

I gathered all my strength and shot up and tumbled in the embrace of a very mistily scented half-naked man-like alien.

He was still holding my hand tight and I clung onto him because the movement and the force of the spinning was so high that I was afraid that I would fall off if I let go. I stayed tightly clutched onto a strange creature who had helped me stay on my purpose.

The dust cloud around us settled. The spinning died away and then there was calm. I felt the man's grip on my hand loosen and then he let me loose. He stood up first, dusting his chest with his hands and ruffling his hair like a dog to get the mud out of it. He spat out some dirt and then looked at me and smiled. He was gorgeous. Some of the creatures here in space were really spectacular.

I sat up and dusted off the grayish mud from my clothes and hair, and didn't feel the spitting was quite necessary.

We were afloat on a mountain; The Mountain of Truth. It seemed, we were gliding through the sky, for there was a large expanse of clouds in all the directions.

"I'm Zi," he smiled.

"I'm Niki. Thank you for helping me through," I was eternally grateful to him for having helped me across. I was certain that I could not have made it on my own.

"No problem," he said, "I know how it feels to be left behind." I could hear a hint of pain in his words; a pain that I could understand as my own.

"Are you here for Zedius too?" I asked Zi. He wore a long rust color skirt across his waist, which was tied with a leather string. His hair was loose and the locks played around his ears. His face had a golden hue to it. His nose was in perfect proportion to his forehead and his jaws. He had a rugged form, chiseled to perfection, not to mention a misty, musky scent that emerged from him.

"Everyone is here for Zedius," Zi smiled. He was beautiful and he was genuine. Though I knew that everyone here had startling varieties of imperfections, I had this feeling that Zi was not evil. I must say I was extremely curious, but I felt no need to ask Zi what he brought to Zedius. He had helped me here and that was an ability that I was grateful for and that was all that mattered for the moment.

"The Great Realization, ha!" I said, looking around. The mountain looked pretty bare - scattered with a few assemblies of the magical willow trees.

Zi started to walk upwards towards the willows and I followed. He had long legs and I struggled to keep pace with him. I heard a waterfall ahead and the sound grew closer with every step. In a few minutes we were in paradise. There was a waterfall splashing down playfully from a gap between two boulders on the mountain above. It fell into a large pool that was surrounded by willow trees that were animatedly in conversation with each other. Their branches were swaying around carrying pebbles, building nests and even imitating each other.

Zi ran towards the pool, while I stood around gazing in wonder. Zi sat down by the pool and leaned inside it as though to drink some water. Instantly, the whole pool came alive with his reflections. His reflection began to spread up to the waterfall, till every drop of the water contained an image of Zi. I was stunned.

I walked towards the pool. Zi was bent over half inside and stayed still. I tiptoed beside him, came down on my knees and bent over the pool that had Zi's image in a million reflections. No sooner than I leaned forward, a wall of water came riding up and hit my face. I shrieked and fell back. The wall of water stayed still and emerged from it a very stern looking deadly man. If there was an opposite of Zi; this was him.

"What are you doing here?" the man bellowed. He wore a heavy metal ring around his bare neck. His ears were frightfully large and his frame even larger. His skin was dark brown and he looked more sweaty than wet. He wore a black cloth around his waist and that's all there was to him. His eyes were nasty, with his brows turned upwards. He looked mean and it was obvious that he did not like me.

"I... I" I stammered and didn't know what to say.

"Why are you here?" he barked and moved towards me threateningly. I instinctively paced backwards still facing him, incase he attacked me while I turned away.

"I ... I am with Zi," I tried to explain that I had come along with Zi and that I was not an intruder.

"Why are you with Zi?" He continued, striding towards me menacingly.

Why was I with Zi? I had no idea why I was with Zi? He had saved my life and helped me through on the mountain. I was just following him.

"I was following him," I answered in my defense, backing away as he approached me. "Why were you following him?" He raised his fist in frustration.

I really didn't know what he wanted from me or what he was getting at, but one thing was sure that all my answers were ticking him off. Why was I following Zi?

"He was walking ahead and so I was following him," I defended. My legs were shaking and my head was reeling with the backwards walk. I was afraid that I would tumble upon something and fall down and this gigantic creature would attack me.

"So why are you here?" The man looked furious. He was ticked off before and he was raging now.

I didn't understand his questions. I had already answered the question, but somehow all my answers led into further questions and now we were back to the same question 'why am I here'?

"Did you come here on the mountain, The Great Realization to follow Zi?" his eyes were blood red and I could see his fist tighten.

"No," I shuddered.

"Then why are you here?" He roared so loud it was deafening.

"I came here to find the truth about my life and my purpose," I trembled, and tears rolled down my eyes as I said that.

"So why were you following Zi?" The man stopped suddenly and his attention went behind my shoulder as I banged into someone. I spun around and an ageless angel- like man with silver flowing hair and a silver flowing beard dressed in a pearl white robe held me gently.

"I will take on from here," he said to the ungodly creature, who bowed and retreated immediately, running in long strides towards the pool where Zi still sat motionless with the water reflecting him back in every drop.

The old man placed his arm around me, nudging me to walk with him. I was numb and sore. That's the only emotion I felt. All my life I had wandered aimlessly, tagging along with people, tagging people along with me, or worse just going with the flow. I had a purpose somewhere, forgotten in my memory lane. I had become so busy in my daily wanderings that if you asked me 'why am I here?' I would be as clueless as I had been today.

I had come so far, so far for one objective - to find out the truth about my purpose and my life. And in a few moments of getting here I was drifting away without a question if my steps, my direction and my company were leading me towards my purpose or away from it. I feel, even back on Earth, that dangerous black man should be standing in our way chasing us back on track, when we drift away from our purpose. If only he had done that to me years ago, I would be living today the life of my dreams.

I looked at the old man. He was angelic. He had grey green eyes and silken flowing hair. His hair melted in his robe and reflected the light every now and then. How far had we walked? I wondered.

We had come to a large clearing and it felt as though we were fast moving towards the top of the mountain. I saw in the distance between a few trees, an orange clad creature with silver hair walk through.

"Thelda!" My heart brightened with joy. If this was only a few minutes ago, I would have been speeding past, chasing Thelda. But my heart sank. I was on my purpose. I had not yet encountered the truth about my purpose and my life. I had not yet reached my goal and this was not the moment to drift away, again. We carried on walking uphill.

The old man stopped and looked at the magical scenery below. He smiled at me warmly. I was too upset with my life but smiled anyway. I could see trees move, new spaces form and there were some clouds below that were scurrying around, it was a lively mountain.

I looked at the sky. It was ocean blue. Not a speck of cloud. It was crystal clear. One could leap up and dive into it.

"I am Saga, I built this mountain, The Great Realization, so that people can see the truth about themselves," he said, stroking his long silvery beard. His eyebrows half covered his eyes and he had to keep wiping them sideways to look at me.

He stretched out his closed hand towards me and said, "This is the channel of the truth," he opened his hand and held forward a round glass object.

"Zi found his channel in the water fall, this is yours," he said kindly.

I was intrigued. The stream held Zi's truth and a round glass held mine.

Saga found a little dry patch and sat down. He spread his robe on the dry grass and spread his hair evenly on his shoulders. He smiled at me and motioned me to sit down too. I sat down cross-legged in front of Saga. To tell you the truth, I was a little perturbed about finding out the truth about my purpose and my life. I had a strong inkling that I had been living a lie in both.

"Let me show you the truth," he said rolling the little piece of glass in his fingers.

Saga held the glass in both his hands about one foot above the dried patch of grass and stayed still. I knew what he was doing. I knew he was going to make some fire. I knew the trick. I smiled. It's nice to know in advance what you are being taught to know. But what I didn't know was that, how creating fire would bring about the truth of my life. Maybe the message would emerge from the flames. Zi's truth was contained in every drop of the water; maybe mine would be imprinted in every flame.

I looked at the sky above, the sun was shining warmly and soon, there would be an image of it on the ground below. I looked at

Saga, his attention was on the glass and then I saw a line of smoke from the dried grass tuft below. I smiled. The smoke spread and thickened and then I saw a spark and then a flicker and then a grand flame.

Saga looked up. The flame grew between us and he smiled. He took his hand and placed them above the flames and to my surprise sucked them all out. A black patch remained where his hand was. He rubbed his hands together to dissipate the heat, wiped the soot on the brow above his eyes and excitedly said, "Now it's your turn."

"My turn?" I was puzzled. I thought he would give me some deep insights with the flame as an analogy, but he was asking me to create some fire, all over again.

Saga handed me over the round piece of glass. It was a small magnifying glass. I looked up at the sky and the sun shone, pleased with what was happening below on the mountain, The Great Realization.

I rolled the glass piece in my hand like Saga had and I stayed still, holding it a foot above the dried grass. I kept my focus on the glass and to my dismay, a large shadow formed around me. Saga knocked my head with his index finger like how one knocks at the door.

"Ow!" I mumbled.

"Where is your focus?" He complained.

"Huh?" I didn't understand him. I looked up and saw that a colony of clouds had obscured the sun. Without the sun, no matter how much I tried, there would be no fire.

"The clouds have come in the way," I pointed up at the sky. "It's not my fault," I defended.

"I didn't say it's your fault. The truth is; it is your intention." Saga spoke kindly.

"You have been witness on my planet that your environment responds to you, to your intentions," he continued. I nodded my head in agreement. The entire planet was alive and aware and had participated in my purpose and in my intentions. I remembered how the grass had led me to my path and the weeping willows had saved my life from Jini.

"Just when it is your turn to take responsibility, you shadow the sun with the clouds!" He exclaimed disapprovingly at my deeds.

"That's not true. I didn't do it?" I protested quite unconvincingly. There was no other explanation for the clouds. They weren't there when I had started. The sky was crystal clear. And now the sun was hidden behind their dense formation.

"Show me what you create and I will show you what you are connected to." Saga glared into my eyes.

"You have the tool, the magnifying glass, but you have no fire. Even a fool will tell you that you have not established the connection with the sun. Show me what you create and I will show you what you are connected to." Saga said.

"Show me your day's worth and I will show you your life force behind it. Show me how you feel and I will show you your intention. Show me your relationships and I will show you your thoughts. Show me your path and I will show you your destination. The truth about your life and your purpose is evident in every moment. Show me yourself in this moment and I will show the truth about your life." Saga spoke straight to my soul, sending shivers down to my bones.

"Your purpose is to deny yours, so that you can be a part of other's purpose. You fear that if you discover your purpose and follow it, you will lose people you are familiar with, you will lose the environment you are comfortable bearing, you will lose your voice that keeps you believing that you are not good enough."

"The sun is there and so is the opportunity," he said, rolling the glass on his fingers. "But you bring in the clouds to shadow that which you are destined for; the fire of transformation. You tag along with Thelda, so you can hide in her shadow. You follow Zi so you can be involved in his purpose and forget about yours."

"The truth about your purpose and your life is that you feed on other's life force because you have stopped creating your own. The truth about your purpose and your life is that you have wronged yourself to the extent that wrong is all you can create. And that would have been ok, but to spread that into the world is an evil purpose, even if it is not your purpose." Saga basically took my whole life and ripped it apart.

Was this the truth about my life? Had I been creating the clouds over my career? If I dared to be honest with myself, I had always had the opportunity of choice. But I chose to bring the clouds and complained about why I couldn't create the fire. I applied for my job at the daily newspaper. I wrote out the application. I went for the interview. I signed the agreement. I did all that myself without any force from anyone. I brought the cloud over my writing career and then cursed my lot every single day of my life. I had the choice to quit every single day. I was not happy at work. But I packed my bag and went to work every single day without any force from anyone. Like I was following Thelda and I was following Zi, I was following other people's purposes every single day of my life. Being in the job was someone else's purpose. Because others went to work, I went to work. My purpose was at my writing desk. But since no one else was there, I followed where everyone else went. And in doing that I not only left my purpose behind, I got lost.

"Your truth is in what *you* want to do in this moment! Your purpose is in what *you* want to create in your life every single day! If you are not doing what you want to do and you are not creating what you want to create then you are a waste of a powerful spirit, like this magnifying glass is. This glass holds the power to create infinite suns here on a planet far, far away. You hold the power to create infinite possibilities of your own choosing. When you create out of your own choosing, then you are living your purpose. Creation out of other's choosing is another word for slavery. Slavery is to sit around another's fire for warmth when you have the ability to create your own." Saga kept me stunned on every word that he said.

"Here," he said, handing me the glass piece over again, "your turn is not finished yet."

I took the glass from his hand. The clouds hung obstinately in the sky hiding the sun. The entire valley was basking in the sunlight, except the patch where I sat. This had been the story of my life for thirty odd years. It was always only me.

I held the glass piece in my hand and held it one foot above the ground. The shadow still loomed on the ground and I knew I needed the sun to make the fire. I tried to shoo away the clouds in my head, but they remained rigid above. I tried to visualize them going away, but they only grew denser. How could I ever lift these clouds from my life?

I tried hard to focus and the harder I focused the more the hope of fire eluded me.

THE PERFECT WORLD // 173

"Maybe it's not meant to be," Saga remarked, shaking his head.

"Maybe you have lived the lie so long that it has become the truth," Saga shook his head with empathy.

"Maybe this is your fate for the rest of eternity," he pressed his lips together, expressing his condolence for my lot.

I could not believe my ears. My destiny had been revealed for me. Is this what I wanted it to be? I had never asked myself this question ever in my life? Is this what I wanted my life to be like? Always over-shadowed by my own clouds of despair, doubt and disbelief? Did I want to live in the lie forever; that I had no choice, that I had no control and that I had no confidence? Did I always want to be a victim of my own limited thinking? Noooo, every single unit of my body screamed. Just like every drop of water had reflected Zi's image, every single living cell in my body reflected my desire to be free. I wanted to bask in the sun of glory. I wanted to live in the truth. The truth that I had choices, that I could control the direction of my life, that I had the courage and confidence to do anything I wanted. I was doing things. I had that ability. If I could only *do what I wanted*, my life would turn around. I wanted to live in the strength of my thoughts, in the belief that I had the power to create infinite possibilities.

"No!" I opened my eyes and glared at Saga. "My turn is not finished yet!"

Saga shook his head and shrugged, implying that I was only wasting my time.

I held the glass piece firmly in my hand one foot above the ground. I cast one glance towards a remorseful Saga and then sealed them shut.

Four green eyes gleamed at me and I felt a tug at my soul. If I need the sun to make the connection, then I had to connect with the sun. I did not need the clouds, so why was I working my energy at them? To create the fire I needed the sun. To have the sun, I had to let go of my need to have clouds too. I could not have both. I had to choose. I had to choose between my job and my writing career. One created a shadow over my life; the other held the potential to light up the world. I had to choose between fearing my future and believing in my future. I could not have both. I had to choose my mental attitude. I had to choose between getting up and making things happen and sitting at home waiting for something to happen. I had to choose my spiritual attitude. I had to choose with whom and with what to make the connection. My choices held in them the potential of infinite possibilities.

I let go of the clouds. I let go of the doubt, the fear, and the bitterness. I embraced the sun, for that is what I needed to build the fire. My purpose will unfold for me the choices I need to make. If my purpose is to build a fire then I need the sun. I should make the connection with the sun. The clouds are not a part of my purpose and engaging them would only bring more doubt and more delays in my purpose. If my purpose is to be an author, then I need to sit at my desk and write. Spending twelve hours at work will only bring more uncertainty and apprehension about my ability to write. If my purpose is to be successful and wealthy, then I need to spend time with those who are. Spending my time and energy with people of mediocre mentality will only bring confusion and reluctance in my ability to create success and wealth. I had to choose. I had to choose in every moment with every person and with every thing. My choices had to be in direct alignment with my purpose, no clouds in the middle at all.

I connected with the sun and its rays poured in on the glass. I could feel the warmth of the sun on my shoulder and I smiled.

I stayed still, holding the energy and guarding it with my soul. It was pure bliss. The joy of alignment is a joy that is innate to a spiritual being. Something stung my hand and I snapped open my eyes and in front of me was the most beautiful fire I had ever seen. The flames were dancing in the wind, breaking into sparkles as they did. I laughed out loud.

Saga was smiling.

"You are always a last minute entry!" He laughed out, slapping his head.

"Not anymore!" I roared with a confidence that had been waiting to explode for my entire lifetime. "Not anymore!"

I was going to be ahead of the game, now and forever.

Saga took his hand and put it over the flame again, sucking them in. He rubbed them together and creased his brow with the moisture-laden soot exposing a brilliant set of grey green eyes.

I saw an orange-clad figure emerge from the trees below.

"Thelda!!!!" I screamed and ran towards her in delight. I could not wait to tell her my experiences with the truth about my purpose and my life and I could not wait to hear hers. I wanted to doubly grow, like she had said we would at the end of our journey here.

I reached Thelda and my eyes went wide with horror. Thelda looked broken. Her eyes were blood red and swollen, as though she had cried incessantly for hours. Her hunch was back and her face had aged as though she was a thousand years old. She was bent over and she looked beat.

"What happened to you, Thelda?" I was shocked. I held her

shoulders and tried to shake her out of the trance she seemed to be in. Her drum was placed against a tree behind her. She had abandoned her drum? I was aghast. That was something she had clutched to with her soul. I darted towards the tree and dragged the drum beside her. The sun shone on us like a spot light.

I lifted Thelda's face and she let out a heart-breaking sob.

"I failed," she said, as a tear rolled down her eye. It shook my soul to see Thelda, the Sorceress cry.

"Don't call me that," she snapped through her sobs. "Don't ever call me a Sorceress again!!" She cried out painfully.

I stayed silent. Thelda had obviously realized the truth about her life and her purpose, and with my experience, I can vouch that is not an easy thing to confront.

"Two hundred and fifty years," she sniffed.

"Two hundred and fifty years!!" She exclaimed louder.

I remained silent. Allowing her the space and pace to gather herself and express her heart.

"For two hundred and fifty years," her voice had a hint of anger, "I have willed illness and despair and devastation and evil for people!"

I was confused. What was she talking about? I wanted to interrupt her. I wanted to shake her out of her trance and tell her that she had lost her mind. She was Thelda the Sorceress who had healed thousands of people, brought them back to health, brought them back to life.

"For me to heal, I needed someone to be sick. For me to give life, I needed someone to be dying. For me to work my magic, I needed someone to be cursed. I needed sickness and death and evil for me to exist!!!!" She barked in total contempt of her entire life.

"Thelda the Sorceress thrived and lived for two hundred and fifty years in total disgrace." She spat out the words with utter hate.

I was stunned. I thought healing another was a noble purpose. What greater purpose could there be than to serve others?

"If I didn't exist, then could it be people would need to learn to get well on their own? If I didn't exist, then could it be that people would need to die gracefully than making a spiritual disaster out of their perishable bodies? If I didn't exist, could it be possible that people would need to find the power and courage within them to fight their own battles? Was Thelda the Sorceress making others weak? Was she the excuse for their mediocrity and spiritual inertia? Thelda the Sorceress was the answer to all their problems. That was the wrong answer. The correct answer is the one that is found within yourself. My presence took their focus away from their own spiritual grandeur and confirmed and sentenced them to being a victim for lifetimes to follow." Thelda was going to kill herself with the shame that she felt for her whole life gone by.

I had to do something. If she could die because she needed a break, then she surely could die because she could see how she had broken her own spiritual honor.

"So you mean that the people who came to you had the power to heal themselves?" I quickly asked Thelda, in an attempt to rescue her from falling apart.

She shot a glance at me and sobbed angrily, "YES!"

"You mean the people who came to you lost and beat, had the power in themselves to turn their lives around?" I questioned further despite her agitation.

"YES! YES! They all had it in themselves. That is where I should have guided them towards; their own infinite power. But I stole that opportunity from them, by using my power to guide them!!!!" She bellowed like a wounded lioness.

"You mean no matter how irrevocable a person's situation may seem, he could do something about it himself?" I pressed.

"YES!" She barked, smacking her head with both her hands.

"Can you show me how? If someone came to you now for help, what would you tell them? If you came to Thelda, what would she tell you now?" I asked her softly.

"Wh..." Thelda stammered. The thoughts in her head stopped. The berating battle in her heart stopped. She looked at me and her head cocked on one side and she frowned, fixing her gaze on her feet.

"If you came to Thelda in this state right now, what would she tell you?" I spoke determinedly to the mighty Sorceress, who in seeing her truth was using it to destroy herself. The truth does not destroy, the truth liberates. The truth does not demean, the truth does all but salvage.

"I would tell myself that it is never too late. I would tell myself that I am fortunate to be here and that I can see. I would tell myself that I am free now, to be free from my need to be a Sorceress. I would tell myself that in laying my false purpose to rest, I could now embrace my new purpose. I can have a new life. I can live *my* life. I can do what I want to do. I no longer have to have people queue up outside my house so I can be busy. I no longer need someone to be small so I can be a Sorceress. I am free. I am grateful," she sniffed and sobbed and grabbed her drum and held onto it with her life.

"I am free," she held my hand and kissed it.

"I am free!!!!!" She yelled out for the whole mountain to hear. "I am free to choose, to be, to do and have anything I want for myself!!!"

"B..But what do I want to do?" She stammered and banged her hand on the drum with frustration and its percussion beat vibrated through the forest. A bolt of lightning ran through Thelda's face.

"I know," she whispered. Her hunch straightened up, her eyes gleamed and her lips parted into a smile that spelt Thelda is back!!! She flung her arms open and her fingers fell upon the drum in rhythmic beats, bringing the whole mountain alive with her piece of music. It was beautiful. Thelda looked like an eccentric drummer with her hair aggressively sweeping to the music and not to mention her robe bobbing up and down like flames gone wild. I smiled. Thelda had found her purpose.

Time stood still and the entire mountain, The Great Realization stood witness to Thelda's truth, her purpose to make music. Every living being on that mountain stood witness to a lie dissolve and the truth emerge from the soul of the beings who tread foot here.

With the last roll of her fingers Thelda took a bow.

"I will play for the world," she swayed her arms around, beating imaginary drums in the air.

"And then you will live a lie all over again," Saga came and stood beside me, facing a shocked Thelda.

"What? Now I can't even play music?" She could spiral down into depression again and I wanted to shush Saga. It took some effort to get Thelda to see the light and now Saga was beating her down again. "Creating music is a great purpose, a spiritual purpose. But creating music for the world is no purpose at all? Does the world really need your music? Is your purpose to have the queues outside your house this way or another? You need to release other people from being dragged into your purpose! The true test of your purpose is even if no one was witness to your creation, would you still create it? Does the flower bloom for you? It blooms for itself, and when it does that, you can't help but be a beneficiary of its purpose. When your purpose to write is for others to read, you are living a lie all over again. Write because you love to. Write what you would love to read. And when you do that, the readers become beneficiaries of your purpose and your passion. Play because you want to, play what you would love to hear. Spiritual creation belongs to the world. When you create out of purpose and passion, people can't help but be beneficiaries of that." Saga spoke kindly and Thelda understood. Thelda smiled and I smiled. She was right. In our journeys apart, we had doubly grown in the end.

"We have to hurry to the top for the announcement," Saga said and turned to walk towards the top of the mountain. I could see movement on top. I could see the clouds scurrying their way to the top, I could see a large cluster of trees moving upwards. I think the curiosity about who would be the chosen one was pulling everyone to the top of the mountain.

Thelda picked up her drum and stretched out her hand to me. We walked hand in hand with Saga leading the way, sharing experiences, growing and rejoicing in each other's. The author and the eccentric drummer were going to be best friends for eternity. There was a major commotion happening at the top of The Great Realization. The grass was denser, the trees were cluttered together, and the clouds were thicker. It seemed as though the whole mountain had migrated up there to witness who will be announced as the chosen one, to assist in helping Zedius bring some calculated imperfections in their own curse of perfection. The trees had made a herd and some of them were so close, they had made a fence with their curiosity. I didn't know that being chosen to assist at Zedius was such a big deal.

"They are all fools!" Thelda, the er, Drummer muttered disapprovingly for the amount of attention that was being given to the chosen one.

It was difficult pushing the trees and the grass and the clouds aside, to find space at the top where all the others stood. The place was a small oval-shaped clearing which held a small circle of beings. In the outer circle were the beings of Zedius, all similarly dressed, Acrodorf being the best looking of them all. Their chosen ones stood in front of them. Saga quickly squeezed his way to the centre and Thelda and I made our way towards Bren and Acrodorf.

I was very happy to see Acrodorf and he nodded at me and smiled, beckoning that he wanted to hear all about my adventures on the way. I missed seeing Bren's expression and I wondered if he knew that the help he had brought from planet Earth had had a change in her purpose. I saw Jini standing directly opposite me across the line of the circle and my expression turned sour. Why was she even allowed here? A being of Zedius stood calmly behind her. I had half a mind to walk up to him and tell him the truth about Jini. But maybe he already knew. I half-wondered what good would evil bring on Zedius in making it perfect? I saw Ray who looked at me dreamily and I averted my eyes and closed them. When I opened my eyes again, he was frowning at me. I smiled. Ray was beautiful and needed to control everyone around him. I wondered if he was working his control on Saga. But on second thoughts, truth cannot be controlled, the truth is the truth, regardless. The little weird creatures were missing. I wondered where they were? Zi stood towards my left. He smiled at me warmly. I was happy to see Zi.

"We have come to the moment," Saga said, bringing the gathering to order, "of truth." He finished his sentence with a deliberate pause of suspense.

"As you can see," he said spreading his arms around, "many have left without the verdict. Sometimes, knowing the truth about one's life and purpose is enough for them to bring closure to their journeys across the universe, so that they can focus their energy and time towards their purpose." Saga explained the absence of the others that I saw by the stream.

"Zedius is at a very critical stage as you all know. And it is important that help falls in the correct hands," he said, casting a glance one by one on all the er, contestants.

"The being who has the right skills to bring a balanced disorder in Zedius is..." Saga said evaluating the implications of his selection,

"Zi!" He announced.

Jini let out an intimidating purr and stood there rooted to the ground. She looked mean. I looked at Zi and smiled. He had helped me across to the mountain, The Great Realization. I liked him. I wondered what he brought to Zedius. I guess, in time I would find out.

"But like always, the chosen one must have an aide," he said looking around for enthusiastic volunteers. No one seemed interested. I guess an aide was a helper - like the valet for the boss.

Jini spat on the ground in response to Saga's request.

"I can help!" I volunteered. I would be more than happy to return

Zi's good gesture. He had come to my aid and it would only be my honor to come to his. And besides, there was not much of a purpose for everyone at Zedius. We would only get our share of powers. That's it. So it was better to spend time constructively with Zi.

"Yo baby!" Thelda whistled at Zi who smiled sheepishly. She rolled her fingers on the drum oblivious to a visibly embarrassed Bren and began to play a celebration piece for Zi. The beings didn't wait for the performance to end, or er, even to start and they began to take off with their respective caretakers. Zi looked at me and whispered, "See you at Zedius."

Zedius; The Perfect World

Bren placed his hand on Thelda as she bowed to an audience that was no longer there. I applauded Thelda's performance cheerfully. She was getting better with every beat. I could sense Bren's impatience, since we were the only ones left on the mountain, The Great Realization.

I would have actually preferred if Zi could travel with us, so I could exchange some notes on the way. Getting to know him would assist in being his aide, but Zi had left the minute Thelda had started her piece with the drum. On another occasion I would have accused the Sorceress to be crazy, but since the Sorceress was gone, the Drummer had to be dealt with sensitively.

"We have to be on our way," Bren said solemnly. I could not tell if he was disappointed that Thelda was not the chosen one. He had traveled two light years to get her here. Thelda the Sorceress had started her journey, but Thelda the Drummer would complete the journey.

Acrodorf seemed undeterred though. He was as kind as ever; unchanged in a changing world.

Bren tugged Thelda towards him as I stepped towards Acrodorf and with the smooth familiar tug we were off on our way out of the Planet of Truth - formless.

No sooner than we were out of the range of the planet, Thelda started off non-stop about her experiences at the mountain, The Great Realization. Bren was supportive, to my surprise, empathizing with Thelda on her transformation into a musician from a Sorceress. I could feel the delight in Acrodorf's soul.

"The surest way to keep a soul sentenced to mortality is by not allowing it to think for itself or create in freedom. Thelda needed to free herself from that. How could she earn her share of immortality if she was the Sorceress who was holding people back from theirs? The Great Realization was very important for her evolution. Though that means that she is not the assistance we had sought, but what the heck, in setting Zedius right, we are also liberating some souls who were kind enough to offer help!" Acrodorf spoke.

"Is Bren disappointed that Thelda is not chosen?" I asked.

"My expectation is not that Thelda will assist in helping us save Zedius. My expectation is that Zedius will be saved and we will have the help that is needed for it." Bren spoke in his defense.

"What about Jini? She is evil! Why is she allowed to come?" I asked Acrodorf.

"She must have been selected for her ability to add some value on Zedius," Acrodorf reasoned.

"But Acrodorf, Jini is evil!" I tried to explain to him.

"Even if she is so, she will have no force on Zedius," Acrodorf reasoned back.

That didn't convince me. I had been the victim of Jini's evil intent and if it were not for the weeping willows, I would have been burnt to ashes. I didn't trust Jini and I hoped that I would have no further encounters with her on Zedius. I put Jini out of my focus and my concern. I focused my energy on Zedius, on Zi, on Acrodorf, on Thelda and on Bren. These were amazing souls, souls with a purpose and goodness so big, that their presence collectively could bring well-being in disorder. A thousand Jinis could not create trouble when a force so good existed, I convinced myself with that thought.

"Look Niki!" Thelda exclaimed.

I looked in the distance and I saw a shimmering round ball speedily heading towards us. It was like a ball of fireworks, radiating, dancing rays of light outwards. I wondered if it were a star or a meteorite and I wondered if there was anything to worry about its speedy approach towards us.

"What is that?" I asked Acrodorf.

"Zedius!" Bren answered delighted.

"Why is it charging at us? Look at the speed with which it is emerging!" I exclaimed.

"Zedius is not visible to everyone, at least that is how we have wanted it. It's a private abode, very private," Acrodorf took over.

The shimmering ball of white fire was too close for comfort and then it abruptly stopped.

"What the…" and before I could complete my sentence, a surprised Niki Sanders was spilled over by an equally surprised Thelda.

The Channel had weird ways of operation. While at Zedius, I could also make a suggestion for a warning system for The Channel, before we snapped in and out of our bodies. Maybe, the beings of Zedius could pass on the message to the creators of The Channel.

Thelda was clutching my shoulder, lest I squashed her.

"Mind the drum please!" She was yelling at someone who had stumbled over it.

"Where are we? What's going on?" I stood up, trying not to step over Thelda as I did. Just a few seconds ago we were in space, formless and lo behold, seconds later we were in the magnetic field of Zedius. It was as though we disappeared at one point and emerged promptly at another. But then this was Zedius, and I had quite expected unusual phenomena here, so I was not really surprised.

Thelda pulled her shaggy hair back and cracked her neck as though I had caused her a great deal of discomfort with my fall. She looked at me and smiled. Even with the little puffy bags around her eyes, she looked pretty, in a crazy way.

Acrodorf helped me up and Bren was in conversation with another being from Zedius. It looked like all the candidates at the mountain, The Great Realization had gathered here. Ray was in an argument with a scantily clad creature.

"We are in the magnetic field of Zedius," Acrodorf smiled. His hair had a delightful bounce to it that seemed happy to be home. I wondered if Acrodorf would take me to his house. I would love to visit.

Zedius lay a few miles below, radiating a silvery white light. Unlike The Planet of Truth it was not bluish green, it was just white light, a ball of mystical white light. I wondered how life was possible on a light source. We were in the magnetic field similar to the one on planet Earth, except that this one was not playing any sinister jokes on us. It was solid and the movement across it was easy. I stared at the planet below and could not wait to set my foot on Zedius.

"Zedius has a protective shield of light. The light helps camouflage it. It is generally mistaken for a star and so other beings pass it by." Acrodorf explained.

"I thought only Earth had a magnetic field," I muttered, looking in the direction of Ray who was visibly very angry at the creature he was communicating with.

"All planets have magnetic fields. Some allow easy access to other spirits, some don't. Zedius has closed access to other beings since a long time, and hence you are here for clearance to proceed further," Acrodorf explained while walking towards Ray.

A whole crowd had gathered here. I saw Zi in the distance behind Ray. I was happy to see him. I wanted to go towards him, but decided to stay with Acrodorf until it was my time to officially be his aide. I saw a whole bunch of creatures that I had met at the mountaintop and I wondered what we were waiting for.

A being of Zedius, raised his hands to bring the argument to an enforced halt. He had a similar form as Acrodorf and wore the same attire. I wondered why all beings of Zedius dressed the same; they were obviously not familiar with the concept of vanity.

"That is Dana. He guards the magnetic field of Zedius. He is special," Acrodorf whispered, as an angry Ray shoved his way past us and stood next to Thelda.

"You all will have access to Zedius, even though only Zi is the chosen one. You volunteered to assist us in saving Zedius and we appreciate you." Dana said and everyone turned to look towards Zi.

"As much as Zedius is grateful for your kind gesture, as per the rules here, none of you will be able to proceed with your powers. What that means is this; for your whole term on Zedius, your powers will be suspended. On your way back, your powers will be returned to you and so will the additional power of the beings of Zedius, to be, do and have anything you want!" Dana spoke like the man with a loud speaker at a public square making some political announcements.

"That's not fair," Ray growled. "Who am I without my powers?" He raged.

"The answer to the first three words is all the power you will ever need!" Bren roared back, controlling the mutiny that was building up just a few miles away from Zedius. His hair rocked from one side to another as he strode up to Dana.

"Who am I? That is all he needs to know, all power lies therein, powers that are innate and cannot be declared or confiscated or stolen." Bren muttered under his breath and gave me a stare as he did.

"Who am I?" I whispered to myself.

"I am opening access to Zedius," Dana announced over the audible dismay of the creatures that scurried around complaining to each other and took me away from the question that held the power to change my life forever. Life is funny. When you finally do ask the right question, you get distracted from the right answer.

"Only the ones that are willing to surrender their powers will be allowed access," he spoke and motioned people to queue up. Bren stayed at guard.

I wondered why these beings were making such a big fuss about rules. They were entering another's home and they needed to respect their rules or norms. I found the attitude to be a little rude and misplaced.

Ray was in a foul mood, scowling. I felt it was such a waste of his good looks and charm. He still had his powers now, but they obviously were not working for him. I think powers don't work on their own. You have to use them to make them work. In complaining and fretting about the problem, he had forgotten he had the power to control, like he had done with me. When people get swayed with emotions, especially anger, they lose their power. Zedius was still miles away, but Ray had lost his power to his own emotional outburst.

I can never forget my friend John. He was a car racer, the best in the Canary Islands. Last year, a very big automobile company hosted the local version of the Formula One. The stakes were very high, the prize money was very big and the competition was tough. At the beginning of the race, one of his competitors said something nasty to him. John was so enraged that he assaulted the guy. He punched his face and then was disqualified from the race. It was very sad that he never got to participate in the race he was preparing for, for months. He had the power to win the race but he didn't use it. Instead, he let his emotions get in the way and lost. Success is the best revenge. Power is in staying on track with your ability and not getting side-tracked with other people's agenda.

Bren's words rang in my head. Who am I? These were the first three words of Ray's question 'Who am I without my powers?' If I know who I am, then that was power enough. I was an indestructible, immortal powerful soul. And if I was that, then I was powerful even if one tried to render me otherwise.

I stayed close to Acrodorf and Thelda. Bren was helping Dana discipline all the foreigners to Zedius. A bolt of lightning ran through my body and I desperately looked around. "Where is Jini?" I muttered to myself. Jini was nowhere.

"Where is Jini?" I asked Acrodorf.

She was certainly there on the mountain. But I could not see her anywhere.

"Don't worry," Acrodorf smiled, his expression calm. "If she would even get to Zedius, she can't do so with her evil powers. On Zedius, every new entrant is harmless."

Acrodorf was calm but I was not. I could not shake off the feeling that Jini was up to something evil. My instinct told me Jini would create trouble. Though I no longer had an affinity for disaster, but something told me that Jini was not done with me yet. I wanted to tell Acrodorf about my experience with Jini, but he was already in conversation with Bren.

The queue ahead was fast disappearing and soon it would be mine and Thelda's turn.

"This is the moment we came together for," Thelda waved her hands ecstatically. "To experience Zedius and to go back with the power to be, do and have anything we desire." Thelda held my arm and shook me excitedly. Even though Thelda had gone through a very painful phase on The Planet of Truth, she had taken to the transformation very well. I guess she had quit being a Sorceress for a long time. She just needed someone to put her on her purpose. Thelda looked happy. She dragged her drum along towards a very surprised Dana.

"This has no power," she giggled, "It's just a drum."

Bren nodded and shook his head helplessly. Dana smiled.

"The minute you are suspended from the magnetic field, you will lose all your powers. You will however retrieve them on your way back." Dana said mechanically as he heaved Thelda and me out together from an imaginary take off point and we went squealing down formless.

The journey downwards toward Zedius was like moving through a very dense space. There was light everywhere and it was restricting my ability to think anything. I felt totally immersed in it. It was as though the light was consuming me. I don't know how long it was, but I heard someone calling out to me.

"Niki!! Get up Niki!!" I heard a voice. It was Thelda.

I opened my eyes and saw a very excited Thelda towering above me yanking at my arm. I shot up and sat up straight. I gasped. How come Thelda was always ahead of me?

I was sitting on a soft ground. I placed my hands by my side and they dug into the silver cool sand. A mist covered the ground and it seemed to rise up in vapors, giving the whole environment a very dreamy look. Thelda's drum was placed in the distance and she was dancing around in the mist around her feet. I looked around and all I could see was a large expanse of smoking misty ground, and, nothing else.

I stood up. The sky above was dark and alive with the whole universe. My mouth was wide open with wonder, as I stared at an overly large satellite with another small one perched by its side. I had never seen two moons. They were white, milky white, pure white. The moonlight poured upon us by two generous satellites. But what amazed me more was a dancing star that was making rounds on the horizon. I was elated. Zedius was nothing short of magical.

I could hear waves crash nearby and I could smell the sultriness of the water.

"How long have I been lying here?" I asked Thelda.

"Not long," she grinned. "This is Zedius baby!" She stretched out her arms and her orange robe looked like a flapping flag. She was inhaling deeply, trying to contain the essence of Zedius in her lungs. Thelda was easy to please. I loved her attitude, always ready for adventure, always ready for life.

"Where are the others?" I asked. No sooner had I even completed the question I heard a flutter of wings and the mist danced around, as Acrodorf landed with Bren following suit.

"Welcome to Zedius," Acrodorf said smiling, adjusting his long-flowing coat. The mist had filled into his coat and was emerging in soft white vapors from his sleeve. The entire sight was dreamy.

I continued to look at the sky for the arrival of others, but no one else arrived.

"We cannot accompany you further." Bren said apologetically. "Since we have to take you back to planet Earth, that gives us very little time on Zedius to meet with the creator and complete our duties while we are here."

"But you are free to be around," he continued, waving his hands in an attempt to tell us that the entire stretch of the uninhabited misty expanse would be an exciting adventure to explore.

"Come," Acrodorf said, "Let me orient you with Zedius," leading us forward, towards, er, nowhere.

"There is nothing here," Thelda drummed as she walked, humming the words, "we are already oriented with nothing," she continued trying to rhyme the words. The drumming was quite, er, annoying and I had this growing suspicion that Thelda would soon try her hand at singing too.

"Oh, my apologies," Acrodorf stopped abruptly, looking around at the stretch of barren silken ground covered in mist, that seemed to stretch till the end of the Zedius.

"Can I create something for you? What would you like?" He said earnestly, trying hard to be a good host.

"A hammock, some pretty young men, a stadium for my show, and a fancy hotel suite to suit the lead drummer of a very famous band," Thelda chuckled.

"No problem," Acrodorf rubbed his hands together. He stood still and the mist grew dense and cool around our feet. The moonlight shone intensely and a light breeze stirred up. I could see Acrodorf's eyes shut tight and the movement of his pupils under his eyelids told me he was creating a visual of Thelda's request. His breathing was heavy and his hair stood still, lest they would disturb his energy. I could see a deep crease between his eyebrows that symbolized the intensity of his focus and then I heard a zooming sound that took my attention towards it.

Two palm trees had zoomed up in the distance. A white rope hammock rocked between them. A large stone-carved cottage sprung up close by. It resembled the luxury cottage you would see in a catalogue of Greek resorts. A large stadium formed into the distance and I was aghast to see four gorgeous butlers come scurrying towards Thelda.

"Unbelievable!" Thelda found the words first.

Acrodorf had created a whole luxury retreat next to a large stadium just by his mere intention. This would be a smashing ability to take back home.

"Do you like it?" Acrodorf said, confirming if he had got all of Thelda's demands right. Bren shook his head in exasperation.

"Yes. I am staying here forever!" She motioned to one butler to carry her drum, as she trotted towards the hammock and plopped on it.

"I have to get you to Zi," Acrodorf said turning to me, twitching his nose to express that I would not be able to join Thelda on her holiday on Zedius.

"You chose to be the aide. You have work to do," Acrodorf shrugged.

"Don't you want to come along Thelda?" I shouted out to her in a tone that this could be her last chance to 'help'.

"Are you out of your mind, Niki Sanders? I am a rock star. I don't hang out with *aides!*" She grinned mischievously and the orange bundle of joy fell off the hammock as she did. Two butlers came speeding to her rescue and soon Thelda the lucky witch was in the arms of a very sexy, scantily clad butler who placed her gently back on the hammock.

"I will see you in the end of our journey, so I can grow. Don't expect great stuff from me, coz I am on a holiday!" She trumpeted again and the hammock rocked violently while the two butlers stood in wait for their next disaster. Thelda wiped the silver mop of hair off her face and winked at me.

"Let's go," Acrodorf tugged at my arm.

"I will join you in a few moments," he yelled out to Bren, who had already stretched out his wings and was ready for take off.

Acrodorf ran forward and I ran along with him. I could see nothing ahead except the same misty ground. In the distance, I could see another Zedian along with another humanoid. I could recognize Zi's figure anywhere in the universe. His large frame and curly locks and his majestic gait were unmistakable.

"Over to you," Zi's host hurried towards us. I had missed seeing where the two of them had appeared from, but that didn't matter. The Zedian nodded in my direction politely and then took off quickly without any formal introduction or goodbye.

"Zi," Acrodorf shook Zi's hand. He looked majestic; one majestic creature in the company of another. The sight was out of a fairytale. One bird-like god man and one man-like god; standing next to each other in a mystical setting. It was a dream.

Zi looked around with the same question 'what are we supposed to do here?'.

"You journey together from here," Acrodorf said to Zi pausing to look at me. "Observe and analyze. You need to help us with a perspective about introducing disorder. When your term is over, your perspective will be conveyed to our creator, Waldon. It will then be decided whether your inputs will bring us the help that we have been looking for, to save Zedius!"

"Observe what?" Zi smiled sheepishly, as though he had not quite understood what Acrodorf was saying. Actually, I had also not understood what Acrodorf was saying. There was nothing around except silvery sand and an inexplicable mist.

"Where are the Zedians? I mean, are we in the wrong area or something? This place looks totally deserted," Zi commented matter of factly.

Acrodorf looked around and shook his head.

"The beings of Zedius are here, they just choose not to be seen." He said softly, lest someone overheard him.

He placed his arm around Zi and started to walk away with him. I followed suit.

"The beings of Zedius have retreated. They haven't been seen in a long time. Look, the entire planet is deserted." He said solemnly.

"It's only us, a few of us, who still believe that there is a way and that all will be well again," he continued.

"But what's wrong?" I interjected. I knew I was the aide and it was probably not my place to ask questions, but since the rules about my involvement were not yet established, I decided to ask.

"The creation is there, at will, as you witnessed earlier with Thelda," Acrodorf paused, glad that I asked the question, "but there is no joy in creation anymore. If you can be, do and have anything you want, at will, then there is no thrill in creating that anymore. Creation has become boring and boredom only brings inaction." Acrodorf took his arm off Zi and explained as I walked along with them.

"So why don't you change the rules?" I asked. I was being a good aide, because Zi looked over his shoulder and smiled at me.

"That's what you are here for; to give us a good perspective. We sit at the epitome of perfection and we are not able to come up with a mistake or loophole or disorder. It is inconceivable to us. That is why we brought you. You give us a perspective and the creator, will decide if that fits," Acrodorf sighed.

"I must leave you here," he said, "because time is running out."

"But what if we fail?" Zi asked. I understood his concern. Zedius, at where we were, was as barren as blank. A perspective would be difficult if we had nothing to observe.

"Then Zedius will be soon destroyed. It has been inert for so long, that it can no longer participate in the universe," Acrodorf said sadly. He opened his wings. His eyes searched mine. For the first time in my entire term in the universe, I saw Acrodorf search my soul for reassurance.

"I don't know what you see in me Acrodorf," I ran towards him before he took off, "but I know it was not my affinity for disaster that you saw."

Acrodorf smiled as his eyes moistened.

"I wish to see what you saw," I whispered.

"You will find that out soon," He whispered back. His cloak fluttered as he spanned his wings and took off into the sky in the space between the two moons.

"Wow," Zi exclaimed, "these are powerful beings, incredibly powerful."

"And yet they need our perspective," I frowned.

"I guess sometimes, when you are too involved in the game, you need an objective view. If your hand is too close onto your face, you can't see it. You need to pull the hand off your face to see it. I guess we are here to spot that hand on the face. I doubt that Zedius needs our imperfections to create a balance. I suspect that Zedius is full of imperfections but because they can't see them, they suffer. Zedius is suffering from a terminal illness called the 'blind eye'. When one turns a blind eye to an illness, it only grows. The state of Zedius is evidence of that." Zi said thoughtfully, still gazing at the breathtaking view of the two moons.

I shuddered. Zi spoke with a wisdom that defied the state of The Perfect World. He was proposing that The Perfect World was not perfect, that it had flaws, but because the beings of Zedius would not accept or acknowledge that, they were suffering. This was a very strong opinion, one that was not even supported by observation and analysis.

"I guess what the Zedians are seeking is the same thing that you Earthlings are seeking; balance. They too seek a healthy balance between perfection and imperfection; a healthy balance between right and wrong; a balance, which keeps both sides equal, perfect, and right. But that balance is maintained on acceptance, on acknowledging both sides. But if one side is in denial of the other, then there is war, there is reclusion and non-creation." Zi continued.

Zi was smart. He had an idea about the state of my world. He was the chosen one and I am sure that the Planet of Truth had revealed the truth in selecting him, but I wondered if any beings of Zedius were here, would they have appreciated Zi's way of thinking. I was his aide, and in being that, I was also the aide of Zedius. I had to find out more.

"Why would you start from the premise that Zedius is not perfect? It *is* the Perfect World. The whole universe acknowledges that. Zedius is not even visible in the universe. It's that special!" I defended Zedius, The Perfect World.

"Who stays in hiding? Who chooses to be invisible? Who chooses not to share their greatness and powers with the universe? Who stays in reclusion and does not want to be seen? Perfection or Imperfection?" Zi stood towering before me. He placed both his hands on my arms and held me tight, as he asked me the questions one after the other.

My mouth was open. The musky odor of Zi's body penetrated my nostrils. The breeze blew his locks on his face and he blinked his eyes to keep them out. I stammered something before I said the words.

"Im..Im...Imperfection!" I shook at my own confession.

"Thank you. Now let's find it!" Zi smiled.

"If we are walking towards nowhere, then it's best to keep walking ahead," Zi said. He was full of wisdom and I suspected that Saga chose him for his ability of deep insight and not for his ability to create trouble.

I walked alongside Zi, his bare arm brushing occasionally on mine, sending a chill down my legs.

"What do you bring to Zedius?" I asked Zi, curious about his abilities.

"I have the ability of hindsight. I don't make the same mistake twice. I have the ability to learn from my past and so I never repeat it." Zi smiled as though he knew that question was coming.

"Wow!" I exclaimed. I sure had spent half my life in only repeating my mistakes. So I spent thirty years living the same stuff again and again. It's like I was actually living only four or five years worth of heart ache and mistakes again and again for thirty years.

'We have company,' Zi said delighted, pointing in the direction of a figure that appeared a hundred yards ahead of us. It was strange that there was a sudden expanse of a thicket of willows in the distance. I stood still horrorstruck, as a nauseous déjà-vu flashed before my eyes. What would be the purpose of a sudden appearance of the willows? And then with a pang of shooting pain in my stomach I knew. Jini!

"Let's go," Zi tugged at my hand and I held him back with all my force. In the distance between the willows I could see Jini, whose evil form and essence was unmistakable even from so far.

"She made it! I knew it!" I muttered, wishing Acrodorf was here.

"What?" Zi looked at me patiently.

"Jini is here. She is evil. She almost killed me at the Planet of Truth. She was not there in the magnetic field. I had watched out for her. But she is here and so are the willows. We have to be careful," I said, hastily wondering if my words made any sense to Zi.

Zi understood. He looked at me deeply and then turned his gaze towards the willows. I followed his gaze. His eyes searched for my truth in the reality that had emerged before us. His eyes fixed at the spot where Jini was, a few moments ago.

"Hindsight is a gift. Hindsight aids survival. Often, people mix hindsight with confused opinions and personal irrationalities. I see hindsight in your eyes. Tell me what happened?" Zi kept his hand on my shoulder to calm me down. His deep eyes were a distraction.

Zi looked so innocent and so young that his looks totally defied the wisdom of his soul and the weight of his responsibility. I guess we earthlings place too much importance on appearances. We make decisions based on looks, we fall in love, and we marry because of looks. And disaster befalls us when we take a peek behind that beautiful face, only to find a confused and shriveled being whose looks had been the sole reason for his survival so far. Looks can be deceptive. The truth lies behind the looks and in Zi's case, I had experienced his truth before being influenced by his gorgeous presence.

"Jini's strength is deception. Her whole demeanor is hypnotic. She has electric energy with which she burns you to ashes. She tried to electrocute me, but the willows that whisked me away from her reach, saved me. She made it to the Mountain of Truth but I don't know how she made it here, because she was not there in the magnetic field," I spoke with a little calm. Zi was in charge here, I was merely his aide and he needed to know everything.

"If Jini made it through the Planet of Truth, then she should be a changed soul," Zi frowned.

"No! I can feel her evil even from here," I protested. I wanted to agree with Zi, but my instinct told me that Jini had an evil purpose for Zedius.

"What's your suggestion?" Zi whispered, putting the onus of the situation on me. For a moment my heart skipped a beat. I was Zi's aide and Zi was asking me for a suggestion. We were on Zedius, the Perfect World and I had found evidence of evil intrusion. This question was a very big responsibility to answer.

"I suggest,,," I hesitated. I looked at Zi and I wished that he had met Jini too, so I could trust his judgment. I looked towards the willows and my suspicion was long converted into conviction. I wished Acrodorf were here. Actually, I was quite fed up of my attitude of wishing someone else would rescue me from my reality. It would be a very stupid request to wish that Acrodorf leave his life and his purpose and mind mine. That was crazy. This was my life and it was leading me to my purpose and my struggle and my victory. In wishing someone else was here to do that for me, I was throwing my life away to be lived by someone else. This was worse than suicide. I was killing my spirit in every situation of my life, that I wanted to pass onto another to handle and solve.

"I suggest," I found my voice, "I go towards the willows and understand what's going on." I could feel the power in my spirit, from the moment I decided to let go of my cowardice.

"I will go there and check if Jini is really evil and if she is, then what is her purpose on Zedius. I will stay in view from where you can see me. If I disappear out of your sight, rest assured that Jini is here to make trouble. And if that is true, then you will be the most important witness to that truth. I don't know how you will handle it from there but if I come back, then I will think with you," I spoke without a speck of fear in my voice and in my soul.

"What if you don't come back?" Zi looked a little perplexed. I guess responsibility does that to you, it makes you…..er….. responsible.

"Then my purpose of being your aide is fulfilled," I grinned.

"No matter what happens, don't die. Else you won't be able to return back to your planet," Zi warned.

"I know that," I smiled.

Jini's form was visible again. Before she could make her approach towards us, I started to walk towards the willows.

"Be careful," Zi hushed, "may the force be with you."

Zedius- The Imperfect World

I walked towards the willows. I wondered if Jini had spotted me. I was out in the open and I had no cover. She was not there in the magnetic field, but she was here now. How did she do that? Was Jini still evil? What was her purpose? Why were the willows here?

I guess mystery brings fear. Ignorance breeds fear. Confusion leads to doubt. The only way to know the truth behind all that you suspect is false and evil, is to confront it. That is what Thelda did. That is what Acrodorf did.

I could feel Zi behind me and I was happy that I was keeping him safe. I dared not turn back, lest that would invite attention to him. He was important for the mission. I could see Jini clearly now. She was standing with her back rested on a willow. Her knee was bent and her foot was resting on the bark. She resembled a lady in the display window in the red light area of Amsterdam, waiting for her prey to set eyes on her, so she could free him of any goodness that was still left in him.

The willows were getting closer. Jini was looking straight at me, smiling with delight.

The willows were swaying in an imaginary breeze. Maybe, they were trying to warn me to stay away. Jini straightened up and stood facing me. I stopped a few meters away from her. She stretched out her arms lovingly.

"Stop!" I frowned at her and I saw Jini's expression twitch.

"Why are you here? I didn't see you in the magnetic field!" I challenged her. If the love that Jini showed was a façade then it wouldn't last long. I was right. Jini's expression changed and her eyes flickered, rapidly changing colors. She started to walk towards me. Her thick mane did not as much as move as she walked. Her hair was like bars hanging from her head. Her eyebrow curled upwards at the edges giving her a very sinister look.

I walked forward and a few branches of the willows swooped my way.

"Darn!" She barked at the willows. Her beautiful face reflected wicked delight.

"If it weren't for these damned willows, you would be dead by now," she cursed at the willows and me.

"How is that?" I asked.

One of the most important things that I learnt in my adventure in the universe is that communication is a powerful thing. If you can just keep the communication going, then you can achieve any objective you want. Non-communication is what leads to wars and disaster and never ending squabbles.

Jini's eyes were blood red. Her beautiful form held no beauty in it anymore. Even though her body and her face were made to perfection, it was not beautiful. Beauty is the domain of the soul.

The soul, its purpose and its magnitude are what radiate from the body and that is what another soul perceives to be beautiful or ugly.

"I can't destroy the willows because they are not connected with me. They are connected with you." Jini spat in rage.

"Huh?" I did not understand. My answer took Jini by surprise, because her expression dropped to confusion and she stood still, staring at me. I feel evil thrives on fear. When you fear something, you give it more power. I did not come to Jini in fear. I came to her in curiosity. I was curious to find out what was going on with her, so I could make sound decisions on how to approach her and my purpose with Zi on Zedius. Sure, I could be her prey and I could be harmed, but then, that threat was evident even without my curiosity about her. Either way, I would have to run for my life, but in knowing her better, maybe I could save Jini, and myself, from her.

"What?" Jini cocked her head on one side, confused with my reaction.

"What do you mean, that the willows are not connected with you?" I continued, as the willows crept in on me with their branches, vigilant for any motion from Jini's side so they could swoop me clear from her.

"The willows," Jini sighed, disoriented.

"Look," she sighed again.

"Ummm," she mumbled.

I was astonished that my question had confused Jini. I guess no one communicates with people who are evil, and so they are not used to being communicated with. People just run away from them without even having a conversation or even making an attempt to understand what's going on. The sad part is that people don't get it; they don't get the simple fact that you can't change something if you don't accept it and understand it first.

Back on planet Earth, when I found that Danny was behaving weird and difficult, I just stopped communicating with him. When a colleague at work was behaving rude and burdensome, I stopped communicating with him. Little did I know that in restricting my communication with them, I had unwittingly embarked on the route to evil with them. Things only grew worse with Danny, not to mention that they grew unbearable at work too. I found myself frustrated, because I did not understand them and their ways anymore. I began to doubt my own ability and purpose as a result of that. I began to quarrel and fight on issues that were not even worthy of being quarreled upon. If I would have had the courage to keep communicating with Danny and asking him the right questions, maybe I would have found out that it was the stress at work that was killing him. If I had had the courage to communicate with my colleague at work, maybe I would have found out that it was his mother's terminal illness that was affecting his attitude. If I had just cared to communicate, to be curious, to understand, I would have found the source of the problem and solved it or changed it. If I had just kept the communication going, maybe I would have understood that their foul temperament had nothing to do with me. And maybe with that understanding I could have changed our relationship for the better.

If I dared to make any attempt to turn Jini's evil around to goodness, I had to understand what made her survive.

"The willows," I could see Jini struggling to gather her thoughts. She was not used to conversations.

"Let me explain," she finally found her bearing. Her eyes glowed blue, her eyebrow straightened up and her face turned beautiful again. I could feel the willows relax their reach.

"All beings have their space," Jini spoke folding her arms. I understood that part. I had shared my space with Acrodorf and Thelda and even Bren. And I knew that you connect with beings with whom you share your space.

"Space is not defined just with proximity to another. It is defined with intention and purpose. If you intend me and if your purpose connects with mine, then you invite me in your space." Jini spoke as she carelessly wandered around the willows, caressing their drooping branches as she did. I stood still in the safety of the one that was connected with me.

I stayed silent. Jini cast a glance at me and I nodded.

"The willows don't intend me and so I can't enter their space. If I can't enter their space, then how can I impact them? I can't! I can only harm you with your permission," she shrugged, making some incomprehensible gestures with her hands as she did.

"You mean I am connected with you and my purpose is connected with yours, and so you can harm me?" I bit my lip as I asked that question.

"Sure," she grinned as her eyes flickered and changed color to black. I wondered what the color signified.

"I don't understand," I stammered.

"You feel me in your gut. You imagine me in your nightmares. You look out for me when you walk. You have me in your space." Jini laughed. She first thrust her hand in her stomach and then bobbed her head animatedly mimicking her words.

"You fear I will stall your purpose. You fear I will create trouble in your journey. You plan my interference in your purpose and you also plan the resolution. You see me create doubt in your purpose and you also create my destruction. You drag me into your reality and then you ask me, why are you here?" Jini laughed aloud, and continued to laugh till her eyes were blue and teary.

The hair rose at the back of my neck. Was Jini asserting that I had led her into Zedius? Was she insinuating that I was the reason she was here?

"You mean, I am the reason you are here?" I shuddered at that possibility.

"Aw poor baby," Jini scowled in pretended empathy. "I brought you here. It's all my fault. How will I face Acrodorf," Jini mocked mimicking my agony, which was written all over my face.

"You are one reason amongst many," Jini smiled her devilish smile. "You have a gift. A gift of perception," she raised her eyebrows in suggested admiration.

"You perceived me," Jini added, with her deceptive smile, striding towards me. "That is a gift not many have, a gift to perceive what's wrong, a gift to perceive disaster. You have that." She pointed towards my heart.

"But your gift becomes a curse for others, when you perceive it and do nothing about it!" Her eyes severed. Jini stood close to me with her legs apart and her arms crossed in the form of a military sergeant about to order war.

My soul wrenched in my body. I had a gift to perceive disaster. It was true. I had perceived Jini. I knew with absolute certainty that she would create trouble. I was so sure that I had even looked out for her. I had warned Acrodorf. But….. I had left it there. When disaster is perceived, then it has to be handled so that its occurrence is stopped. What kind of gift is it to perceive disaster and then watch it come true? That's a curse. I could have done something about it then, when I had the chance. I could have put my foot down and involved Bren and maybe some others. But because I doubted my own ability, I let evil prevail.

I had great perception. I had perceived that my colleague Mark was swindling money in the company and I did nothing about it. After he had created a million dollar loss to the company and he was fired, I took glory in my perception that *I always knew it*. What good did my perception serve, if I could not protect my company from a loss? I had perceived that Danny would leave me. I knew it from the day he started immersing his attention in his work and taking it off our relationship. I knew there was trouble, but I did not work to set it right. I left it to meet its prophesized reality. When Danny left me, I took pride in my perception that *I always knew it*. Perception is a gift, when you can create alternate realities from the evil ones that you perceive. The future is not written in stone, it is created everyday. The future is a consequence of a present action. Because I failed to take action on my perception in the present, I participated in the creation of evil.

I brought Jini here with my perception? This was too much for me to handle. How would I face Acrodorf?

"For me to be here, I needed a gateway. I needed someone to invite me here, even if it is just from their thoughts. You helped. Ray helped. Zi helped amongst many others. When evil becomes a mass preoccupation, it opens gateways for me," Jini would not know this, but I was relieved to hear that others were responsible for her presence too.

"When you doubt goodness and greatness including your own ability to create the two, you give me space in your universe, you invite me in your world. So here I am," Jini bowed at the magic of evil, that we had collectively created with our thoughts.

"I didn't see you in the magnetic field. How did you get past Dana? How did you get past the magnetic field with your powers?" I was curious to know how Jini managed that.

"Just because you didn't see me, does not mean that I was not there. I was there all along. You felt my presence, didn't you? You knew I would be there, wouldn't you?" Jini grinned. "And Dana sees no harm in me for I have no powers really. Evil is innate to me. I am evil. How can you take that away from me? It's not an acquired ability, it is me. Jini is evil. Evil goes where Jini goes. With my looks," Jini paused and winked cunningly, "even the devil would not suspect my intent. Besides, we were supposed to leave our powers behind, not our intentions. And the truth is that, intention is all the power you will ever need to create," Jini paused, "or to destroy." And with that, she burst out laughing at her own joke.

I shuddered. Jini must have worked really hard to deceive the being of Zedius, who brought her here into believing that she could even assist in saving Zedius. Wait a minute! I didn't bring Jini here, a being of Zedius brought her here, someone she had very cleverly deceived. So, why was she putting the responsibility of evil on my shoulders? I guess evil people are so, because they kill you first with guilt. They make you believe that it is all your fault. And when you beat yourself small with that remorse, they kill you effortlessly. Jini was trying to break me. I could see that.

Jini was done with her conversation with me and I knew her next move was to kill me. I had to keep her engaged. I was not done yet in understanding her or her purpose.

"How did you escape the Planet of Truth? Did you not find your truth there?" I asked her, hoping she would bite my bait.

"Hmmmm. You are clever. Very clever." Jini complimented. She found a large protruding stone besides a small willow on the right. She perched herself on it. I could have a clear view of her and I was hoping that Zi had too.

"The Planet of Truth shows you the truth about you. You were living a lie and the truth liberated you. I am living the truth. The more I see it, the more I live it." Jini spoke lazily from her perch.

"What is the truth about you?" I was curious. Jini was evil; that was the truth. If that was the truth that I had discovered about myself, I would be devastated. I would change that. The truth must aid goodness. The truth must aid creation. What kind of truth was Jini talking about?

"I am evil. I destroy. I deceive and then I dominate," Jini spoke matter-of-factly interrupting my thoughts.

"And you are okay with that?" I asked, confused on how anyone could be at peace with being evil.

"That's my purpose!" She exclaimed logically, tossing her hair on one side as she did.

"If my purpose was to create, then evil would be a problem and the Planet of Truth would serve me good. But my purpose is to destroy, so the truth that I am evil serves me and gives me more power," Jini grinned.

Jini was going to spell disaster on Zedius. She was not like the lion that I had met on The Game. Couga was unwittingly playing a game he did not like. But Jini was purposefully in the game of destruction. And when one is on a purpose, it's almost impossible to change their mind.

"I have waited for so long to be here on Zedius. Zedius opens access to others. It was extremely difficult to get here. My mission will finally see its light," she smiled wickedly.

"Your mission?" I quizzed.

"Zedius will no longer be the Perfect World!" She exclaimed, clapping her hands. "Zedius will belong to me, to us," she waved her hands, first pointing to herself and then to the sky above.

"What do you mean?" I looked above, and there shone a clear sky full of heavenly bodies.

"I come from The Planet of the Original Sin," Jini said standing up abruptly. "My kind has eyed Zedius for a long, long time. It would be incredible to be, do and have anything we want. That kind of power would be magical in the hands of evil. The whole universe will bow to our mercy." She bared her teeth in contempt as she said that. Her eyes flickered blood red again.

"I will break the magnetic source first at the poles. That will destroy the magnetic field and open access to my kind," she said, pointing towards the sky again, to indicate that her kind were standing in wait for her to break the magnetic field. "And then Zedius, the Perfect World, will be our domain, our planet," she coughed in sadistic delight.

"But for that I have to get rid of you first!" Jini rubbed her hands as though to activate the electric charge in them, tilted her head sideways and began to walk towards me.

Before Jini could even take a few steps forward, the weeping willow scooped me up with its branch, away from her reach. I swayed with its grip tightly around my waist. I could see a shocked Zi and I motioned him to stay still with my hands.

An angry Jini was holding the bark of the willow with her hands, with electric currents sparking out of her body. The color of the tree began to change from green to yellow to brown. I could hear the branches creaking. Jini was electrocuting the tree, sucking the life out of it.

I heard a frantic whisper, "Leave your body."

The whispers grew into echoes. The tree was talking to me. It was whispering and telling me to leave my body. I didn't understand. The willow began to dry up and its branches began to disintegrate and turn into ash. I felt the grip loosen as the whole tree came crashing onto the ground. Before my feet touched the ground, another willow whisked me. There were half a dozen willows and it was only a matter of time, all of them became victims of Jini's wrath. This had to stop.

"Stop it, Jini!" I raged from the top of the tree.

"Put me down!" I ordered the willow. My command made the willow tremble and the branch lowered, till I stood upright with Jini a few feet away from me.

"Leave your body," the willow whispered.

My act of kindness towards the willows had no impact on Jini. She looked as mean as ever and her every move spelt only one purpose, destruction.

Zi had warned me not to die. I knew what dying on another planet meant, that I would never be able to return to my planet again. If

I died here, there was a chance I would be sent to The Game, to serve as game for the trespassers who found their way accidently into the universe out of their turn. But right now, death seemed inevitable. I was only saving a few willows their life in the bargain.

Jini took cautious steps towards me and the branches of the willows were crashing against each other violently in total resentment of what was to follow as a consequence. Jini spread out her hands and I saw the sparks fly. Her stride grew bigger and with a well-practiced crouch, she leapt towards me.

I ducked out of her way and Jini crashed right behind me, creating a dent in the misty ground as she did. She stood up in a flash and opened her hands again. This time she would not fail.

"You will die in my hands," she said mockingly.
One branch of the willow came speeding in my direction and wrapped itself around my neck.

"Leave your body," it whispered so loud that the sound rang in my head.

If I left my body, my body would die. Why was the willow suggesting that I die? Did they not know the rules of the universe? They certainly were on my side, saving me from Jini. Then why were they sentencing me to eternal bondage on The Game? Or, could it be possible that they knew something about dying that I didn't? I had only two options that lay in front of me. Actually all through my life, I had only two options in front of me, live or die, love or hate, do or don't, rise or fall, lie or truth. Any other option besides that was compromise. I had lived in compromise all my life. I had not really lived and I had wished I was dead on many occasions. I had never really loved and I didn't want to admit to my hate. In my juggling between do or don't, I usually did what I shouldn't have. In my haste to rise and in my fear of falling, I stayed where I was.

In lying I tried to find the truth and I usually covered the truth with my lies. Jesus Christ!!!! I had not lived at all. I had compromised.

So one more time, I had two options and this time round, unlike all the others, I could see the two options for what they were. I could either die at the hands of Jini whose purpose was that I die, or I did what the willows suggested, leave my body and er, die. The only window of doubt here was that the willows' purpose was my survival, and if they were asking me to leave my body, then that must be a part of their purpose; my survival.

Jini crouched back and heaved herself towards me.

"Leave your body. Collapse your awareness and leave," the branch growled, as it snapped loose from my neck.

I closed my eyes, shrunk my awareness to one tiny point just like I had done to hide from The Game. And then with a huge bang I exploded. Like the willows had suggested, I left my body.

I watched Jini's hand barely brush past my face, as my body fell down lifeless. I had left. I had dropped my body. A surprised Jini stumbled forward and spun around and stood next to my lifeless body, confused. It took her a few moments to gather that I was dead.

"What?" She said, as she narrowed her eyes and looked at my limp body lying on the misty ground. She looked at her hands and smiled at the impact of her touch.

"That was easy," she looked extremely pleased with her power to kill in one slight gentle stroke.

I was surprised that Jini did not suspect that I had left before she had killed me.

"With you out of my way, no one will suspect my presence or my intent on Zedius. I will break the magnetic field at the North Pole and take over Zedius, while you celebrate your immortality on The Game," Jini laughed mocking over my body.

She looked around, I suspected she was looking for Zi, and then very cautiously started to walk away from the willows, casting one last glance at my body.

Maybe this is what the willows wanted. If Jini would have electrocuted me, she would have made sure that I turned to dust, but my body was intact. The only problem was that it was a dead body. But wait a minute; I had heard dozens of stories of the people who came back from the dead. People who died but came back. If leaving my body was possible, then I could also retrieve it. Maybe, I could enter back in my body. I suspected this is what the willows had perceived, when they told me to leave my body.

"Not now," I heard the same whisper.

The willows were talking to me. They were talking to me, even when I was no longer in my physical form. I thought the willows were just trees, but they were spiritual beings choosing the form of the tree to serve their purpose. All life is like that, spiritual and purposeful.

"Jini may come back, let her leave. We will watch your body till you can come back," the willows whispered. I saw their branches reach my dead body and heave it up from the misty ground. They cradled it and then spun a cocoon-like structure around it, keeping it safe till I returned.

I had to get help. I had to get to Acrodorf. I had to warn Zi. I had to protect Thelda. Heck, I had to do something and I no longer had my body.

I hovered around and saw a devilish Jini run forward, I suspected, towards the polar region, to break the magnetic field of Zedius. Where was Zi? No sooner than I had intended him, I saw Zi rise from the misty ground from where I had left him. The mist had served as his cover. He had lain hidden in the mist the whole time that I was with Jini. I wondered if he knew what was going on. I wondered if he had understood that Jini was intent on destroying Zedius. I wondered if he knew that he was going to be responsible for Zedius. His status from being an assistant to help save Zedius had just been upgraded to being the savior of Zedius.

"Zi!!" I yelled. I watched Zi totally fixated on Jini and broke into a run after her.

"Zi!!" I yelled again, "Can you hear me?"

But Zi continued his pursuit of Jini. Zi could not hear me. If Zi was following Jini, then he knew that she was evil. If Zi was not aware, then he would have waited for me to return from the willows. Zi knew.

That was a good sign.

I had to get to Acrodorf. I had to get help.

"Come back," I heard the willows whisper.

"I can't come back yet. I have to get help. I have to get to Acrodorf!" I was frantic. If I retrieved my body, I would never be able to find Acrodorf, but as a spirit I hoped I could.

"You don't have much time to come back. If you don't make it in time, you will die," the willows whispered with a very apparent hint of concern.

"I have to get to Acrodorf. I can't let Jini destroy Zedius," I tried to reason.

"You don't have much time," The willows whispered with a sense of urgency.

"How much time do I have?" I questioned, trying not to waste any more time in this conversation.

"Maybe five minutes…."

Before the willows could complete the sentence, I was off in search of Acrodorf.

"Acrodorf!!!" I screamed, a voiceless scream and envisioned the sound to ring through all of Zedius. My awareness grew in all directions encompassing the whole planet, in search of the soul that had saved mine.

I knew as a soul, I could travel faster, almost at the speed of light, if I did not need my body at the destination.

"Acrodorf," I called out from the depth of my soul and the next instant I saw him. I didn't really see him, but I felt his presence. In the distance, there was a large block-like building of solid gold floating in the mist. I got close enough to see that it was a palace, a golden-block carved as a palace, but it had no doors or windows or any entrance of any sort. It was just a solid block of gold that shone in the moonlight. The two moons generously poured their moonlight on a large terrace that was jutting out of one of its sides. The dancing star circled the sky religiously in turn, as though staying guard to ward off imaginary trespassers.

I could see Acrodorf. He was seated on a bar-like stool made of a grayish shiny stone. In fact, all the beings of Zedius that had gone across the universe had gathered here in a semi-circle, seated on the same grayish shiny stool immersed in intense discussion.

The palace was floating along on the mist, making it look like a ship in the middle of the ocean.

One being of Zedius was seated in the centre on a large throne-like chair. He looked like royalty. He looked magnificent. His blackish greenish eyes had youth and glow in them. His skin was supple and he looked young, fresh and strong. His large black cloak lay rolled besides the chair. His hair was short and danced behind his ears. His wings were extra large that lay neatly folded on his back. His face was serene and charming, befitting a creator. He was silent and was looking intently at Bren.

Bren was standing next to the throne speaking to him.

"Thank you for your trust, Waldon," he bowed to the being that emanated a strong power.

"Acrodorf and I will do the best that we can do, to lead the change that Zedius needs in order to be restored to its full glory," Bren's look was serious, but his delight at being bestowed the responsibility was unmistakable from his body language.

I understood what was going on. In my spiritual state, the context was perceived without any periphery explanations. That energy that emanated from him was unmistakably that of the leader. I guess when you are in the presence of power and authority, you don't need to be told, you can spot the royal blood, you can spot the leader, by the energy the emits.

"Come back," I heard the willows whisper, "You have only a couple of minutes left."

My urgency grew.

"Acrodorf!" I tried to communicate with all my energy hoping that he could hear me or sense me. Acrodorf looked on towards Bren, without any sign of awareness of my presence.

The body can sometimes be a spiritual hindrance. As long as we were spiritually connected without our bodies, our mere intention was felt and communicated and now with the body, sound and presence became the medium of communication.

Though time was ticking on my body, I was not giving up.

"Acrodorf," I tried again focusing my attention on him. I was so close to him that I could hear him breathe, I could hear his heart beat. I could look directly into his eyes and through his eyes, but he could not hear me.

"Come back," the willows wailed this time, "You have only a minute left before you die!"

"Acrodorf!!!" I growled desperately into his soul and to my relief, I saw his expression change. Acrodorf flinched at first and then spun around.

"Niki?" He looked baffled and a little startled that he whispered my name.

"Acrodorf, it's me. I am here. Jini is here to destroy Zedius. You have to get to the North Pole." I blurted out.

Bren looked towards Acrodorf and frowned.

"Niki," Acrodorf frowned and looked around much to the dismay of Bren, who did not seem pleased with Acrodorf's distraction.

Two other beings of Zedius had now joined in the conversation with Waldon and Bren saw that as an opportunity to slip around Acrodorf.

"Come back, Niki," the willows shrieked, "your time is up!!!!"

"I feel Niki," Acrodorf leaned towards Bren. My soul began to tremble at the thought that I would die on Zedius. It would only be a matter of time that I would be spotted by The Game and be pulled into it. I didn't know what horrific destiny lay on the other side of my death on a foreign planet and I tried to keep my focus on my purpose.

"Acrodorf, listen to me!" I pleaded.

"She is half a planet away with Zi. We are needed here. You are needed here," Bren said sternly, trying to brush away Acrodorf's hunch.

"Acrodorf, I am here. I am as good as dead, but I am not leaving without you. I cannot survive anywhere in the universe if you don't. Acrodorf ! Can you hear me?" I begged against the stern command of Bren, who was preventing any communication that I could have established with Acrodorf.

I would not leave without him even if that meant that I would die on Zedius.

"But I feel her. That's not ordinary. We are not connected. I must find out what's going on," Acrodorf reasoned back.

"But we have an important task here. It's our opportunity now to lead Zedius to the change that it needs. We have finally been chosen to lead. It is our turn to take the seat next to the Waldon and you want to leave? Waldon has chosen us. Do you know how big a responsibility that is?" Bren was appalled that in this moment of great responsibility and glory, Acrodorf seemed to be concerned about A Niki Sanders from Planet Earth who was merely an aide, with a potential affinity for disaster.

"Acrodorf," I tried to push my intent through to him as I watched him fight his instinct. I reduced my awareness to a tiny point and then exploded into Acrodorf. Acrodorf stood up with a jerk.

"She is here. Niki is here," he said frantically. Waldon stood up and walked towards a much-rattled Bren.

"There is no way that she can communicate with me from so far," Acrodorf shook his head "I can't help but feel she is!" He exclaimed, "I need to find out!"

"What's going on?" Waldon put his hand on Acrodorf's shoulder.

"Come back," the willows shrieked in pain, adding to the tension in the already tense situation.

"I must find out what is happening. I feel Niki. There is no reason for me to, but I do. Bren will take over for me until I return, which will be soon. Please pardon my absence," Acrodorf said hastily to a much-surprised crowd.

Waldon frowned and looked deeply into Acrodorf's eyes. Acrodorf opened his wings, getting ready for his flight.

"I feel what you feel. And what's more, I feel that something is not right. And this is more than the energy of a reclusive Zedius, it is the energy of evil," Waldon said to a totally startled audience.

"I have never felt this way before. There is a perceivable shift in the energy of Zedius," he frowned and looked at others wondering if they felt it too.

The words of Waldon were enough to confirm what Acrodorf felt and without as much as a goodbye, he darted towards the sky.

"Come back," I heard the fading whispers of the willows. Acrodorf had taken flight towards the other side of Zedius. I saw him zooming towards the dancing star and I sighed with relief.

The next instant, I returned to the willows. They were cradling and gently rocking my body, keeping it warm and in motion. The willows picked up my presence and I could hear their whispers sounding like sorrowful lullabys "Come back."

The willows parted their branches exposing my body, which had turned a light shade of blue.

"Am I too late?" I asked, worried at the color of my body.

"It's been over twenty minutes," one willow whispered sadly.

"But if she is still here and not yet summoned by The Game, then maybe its not too late," another willow reasoned.

I had no idea on how to claim my body. I had no idea on how to enter it again. And even if I was late, I was happy that Acrodorf was on his way. I was happy that Waldon had picked up on Jini's energy. Help was on the way for Zedius, and maybe that was my purpose of being here. And who knows I would be of good help on The Game. I choked at the thought.

"Collapse your awareness and reclaim your body," one willow placed a branch over Niki's chest and brought my attention back to the little hope that loomed over my body.

228 // PRIYA KUMAR

I collapsed my awareness and focused my intent on my body. The entire space blanked out of my awareness and I felt the solid weight of my lifeless body around me. I struggled to open my eyes. My eyelids were shut together and I had no strength to open them. I felt very suffocated in my body. It all felt silent and still and dead. I felt an explosive urge to get out. I could not breathe, my heart was not beating, and my blood was not flowing. I was dead, certainly dead. I was just about to get out of my own corpse, when a branch of a willow came crashing down on my chest. And then the willow branches began to rain on my chest, beating and pumping it. I tried with all my might to get my heart to move, but the weight of inertia was building up.

"Come back," the willows were growling as they were beating their branches on my body.

It's so easy to wish you were dead. All my mortal life on planet Earth, when life got tough I wished I were dead, as though being dead would make life easy. Though in this moment my body was dead, I was not. I had full awareness. And as long as I was alive and my awareness was alive, death really did not close the door to responsibility. My body was dead, but that did not dim the responsibility that I carried to help save Zedius. Death is not the answer to a problem, life is. And for the first time in my life, I wanted to be alive so I could face evil and the challenges it posed and set them right.

"Come on," I rumbled in the body of Niki Sanders that was motionless, except for the vibrations of the branches that were pumping her chest.

And then the branches went still.

"They gave up?" I muttered in disbelief. So I was really dead.

But before I could react, the branches swayed low and with one forceful thrust they flung my body up in the air so far, I felt I could touch the sky. My body shot up over thirty feet above the ground as I tried to keep up with it. And then with a little jerk, it started its fall towards the gravity of the misty ground below.

"Oh no!" I exclaimed. In a few seconds, my brains would lay splattered in the misty ground, emitting a crimson red mist.

"Come on!!" I shuddered in my body with all my strength. If I were to live, then this was my last and only chance. I expanded myself in my body permeating every muscle, every vein, every drop of thickened blood and then with all the energy that I had, I burst out into every single cell of my body. With a loud gasp I shot my eyes open as I felt my body speed downwards towards the rock that Jini had sat upon.

A few inches away from the ground, the branches of the willows greeted me in their embrace as they flung me gently, this time in sheer glee that I had come back.

My head was exploding and I had an incessant cough. The willows rocked me gently before they put me down on the ground. My whole body was sore and swollen and I could barely keep my eyes open. I had a splitting headache and I could hear my heart beating frantically. I tried to stand up, but I could not.

"I have to get to Thelda," I muttered inaudibly.

Acrodorf was on his way to find me and I had to find Thelda while I could. I had to warn her. I didn't know what fate awaited Zedius and I had to get Thelda out of here.

I lay on the misty ground, limp in my body, but totally alert on my purpose. I strained my hands and my legs and tried to crawl forward. My head was exploding and I could barely see. I think being dead was a better state. The body came with a price of pain and no matter what my spiritual state, once in the body, I was a slave to its idiosyncrasies.

Acrodorf would be here soon and I would survive to tell him about Jini. That was all that mattered.

I crawled on the ground dragging my aching and half-dead body along.

I could hear music in the distance, drums. My heartbeat altered at that sound. Thelda. That had to be Thelda. The music was beautiful, almost enchanting. I could hear the melody fill the emptiness that surrounded Zedius. I could feel the vibration in the ground. And as magical as it may sound, I could feel some energy return to my body. I hastened my crawl.

A few meters ahead I saw a sight that made the hair on my body rise.

The Sacrifice

I tried to sit upright to actually believe what I was seeing ahead of me. In the middle of the open stadium that lay ahead, Thelda was playing the drum. She stood in the centre and her orange robe was dancing with the movements of her hands like a raging fire. Her hair was blown back in a breeze that was certainly not blowing in the place that I was crawling. Her eyes were closed and she was totally immersed in the music that she was creating, as though the music was emerging not from the drums, but from the depths of her soul.

The stadium stood ahead of me like an open mouth and the music reverberated from it so captivatingly that it began to pump life energy into my body. I tried to sit up. My head kept slopping down with the weight and the pain and I struggled to keep my gaze fixed on Thelda. She was magical.

The music was drawing me and I felt a growing impulse to move towards her. I struggled to move forward despite the pain and the slumber that my near-dead body was bearing upon me. I inched forward slowly. A being of Zedius appeared from nowhere and hurried towards the stadium. My heart flipped with joy. This was not one of the beings whom I had seen at the golden floating palace with Acrodorf, this one was different. But before I could even muster up the energy to call out to him for help, another being of Zedius appeared, just like the earlier one, out of nowhere and hurried towards the stadium.

"Excuse me," I barely could move my lips and the words just stayed in my mouth. In the next few moments I sat helplessly, witness to hundreds and hundreds of beings of Zedius just appear out of thin air and hurry towards the stadium, as though they did not want to miss even one note of Thelda's music. I felt the surge of energy grow in my body and I staggered my way up.

I guess music and creation does that to you, it touches your soul, it heals your pain, it brings life to the dead, it brings joy to the miserable. Music, like all creation, does that to you, it touches your life.

I stood upright with a newfound energy. It was only for a few moments before I collapsed into the mist again. I still had a terrible hangover of the pain and the deadness in my body and I still had a heavy head. I had bouts of energy that found its source in Thelda's music. I was blown away by the stadium, full of beings of Zedius who were mesmerized by the passion with which Thelda was creating one soulful melody after another with her drums.

These beings of Zedius had stayed in reclusion for millions of years. Acrodorf had said that the beings of Zedius had withdrawn. He had said that, because everyone on Zedius had the power to be, do and have anything they so desired at will, creation had become boring. If you could have anything you wanted at will, then there was no joy in having it anymore. But here they were, out of their self-sentenced sabbatical, live in concert with the Sorceress turned Drummer.

Creation is a wonderful thing. It brings life, it brings joy and it brings well-being. Music is a wonderful example of creation. And Thelda's music was fit for the Gods, not to mention the beings of Zedius.

When one creates from one's soul, it draws people. People are drawn to the energy of that being. They are drawn to the expression of his soul that found its way in his creation. I never understood the mania that followed singers, musicians and artists of every kind. I guess every artist has a magnetic impact on other people through his creation. Anyone who creates out of his soul, has around him a force that attracts people out of their homes and their miseries.

Where was Acrodorf? Despite the soulful music of Thelda that was resurrecting my body, I could not help but have flashes of terror, each time I thought about Jini and her mission and about Zi who had gone after her. Acrodorf was taking too long and I just hoped that he wouldn't be too late.

I wanted to go up to Thelda and warn her. I wanted to get the attention of any one being of Zedius, and inform them of the danger that awaited Zedius, but I just could not get my body to co-operate with the mission of my soul. It was a herculean task to crawl a few feet. I could barely whisper and my voice would certainly not find its way above the music that vibrated in every atom around me. I struggled on, towards Thelda. Maybe someone would notice me and come to my rescue, but all eyes and attention were hooked on Thelda.

A strange phenomenon was happening on Zedius. On one end there was Jini, whose evil purpose brought her to destroy Zedius. On the other end we had Thelda, whose purpose of creation was bringing Zedius together. This would probably be for the first time in the history of Zedius that destruction and creation were found in the same space.

Actually, creation and destruction *are* found in the same space. Which one will be active, is the choice of the person holding that space. At all times, I had the option to create my relationship with Danny or to destroy it. I sometimes created the relationship, doing my best to make it work. I would try and forget all the hard feelings and tried to focus on the goodness and love that did exist between Danny and me. At other times when my impatience and irrationalities took over, I destroyed it by being unreasonable and giving up. Between my self-inflicted battle of creation and destruction, it was only a matter of time that one lost and the other won.

My thoughts were broken by a shrill batter. It was followed by ear-splitting gasps from the stadium. My heart sank and my body froze at the thought of Jini's mass massacre in the stadium. I spun around from my perch with all my strength and I saw a horror struck Thelda standing motionless in front of her drum, er, torn drum. The crowd was still gasping as though someone had pulled the plug from their lifeline.

"We want music," I heard a scream and then it turned into a holler, "We want music."

This was the first time that Thelda had opened her eyes and she looked around at a stadium full of beings of Zedius. Her dream to be a rock star had been granted. Her desire to be a famous drummer had been fulfilled. Zedius had the power to allow you to, be, do and have anything you wanted, but this fulfillment was different. Thelda had achieved her dream not at will, she had created it. She had earned every single heart that begged her for more. A strange phenomenon was happening on Zedius.

This was my time to bring some attention to the ill fate that waited in the hands of Jini. I frantically started to crawl towards Thelda.

The stadium was echoing with the chant "we want music" followed by a clap. Thelda was ecstatic. She bowed in every direction in sheer euphoria. It took her a few moments to understand that the unrest was building up for her music. She looked down at her torn drum and then raised her hands to the crowd motioning them to stop the ruckus.

"The drum is broken," Thelda cupped her hands together and shouted as loud as she could.

"The music is no more," she continued. A long spell of silence prevailed in the stadium. I didn't understand the silence.

"I can make the music," one being of Zedius volunteered. He stood up from the crowd, opened his wings and flew in the centre next to Thelda.

"What kind of drum do you have?" Thelda looked around him, not at all happy at the thought of having a competitor, even before she had established herself.

"I don't need a drum to create music," the being of Zedius smiled mischievously. Thelda should have known better. We were on Zedius, where you could be, do and have anything you wanted, at will. The look on Thelda's face was to die for. She looked heartbroken and excited at the same time.

The being of Zedius took centre-stage as the audience sat in wait for his creation. He closed his eyes, raised his arms like Thelda did while playing the drum and played back the same music on an imaginary drum. He played the same melody that Thelda had put her life in, at will.

Within a few moments of the replay of Thelda's music, there was a thunderous 'boo' from the audience. The music stopped abruptly.

Before the being of Zedius could react, Thelda spoke first.

"This is piracy! It's robbery. You stole my music!" She bellowed and the crowd bellowed with her.

This was utterly insane. Zedius was under threat to be destroyed and these beings of Zedius were involved in issues of piracy and original music. If they only knew that bigger problems awaited them, they would have long past left to save Zedius.

"But I am creating it," the being of Zedius complained. He looked around and no one seemed to support his logic.

"Create your own music," Thelda said waving at the crowd, who echoed back in unison, "Create your own music."

The being of Zedius glanced at Thelda and shook his head. He hastily flew back to his seat and the crowd thundered again, "We want music."

"I need a new drum," Thelda sat on her drum to make the point clear, that there could be no music without the drum.

"Here is a drum," one being of Zedius appeared right behind her holding an exact replica of Thelda's drum. Thelda staggered off hers startled. She took the drum and alternated her glance between hers and the new one that was offered to her. They were identical.

"What skin is this?" She asked, spreading her hands over the hide, trying to feel the music within it, while she gently tapped her fingers on it.

"Er, I don't know," the being of Zedius blurted, "Is this not good?"

"I don't know that. I want to know what hide it is. Is it deer?" She queried, inspecting the drum thoroughly.

"Maybe," the being shrugged.

Thelda frowned. "This looks the same." She compared. "What wood is this? Where was this made? Does this drum have a story?"

The being of Zedius was spinning with confusion at the questions. I guess he was so used to creating at will, that he had forgotten the real meaning of creation.

"Look, music is not just about *a* drum. It's about a *certain* drum." Thelda explained to him as the whole stadium full of beings of Zedius eavesdropped.

"This drum," she said tapping hers, "was made by the Cannibals in The Game. It is made of deerskin and the wood is from the trees they felled. The drum was used to make music in sacrificial ceremonies. The last music that was ever played, was for the spiritual liberation of the whole tribe. This drum has a story. It has a life. It has a journey. It has traveled across the universe to have the next tune of spiritual liberation be played on it. This is not just a drum, it's an instrument in my creation, its an aide to my soul." She explained to a totally zapped fellow of Zedius.

"Your drum is an imitation, it is fake. You call that creation at will?" She scolded him for having tried to play with creation.

"That's why you suffer. Creation is not about conjuring up a drum. Creation is about first needing a drum for a purpose, the purpose your soul seeks. Creation is about then finding the right tree that will fit your purpose and using its wood and carving it into the base. Creation is about finding the right deer whose purpose is as eternal as music. Creation is about earning the right to fell the tree and to skin the deer for the purpose of healing others through the music you will create out of that. Creation is then in knowing that the drum you have is not just a drum, it is two souls, the tree and the deer that have gathered in unison with yours for a purpose higher than all the three put together, to heal, to liberate, to spread happiness and love. And that is the first step to creation of music." Thelda looked up at the sky and then at the being of Zedius who quickly retreated with his drum.

"You want music?" Thelda mused at the crowd.

"We want music," they roared back.

"Then create *a* drum," she giggled at them. "Fell a tree, carve the base. Hunt a deer, skin the hide. Bring the two together in perfect unison. Create a drum that is worthy of healing Zedius," Thelda waved her arms.

A murmur broke loose in the stadium. Little groups and gatherings formed instantly. Hurried discussions erupted and echoed. And then a few beings of Zedius began to dart and fly off in their virgin attempt to *create* a drum.

The crowd in the stadium became scanty but some beings still stayed put for the much-awaited show.

"Create while you wait!" Thelda exclaimed to the ones that remained. "You could build a stage here. Add some lights and maybe some fun acoustics." She laughed at a very surprised idle audience. I guess the beings of Zedius were not used to being pushed around. When you have lived all of your living life creating at will, then creating in the true essence of creation seems a drudgery.

I was surprised that the beings of Zedius left their seats and dispersed. Thelda the overly demanding Sorceress, lost her audience and fans to her unreasonable demands for creation.

"Thelda," I whispered out as loud as I could. I saw Thelda looking around for me. She had heard me. I was camouflaged by the mist so she could not see me. I think that the last thing that I would expect out of Thelda would be to search for me on the ground.

One being of Zedius tripped over me and spilled a whole stack load of wooden logs as he did. I was surprised that they were coming back, with equipment, with tools, with materials, to create a stage and the fancy acoustics.

"Thelda!" I needed to get to her before the others did, but in vain. I had to get out of the way before more beings of Zedius appeared with more materials and before I would get killed in the stampede.

The mist was not helping. I dragged my body towards the little stone luxury cottage. I had no strength to make it to the cottage, but I leaned against the tree that held the hammock at one end. Here at least I was safe and I had a clear view of the commotion that was led by Thelda the Drummer.

"I got this from my friends on a planet nearby. I think this wood will be sturdy for a stage." A being of Zedius quickly collected the logs as a few others joined in with more.

"Does anyone here know how to put a stage together?" He yelled out.

"I have the tools," One fellow answered and soon the entire stadium resembled a construction site with dozens of beings of Zedius flying around with materials, tools and help. It was extraordinary to watch beings at work, creating a stage and a set-up for the music they wanted to hear.

I don't know how much time passed by. I was having spells of amnesia. I was getting so involved and fascinated with what was happening here, that I was forgetting my purpose of being here, to warn Thelda and the beings of Zedius and to get help. My body was not even fit enough to make a point, let alone hold on to a thought.

I knew that the stage was set and the musician was set when I heard a loud roll of a drum.

"This is it!" Thelda squealed. "This is THE drum!" She said, tapping her hands on the skin and delighting a house-full audience.

"What's the story?" She asked the being who had presented the drum to her.

"It's a long story," he said bashfully. "I went to Sonar. The planet behind the two moons," he said pointing towards the two moons suspended in the sky. "I got the best wood they had ever grown. Grushe here," He said, pointing to a very excited being in the front row of the stadium, who waved back at the mention of his name. "Grushe, chiseled and carved it," he smiled. "Stef there," he said, pointing to the being next to Grushe, "Went to Dice to hunt the deer......."

And the story went on and on, about how almost everyone there had contributed in some form or the other in either creating the drum or the lighting or the stage or the sound or the peripheries that added to the creation of music.

When all the stories ended, the din started again, "We want music."

Thelda took a bow like a drummer whose sole purpose was to enthrall her audience; she set her fingers to the drum and rolled out a rythm that could liberate your soul forever.

I watched the beings of Zedius. I watched the crowd immersed in the melody. I watched Thelda become the melody. This was not the same Thelda and this was not the same crowd. These were creators, creators who could create from their purpose and desire. These were creators who could create from their soul. Creation at will is the surest way to sabotage the soul's ability to create for a purpose. Though Thelda was creating the music, every being of Zedius present there had a hand in that creation. Some had created the drum. Others had created the stage. Someone else had created the lighting that added more magic to the music. Some contributed to the sound effects that enhanced the music. The listeners created a strong desire for the music that gave it purpose to be created. Every single being there was a creator, of the music.

Every single person is a contributing source in the final creation. So it may seem like the author was the creator of a book. But along with that one creator, there were hundreds of others involved in its creation. The author created the story, the designer created the cover, the printer created the copies, the distributor created the supply, the reader created the demand, the PR created the hype, the media created the awareness. Creation is not an individual phenomenon. Creation is not an isolated event. Creation is a planetary drive, a drive that had gone missing from Zedius for a very long time.

I was working in the sales department of a daily newspaper. I never thought I was a creator or that I was even creating anything. I was just doing a job. If the being of Zedius who created the stage for the music to be created on, could be a creator in his own right, then why was I behaving like a foul employee? I was creating the business that would ultimately help in the creation of the magazine. There was not just one creator, creation was a collaboration of co-operation.

To a naïve soul, it would seem like Thelda was at the centre of the attention and it seemed like Thelda was the creator of the music, but it would take an evolved soul to perceive that every single soul in the stadium had a hand in the music, that emerged from Thelda's hands and spread into the soul of Zedius.

I felt two hands on my shoulders and I jolted out of my thoughts.

"Niki?" It was Acrodorf. My heart pumped faster and I felt some energy return to my body.

"Niki!!!" Acrodorf said trying to hold me up. His eyes were narrow and his expression was that of disbelief and shock merged together.

"What happened to you?" He looked at me intensely and then cautiously looked at the raving crowd growing to Thelda's rythm.

"Jini is here," I struggled in whispers, trying to stand upright. I collapsed in Acrodorf's arms.

"Listen to me. I am fine. Jini is here. She is going to break the magnetic field at the pole, so that her kind can enter and take over Zedius and its powers. Jini's purpose is to destroy Zedius and make evil prevail in the perfect world!" I spoke in spurts and shivers. Acrodorf hung onto every word patiently, with his expression growing graver and graver, till the last word was uttered.

"You were right," he pursed his lips, he held me tighter and said, "We have to get to Waldon and Bren, but I'm afraid I won't make it to them. She must have headed to the North Pole," he looked ahead estimating that Jini would have headed for the North Pole of Zedius since it was the closest from where we were.

"We need this performance to stop," Acrodorf said urgently.

"Wait here," Acrodorf said, laying me down on the mist. I saw

Acrodorf hurry towards the stadium.

Through the mist and the tears, I saw Acrodorf fly above the stadium and land next to Thelda. Thelda was oblivious to his presence and so were the audience in the stadium. They all were connected to their creation, Thelda's music. Acrodorf stood there dumbfounded. Every now and then a cloud of beings of Zedius formed above the stadium, flying, somersaulting and sailing to the beats of the music. The sight was magical. I could not figure if Acrodorf intently did not want to disturb the concert or he too was mesmerized by it.

A few seconds later, Thelda drummed the outro (the ending) and with the last note she lifted her hands and took a bow to a wild, howling and shrieking audience. It is only when Thelda turned towards Acrodorf to bow to the audience on her left that she yelped out, alarmed.

Acrodorf immediately pulled Thelda into his arms as a symbol of his appreciation of her music. It took him a while to figure that the entire set-up was created with force, effort, vision and collective purpose.

"Beings of Zedius......." I heard him address the crowd, like a politician, a presidential candidate addressing his constituency.

I heard Acrodorf passionately appraise them of the crisis at hand and I heard the shock emerging from the audience. Acrodorf's last word was met with a clamor that spelt unity, that spelt purpose, to save Zedius from the evil threat of Jini.

I saw the beings of Zedius fly off in different directions. The sky was full of them, darting off in all directions like an exploding star.

"Niki, are you alright?" I heard Acrodorf's concerned voice. I had no strength to tell him what had happened with Jini. Acrodorf lifted me up and I could not hold myself in standing position. Thelda came hurrying in behind him.

"Niki, you missed a legendary performance," she said excitedly embracing me and shaking me enthusiastically. I smiled feebly and then collapsed onto a very shocked Thelda. Acrodorf came to my rescue and held me from pinning a totally startled Thelda on the misty ground.

"What's the deal with this passion?" Thelda joked, totally oblivious to my state. Acrodorf held me tight. Thelda was not in the least affected by the news that Zedius was in danger. Maybe she knew and maybe she chose to be happy and excited in the moment.

One being of Zedius came and stood behind Thelda, er, as her aide. She was a rock star and she only deserved to be waited upon.

"I need to hurry to the North Pole," Acrodorf looked at me with worry. I don't know if the worry that I saw in his eyes was only for Zedius. I suspected and would have loved to believe that part of the worry was also for my life.

"I will come too," Thelda said enthusiastically. "My powers and my presence would only be of help," she chirped. Thelda was not the chosen one in assisting to save Zedius but Thelda believed otherwise.

"I can take you," the aide jumped in.

"Let's go then," Acrodorf said. He spanned his wings and then looked in my direction. I was near dead. My spirit was doing a lousy job at keeping my body alive. If someone else had been in my place, like the near dead instances that I had heard about, then they would have spent a month in coma doing their best to get their body started and going, before they crawled for miles getting help for Zedius. I was as good as gone. I had just needed to survive until Acrodorf could reach me and get help. My purpose for being alive was fulfilled. My purpose of being here on Zedius was accomplished.

"Come with me," Acrodorf read my mind. He bent forward and lifted me in his arms. Acrodorf was not going to leave me behind. Thelda was delighted that I was going too and we all took off towards the North Pole of Zedius.

Thelda was perched neatly in the arms of her aide, and was not happy with the fierce wind that was cutting through, as we took flight towards the two satellites. Thelda tried to open her mouth to say something, but the wind gushed in and forced her to keep it shut. I knew that Thelda wanted to fill me in with her infamous performance. I wanted to tell her that I was there, or maybe on second thoughts I would like to hear Thelda's version of it.

The wind was piercing my eyes and I decided to keep them shut. I was in the security of Acrodorf's arms and all that mattered was that I had contributed in his purpose. This was the closest that I had been to Acrodorf, physically. Making a physical connection with a being from The Perfect World sent chills down my limp spine. His body was warm, er, hot. His skin was baby smooth and emitted a faint spicy smell. His heartbeat was loud and his chest throbbed against my face. Acrodorf was near human, except that he was not.

Acrodorf's grip loosened suddenly. I felt a jerk and my body arched into a fall as the gravity of Zedius pulled me towards it. I shot my eyes open and I could see Thelda falling down, her orange robe blown upwards like a parachute. Her aide was speeding behind her with his arm stretched out to catch her. I was also headlong in a free fall, before Acrodorf caught my arm and held it tight. Now we both were falling downwards. Acrodorf tried to regain his balance, flapping his wings hard. The greenish black feathers began to break away. It was only moments before he gathered his strength, steadied his flight and hauled me up with his grip. I craned my neck just in time to catch Thelda being swooped away by the aide. I was relieved.

Another jerk threatened to heave me loose from Acrodorf, as we somersaulted into the sky out of control. The jerk was so solid that I felt the satellites shift in position too. The distance between them had grown drastically.

"The magnetic field is disintegrating," Acrodorf growled in my neck. "Hold on tight," he shouted, his lips pressed against my ears. The wind was cutting into his face making it difficult for him to speak.

I held tight onto Acrodorf. His hair spun around my neck and my shoulders, making a tight web around me to prevent me from falling off again. I dug my face in his neck and tried to keep a grip with my hands on his arms.

"We are there!" the words vibrated from Acrodorf's lips into my ears. I could feel the tension in Acrodorf's muscles, as he started his descent towards the horizon, which held a magnetically charged bluish area. The space was heavy and charged. I could feel tremors in the ground that were finding their way up towards us, threatening to steal me from Acrodorf''s grip, as he struggled to keep his balance and his hold on me. I looked around and Thelda and her aide were nowhere in sight. My heart sank. I hoped that Thelda had not fallen off with all these magnetic tremors, that were becoming more and more violent with every passing second.

Acrodorf landed us on a misty electrically-charged ground. He laid me on the ground that was trembling wildly like a feverish puppy. Sparks were flying out from the mist at many places. The North Pole was lit up like day, because it was the closest to the two satellites. A blue color prevailed the mist and shone with silver electric sparks every now and then. I could hear the rumble from within the ground and I could hear it creak. Acrodorf ran towards the dark blue spot far away, I suspected that was the magnetic source. The ground creaked in the space between us and with violent tremors it split open in the distance between Acrodorf and me, making a divide between us. Acrodorf was half-running and half-flying towards the magnetic source.

The tremors were very violent and the ground below me began to sink. I wanted to cry out to Acrodorf - but getting him back to save my life at this moment would mean the destruction of the entire planet.

In the end, we all have our own battles to fight. I had to battle for my life and Acrodorf had to battle for Zedius. Which one was important was not the issue. The issue was that, as long as each one of us fought our own battles, then our lives and the world at large was safe. When people learn to take responsibility for their own battle and their own struggle, then everyone wins. I wished I had learnt this lesson earlier. I wished I had known this truth earlier. I had only blamed Danny for not fighting my battles. I had made him feel small for not making me his priority. So I never grew in learning to take care of my life, but I kept him crushed with the guilt of not being able to be there for me, for the things that I needed him to tend. My expecting that from Danny, had not only lost him many opportunities for his own progress, but eventually I had lost him too.

The ground below me sank as did my heart in remorse, at the stupidity of my life on planet Earth. The ground sank and tilted towards the crevice, the large gap that had formed between me and the dark blue spot in the distance. My body began to slide towards the gap slowly. I could not get up and crawl away. My energy had sapped out and I was beginning to drift in and out of consciousness. Soon I would be swallowed by the planet, the Perfect World.

The tremors became waves as I slid. I knew the end was a few feet away. I tried to get a hold of something, but there was nothing except the smooth silvery sand. I tried to dig my hands in it but it wouldn't stay. I could see the big mouth of the crevice and I gasped and made one last futile attempt to dig my hands and feet into the mud. With my face dug in sideways, I dug my fingers and toes into the sand and thankfully, my slipping came to a halt about five feet away from the crevice.

There was hot vapor emitting from it and a creaking and groaning sound kept coming in lazily at intervals. My hands and my neck ached with the weight that they were holding. I don't know if I was dying or dead, but I could not feel my body anymore. I felt no body sensation of pain or struggle. I felt a relief. I could see myself lying on the misty ground motionless. The gap lay in wait for my hands and feet to loosen the grip, so that it could relish me and send me off to The Game.

I was drifting between life and death. I saw Acrodorf near the blue spot. It was a very dense place, you could see nothing but a dark blue electric cloud, that was sitting right at the top of Zedius holding its magnetic field. I could see Jini. I could feel the fury build up in my soul and I could see my body tremble on the ground.

Jini was lying on the spot near the dark blue magnetic field, with her hands stretched above her head, her fingers dug into the ground. She looked up and cursed and then dug her head in the mud, putting extreme pressure on her hands and then there was the tremor again. The dark blue cloud shifted and became a shade lighter and thinner as she did that. Jini was breaking the magnetic field.

Acrodorf stood dumbfounded. I could feel his soul. He turned around and looked towards me and frowned. My body was far away breathing its last and I was here with him. I could feel his soul. Acrodorf didn't know what to do. He wished Waldon were here. He wished Bren were here. He could not attack Jini or as much as touch her, because she was connected with the magnetic field and had so much electric energy flowing through her, that she could electrocute any living matter to ashes in seconds.

I looked around. Where was Zi? Had she killed Zi? No sooner than I had thought of him I saw a wounded Zi trudging towards Acrodorf. Acrodorf ran towards Zi, horrified.

"Don't touch me or come near me!!!" Zi shouted. There were burn marks on his face and also his body. He was walking with a painful limp.

"Don't touch me," he warned again, "Don't come near me."

Zi's head was hung low and he was walking with difficulty, clutching his knee with his hand as he did.

Acrodorf stopped short, helpless. He could not attack Jini and he could not help Zi.

"I tried to stop her," Zi tried to explain solemnly.

"I tried my best," his voice quivered as he spoke.

"I could not stop her, but I sure did delay her in her mission." He had tears in his eyes as he spoke. Zi was asked to assist in helping save Zedius, and that is exactly what he had done. If he would not have been here, Zedius would long past have been destroyed in the hands of evil.

"What happened to you?" Acrodorf asked Zi. Jini raised her head and glanced at the two. Her eyes gleamed like the headlights of a speeding truck emitting rays of bright red as she looked towards them. One red dot settled on Zi's chest and another on Acrodorf's.

"DUCK!!" Zi shouted and fell on the ground with Acrodorf following suit, as a lightning bolt of heavy electric current cracked through the space where they had stood.

"If her current touches you, you will carry it to destroy others!" Zi trembled as he tried to stand up.

Oh My God! Jini had loaded Zi with her current and now he was carrying it. That is why he was telling Acrodorf not to touch him and stay away. This was insane. Jini was not just breaking the magnetic field, she was also breaking the electrical field of the beings who came in contact with her.

Zi had tackled Jini all the way to the North Pole. I had great admiration for Zi. It takes immense courage and compassion to be able to battle with evil hands-on, to risk one's own to save a million others. I had done the same thing. I was acting more out of duty and responsibility, out of natural instinct. And I knew without a doubt that Zi had done that too. He was not doing a favor on Zedius by helping it and protecting it. He was doing it, because that was the right thing to do. I guess what people admire is that sense of responsibility, that state of compassion and selflessness behind the action.

The ground trembled again and the magnetic field became lighter and visibly thinner. A being of Zedius came zooming down awkwardly from the sky and fell down close to Zi. It was Bren.

He was clutching his right wing agonizingly. His face turned white with shock as he saw Jini lying on the misty electric ground, hell bent on breaking the magnetic field of Zedius.

"So it is true!" Bren said frantically. He started to pace around on the shaking ground, trying to come up with a solution to get Jini off the ground. The magnetic field was already weak. It was affecting the gravitational balance and that is why Bren had fallen down. He was just in time to make it here, because now the beings of Zedius would no longer be able to take flight.

Why couldn't they create something at will? Why couldn't they use their powers to be, do and have anything they wanted to save themselves and their planet? They were creators, why wasn't their creation coming in handy to save their lives? If they couldn't do this, then what good was any of their powers?

"We were not prepared for this!" Bren exclaimed, answering my doubt. "Zedius was built on the premise of goodness and perfection. Evil is foreign to us. It is unthinkable and incomprehensible. We survived its influence for millions of years and never suspected that we could ever be victims of its power."

Acrodorf was heart-broken. It was evident on his beautiful face. Bren and Acrodorf stood by each other in support.

"The Perfect World was perfect, because it had no provision for evil or challenges, challenges that do not follow your rules. You failed not because you aspired to be perfect, you failed because you aspired to create perfection in isolation." Zi spoke in heavy puffs.

Zi was right, *that* was the problem on Zedius. I don't know if he knew that, but he had nipped the problem in the bud. Jini could be here on Zedius, because Zedius had no provision for evil or challenges. And because the beings of Zedius were not aware of evil, that did not mean that evil was not aware of them.

Goodness does not mean that you ignore evil and turn a blind eye towards its existence. Goodness and greatness is a responsibility. For goodness and greatness to persist, it must be guarded against evil. If all good people must suffer at the hands of evil, then goodness no longer remains an aspiration. What is more is that, if goodness is not strong enough to fight evil, *it becomes it.*

Back on planet Earth, I did not have a good reputation with compassion or care. I was known to be the insensitive one at work. I was not always like that. I was enthusiastic and full of life. But my colleagues at work would always put me down. They would always criticize my projects. They would take credit of my work and undercut me on the recognition I deserved. Though I left that organization, I carried their malicious behavior with me into my new job. I became cautious of people. I did not trust people easily. I doubted the help that was offered to me. I got defensive even when people gave feedback on my work. Slowly and slowly the enthusiastic and passionate Niki Sanders became exactly like the malicious colleagues she had failed to fight and overcome. Goodness needs to prevail and for that it must make provision for understanding and overcoming evil.

It was a miracle that Zedius had survived the influence of evil for so long.

"Evil has kept a firm eye on Zedius for a long time. Jini and her kind have been keeping watch, waiting for an opportunity to set foot on Zedius." Zi continued with his perspective and Bren was rooted at every word he spoke.
Zi sat down on the blue electric mist, shifting his eyes from Jini to Bren and then to Acrodorf. Surprisingly, Jini lay still as Zi spoke. I guess even she was curious to hear Zi's perspective.

"It took Jini to bring your flaws to surface. It's a pity she does not believe that her act of evil has been the greatest act of goodness for Zedius." Zi panted.

I could hear the strain in his voice and I could sense his struggle to keep his body alive. Zi was the chosen one and his words were evident of that trust the beings of Zedius had in him.

Trust is a tricky thing. In trusting Zi to give them a perspective to save their world, the beings of Zedius had to digest the fact that they were wrong. Sometimes people confuse trust with praise; because I trust you, you should tell me that which I would be pleased to hear is not trust, that is flattery. Because I trust you, I expect that you tell me the truth even if it hurts me, if it aids my survival and progress. Trust is a big responsibility that weighs heavily on both sides.

Zi stood up abruptly and began to walk towards Jini. She had not moved ever since Zi had started to speak. Acrodorf and Bren moved closer to Zi, expressing their unsaid support. The ground shook again as Jini raised her head and bared her teeth in Zi's direction.

"Alas, your perspective came a little too late! I will take over Zedius!" She grinned with her eyes flashing red and the ground beneath began to crack as Jini flung her hands up and then bore them into the ground, sending up sparks in the mist that surrounded her body.

"There must be a way," Acrodorf looked at Bren, adding to the urgency at hand. The tremors were making it difficult for them to even stand without staggering. With the weakening magnetic and gravitational force, it was clear that no more help could reach them. To make things dramatically worse, the smaller moon first trembled and then large cracks in its centre were visible even from where we were.

"We need to act fast," Bren spoke helplessly looking around for Waldon to magically appear and save Zedius.

"I know," Acrodorf said in sudden cognition.

"Waldon had said once," he spoke solemnly looking sadly into Bren's eyes. Bren leapt up and held Acrodorf from the sudden jolt that emitted from the ground, as Jini dug her hands in the ground again. There was thunder and lightning in the sky and the smaller moon began to shake like a leaf.

"The only one source of electric energy to counter Jini's evil emission,,,,," Acrodorf hesitated, "is that of the spirit."

Acrodorf and Bren gasped together.

"Only a soul can produce an infinite mass of energy, that can construct the magnetic field, counter any evil force, and hold planets together. That is the only way to save Zedius. The magnetic field will soon collapse and there is no way we can build it back in time, before the evil beings of Jini's abode enter Zedius. But, if one of us drops our body forever and connects with the magnetic field, then the electrical energy of the soul is powerful enough to restore the magnetic field or even hold it till eternity. But that means that the soul will serve as the source of energy for the entire term of Zedius or until the magnetic energy is restored." Acrodorf said, and my soul trembled.

"Maybe this is my salvation." Bren put his arm around Acrodorf regretfully, "Waldon had warned us of this day, but we did not believe him. Waldon had warned us repeatedly that our powers were killing us, but we chose not to let go. We failed. We failed Zedius."

"Waldon has chosen me to lead Zedius to the change it needs. So I must make the sacrifice." Bren stepped forward.

Acrodorf pulled Bren back instinctively.

"Wait!" Zi yelled. He was standing very close to Jini. There was a force that was pulling him back and he was fighting to keep his foothold. His body was arched forward fighting the force that was pulling him back, towards Jini.

"Sacrifice is not salvation. Sacrifice is compromise. Sacrifice does not make a being powerful, it only weakens his soul. If you sacrifice in regret, you will live in it forever, for your sacrifice will be the reminder of your inability to set things right!" Zi shouted over the force that Jini was emitting.

My body shivered with the constant attack of the tremors that were building up in the ground below. I was struggling to keep my body stable.

"You want salvation? Straighten up the mess you made! That is real salvation. How else will you learn? If you don't learn that, you will only make a mess of further worlds you create." Zi staggered, keeping his foothold. Despite the disaster that was wreaking havoc around us, Acrodorf and Bren paid heed to every word that Zi spoke.

"What must we do now?" Acrodorf spoke. It was critical that they came up with a plan quickly to stop Jini, for in a few moments, the magnetic field would be broken and that would be the end for all of us.

"I will hold the magnetic field. Free Zedius, and then free me. I will stay here in the magnetic field as a debt to the freedom that you have owed Zedius for a long time. With you gone, Zedius will fall for sure. If I hold the magnetic field, then you have a chance to restore your planet in the glory you had first envisioned." Zi towered behind Jini and my soul trembled.

Bren and Acrodorf gasped. They were speechless and so was I.

"Free Zedius, and then free me! I am electrically charged with Jini's evil anyway. Let it be me!" Zi yelled out loud over the thunder and the lightning that was cracking and breaking in the skies above.

Zi was standing a few meters away from them and I could feel his power. His electric field had already been touched by evil. He was a walking talking good version of Jini but with the touch of death. His choice to serve in the magnetic field was going to give him and Zedius a second chance.

"Noooooo" I screamed, as my face near the crevice lifted with a feeble version of 'no' that my soul had emitted with all its force.

Zi jumped onto a shocked Jini. She lifted her hands out of the ground and crawled up like a wounded lioness. She snapped her hands towards Zi who leapt around them, caught her by her hair and hauled her off the ground. Jini squirmed and scratched Zi's arm and a lightning current went through his body and the ground trembled again. Zi screamed in pain. He did not let go of Jini's hair and yanked her with the last traces of energy and life that remained in his body. Jini tried to heave herself up and her hands fought around to grip him. Zi was sparking like a metal pole live with electricity. It was only moments until he would turn to ash with the amount of electric current that was flowing in his body. Zi screamed out loud and his voice pierced the depths of my soul. Jini screamed and her voice thundered in the skies.
"Jini came here to take over Zedius. I am granting her that wish! She has been an aide in saving it and she deserves it." With his last breath and his last store of energy, Zi hauled himself along with Jini full body into the dark blue area that held the source of the magnetic field. There was a loud explosion that shook the

entire planet throwing Acrodorf, Bren and Waldon to the ground. My body inched a little towards the crevice with the sand sliding slowly from my frozen grip.

Bren and Acrodorf were horror struck at the scene that had just occurred before their eyes. Bren ran towards the spot where Jini was lying. The mist was not flowing over the impression of her body, making it look sinister. There was a mark of evil that she had left over the spot, boring dark holes into the ground with her fingers.

The dark blue spot, the source of the magnetic field was alive with sparks and electric spurts. Two souls, Zi and Jini, representing goodness and evil, were now the source of the infinite electric energy that would now surround Zedius.

Bren and Acrodorf looked at each other and then the magnetic source with disbelief. They had not expected such a move from Zi. My soul trembled. I had not expected such a move from Zi.

Zedius shuddered and raged as Bren and Acrodorf went tumbling over each other. The ground began to turn solid, the dark blue spot turned blackish blue. The sky cleared up. The satellites were pulled back together. The crevice began to seal up. The moonlight poured onto Zedius with extra shine and brightness.

Jini had come to destroy Zedius and had been enrolled in the purpose of protecting it from evil for the rest of her term there. Zi had come to assist in saving Zedius and he took over that role, until the magnetic field of Zedius was restored.
I guess evil, like goodness cannot be destroyed. It can only be transformed.

It was a heavenly phenomenon where goodness and evil were bound together in service to Zedius, the Perfect World.

As the magnetic field and the gravity resumed with even more vigor, the sky filled up with beings of Zedius, who rained in on the North Pole, frantic about the disaster that had passed them by. There was a major commotion, they all wanted to know if they were late and what they could do to help.

Bren took the lead and explained the tragedy that had befallen them and how Zi, the Chosen One along with Jini, the Evil One had saved them from her curse. A bewildered crowd cheered for Zi's act of service and victory over evil. They all gathered together holding hands, making a circle that spanned through the North Pole. Bren explained to them Zi's perspective and there was a heavy silence, a silence that was loaded with realization. The silence was laden with the truth that the beings of Zedius would need to change the way they perceived power. The silence was bordered with acceptance. And then with their combined energies they paid their respects to Zi, and his acknowledgement was evident in the warmth and energy of well-being that spread through every single atom and living cell on Zedius.

"Niki!" Thelda was shaking my lifeless face.

"What is with this girl?" She muttered. Thelda lifted me up and looked carefully at my blue face.

"Niki!!" She shrieked into my face. For the first time in our whole journey together, Thelda freaked out. The Drummer did not know how to react to death anymore. Thelda the Sorceress who brought the dead back to life was gone. Thelda held me tight, "Come back!" She yelled.

Little did Thelda know that that is exactly what I had been trying to do for half my term on Zedius, to come back to my own body. But my body was lifeless.

"Focus! You are not dead. You have a purpose, focus on that! You have to witness my performance, focus on that," she whispered as she cradled my head in her arms. I giggled, but my face lay still.

"I am not leaving without you, kiddo. And I sure don't want to get into The Game once more to get you out of there," her voice choked.

Acrodorf shadowed over her. Thelda offered my face to him, signaling that it was now his turn to bring me back to life. Acrodorf bent over. He placed my head on the ground and the mist covered my face. He turned over his shoulder and was relieved that Bren and some others were walking in his direction.

"You created two butlers! You built a whole stadium! You put a whole world-class concert together!! Save Niki Sanders!" Thelda cursed at all the beings of Zedius who were gathering towards what looked like, my funeral.

There was silence. There was thick silence. No one spoke. I guess creation is not about creating 'things'. It's about putting 'life' in 'things' you create.

My soul shivered at the sight of over a hundred beings of Zedius who kneeled down on the ground where I lay, near-dead in body, but as alive as a new star in spirit. They placed their hands on my body and on each other and then a strange vibration filled the space. Thelda jerked backwards, taken aback with the force of energy that was flowing through the beings of Zedius into my body. I saw my body vibrate and twitch and then I saw it lift a foot above the ground. The beings of Zedius stood up as my body lifted four feet above the ground and stayed still. I could not help but get in it to feel what was going on. My head felt heavy and my blood flowed weakly. I felt pain and pressure on my body and my heart was beating faintly. The vibration grew over my body. I felt the pain lessen, the heaviness lift from my head. The blood began to flow, bringing sensation of life. My heart began to beat frantically. I opened my eyes feebly. After a few moments of blur, the sight was magical. A dense crowd of beings of Zedius was holding me afloat with their energy. They were sharing the energy and intention to help me bring my body back to life. I felt a spark and bounce and then I smiled weakly, my lips peeling off each other as I did.

Acrodorf smiled and a hundred of the beings of Zedius sighed in relief. I could not wait to be put down and struggled to my feet as they did. I had energy and I had strength. My body did not feel as tight and solid. It was lucid and flowy. I could move my arms and legs. I had control over my body and I felt light. I leaned onto Acrodorf, trembling with a sudden burst of life force and he held me tight and kissed my forehead. A hundred beings of Zedius huddled together, holding each other, spreading their energy towards me.

Intention is a powerful thing. Intention is what people know as prayer. Intention is the medium of all healing. Intention is the birth of love and all emotions alike. Intention is the single source of creation of life. And when intention unites on a mass scale, it can pump life into a block of stone, let alone a near-dead body.

"I want music," Thelda trumpeted above the celebration of life that had erupted at the North Pole of Zedius.

A startled crowd looked at Thelda. They were still in a trance with their energies focused on bringing my body back to life. Thelda was waving her hands and head banging at an imaginary drum.

"I want music," she grinned at the bemused beings of Zedius.

"Then let's go and create a concert, fit for a New Zedius!" One being of Zedius clapped his hands signaling his consent. He was the same being of Zedius who had been accused of piracy, when he tried to re-create Thelda's music.

In the next few instants, the beings of Zedius went buzzing towards the sky flying off in the same direction, like a school of fish running away from its predator.

Acrodorf and I were the only ones behind in the essence of Zi and Jini, whose souls were radiating through the dark spot, holding Zedius safe.

Acrodorf tugged at my arm and we walked towards the magnetic source, towards Zi.

Zedius – The Soul of The Universe

There was a sudden calm at the North Pole. The ground had leveled up, the cracks had filled in, the energy had resumed, the satellites were in place and the dancing star was doing its rounds as usual. A bluish hue filled the otherwise grey sky. It seemed to spread over the entire Zedius.

"What started out as a mission to bring perspective to Zedius, turned out to be a mission to save Zedius. And really, it was about time. This realization was long over-due." Acrodorf sighed.

"Zi is an amazing soul," Acrodorf stood near the dark blue cloud staring at it. "Saga is always right. The Planet Of Truth sees more than it tells."

"So what happens now?" I asked Acrodorf. He turned towards me and drew me close. I had developed a high affinity for Acrodorf. Beings like him were rare; so calm and yet so high on purpose.

I guess when you work together with someone and consider their well-being along with yours, you can't help but develop affinity for them. Acrodorf had considered my good and my well-being at every step, in every decision he took. He did not put me down when I was in doubt. He did not mock me when I was weak. He did not withdraw his support when I failed. He was patient and understanding in all I did and didn't do. When you have a friend like Acrodorf, when you have a colleague and a partner such as him, you can't help but have affinity for him. I had developed an intense bond with Acrodorf.

"Zi stays here as the magnetic and electric energy on Zedius, till Zedius restores its original powers. That could be another hundred years maybe. He is now the soul of Zedius," Acrodorf squeezed my hand. I could feel his emotions towards Zi and what he had done to save Zedius.

"Since he died here, then does he go to The Game?" I felt bad that Zi would pay a very heavy price for his sacrifice.

"No," Acrodorf looked at me and smiled. "Zi did not 'die'. Zi saved our planet. The universe recognizes that. We live in a fair universe. Zi will have the option to stay with us here on Zedius or return to his home planet once he is back."

"Is that why The Game didn't come after me when I 'died' and came looking for you?" A sudden realization dawned upon me, which explained my initial fear of being sentenced to The Game, in failing to reclaim my dead body.

"You died…. to look for me?" Acrodorf spun towards me. He gazed into my eyes and I did not need to answer, I did not need to tell. He held my hands folding his on mine. He read my soul. He saw my intention. Acrodorf pulled me into his embrace and held me till what felt like eternity.

"What happens to Jini?" I mumbled above the wild beating of his heart. I was curious if she would change, if her soul's purpose and fixation from evil would change.

"No soul is evil." Acrodorf smiled and let me loose. "Evil is an acquired fixation on destruction. Hopefully, Jini will be able to discover herself and her innate power of goodness and creation, while on her term on Zedius. Zedius did serve her well after all. Zedius *is* the Perfect World after all; a planet which brings creative purpose even to the evil ones."

Jini was convinced that she was evil. I had witnessed her certainty. Jini knew evil was innate to her. Maybe she was about to discover the other side of evil; goodness. Maybe evil was not innate to her. Maybe all evil are mistaken and misled souls. If that weren't true, then Zedius would have fallen to pieces right now. I guess the obvious is what is evident and what is evident is mostly true. Evil is not purely that, it is goodness gone astray.

I had gone astray with goodness. I had lost my joy and my enthusiasm and my ability to love for the sake of love. I had become bitter and unbearable. But like Jini, I had convinced myself that this was me. I had begun to believe that I was no good and I was destined to suffer. I had built my identity around the lie that I was a loser and that I would never be happy to the point that I expected disaster. I was wrong. I had discovered that I was goodness in abundance. I discovered that I was strong and aware and caring and courageous. I had discovered every single trait of goodness that there was, I had in me. I had discovered my truth and I hoped that Jini would uncover her lie and see the goodness that resided in her.

"You look better now," Acrodorf commented as he looked into my eyes.

I felt better. I felt alive. My comatose state was gone and my energy was back.

"Thank you for watching over me," I whispered looking into Acrodorf's eyes.

Acrodorf held me close in acknowledgement.

"I don't want to miss the concert," I smiled and Acrodorf smiled back. He spanned his wings and lifted me off my feet. "Let's take you to the concert then. It's time to celebrate."

I held onto him tight with his hair gleefully wrapped around my neck. The flight to the concert was low and easy paced. It took a long conversation soul to soul, filling Acrodorf in on my journey as body and as soul until I was revived and brought fully back to life by the beings of Zedius.

"It's not an ordinary gift to communicate as soul to body. It's natural for a soul to communicate with another in its natural state. But that you communicated with me as soul while on Zedius, is an extra ordinary thing." Acrodorf commented. He put me down gently near the luxury cottage of Thelda, the rock star.

The stadium was full, the rythm of the drums was overflowing. Acrodorf and I looked at each other as we heard two voices singing to the music. There was the sound of drums and a few other instruments that were stringing and beating out a music of celebration, fit for a new Zedius.

Acrodorf smiled with satisfaction. His planet, his home had sprung to life. The beings of Zedius, who could create at will, were now creating with life force, for a collective purpose.

We strolled towards the stadium and decided to stay in the periphery as witnesses to a new world that had come to life in the past few hours.

This is the kind of world I wanted to build with mine. I guess, each one of us on planet Earth have had this vision of joy, of co-operation, of support, of co-existence and a common purpose. At some point or the other, each one of us have craved for a perfect world, where all is well, where there is trust and compassion between people, where creation is the pre-occupation of all and the well-being of all concerned is their highest priority. Zedius like planet Earth had craved for it too. If each one emerged and became an active participant in creation, then that was the first step to creating the perfect world. It is when people live in reclusion and non-participation, that even the perfect world can self-destruct. If I had become an active participant, a contributing participant at work and in my relationship with Danny, then I could have laid the foundation of my own perfect world. If I had the courage to stand up for what was right and to make right what was wrong, then my world at work and with Danny would have been perfect. I had learnt now all that I had already known, but forgotten. For if I had not known it, I would not have yearned for it, I would not have been miserable in its absence. I knew now and I would build a better world for myself. In the universal context, it is never too late, for we all have eternity on our side.

The concert finally did come to an end. The applause was non-stop and an eager Bren had to take centre-stage to bring the mania to a halt.

"Zedius has come to life. The Perfect World has been overhauled and our own imperfections have been brought to the surface." Bren spoke and his voice echoed through the stadium.

Bren was right. Perfection is the overcoming of imperfections. If the flaws are denied in the arrogance of perfection, then the downfall is a natural consequence. Zedius was evidence of that, my life on planet Earth was evidence of that.

Bren whispered something to Thelda and I saw her face brighten. She straightened out her robe, combed her hair with her fingers and looked onto the crowd, her eyes searching for someone; I suspected it was me she was looking for. I smiled. Thelda wanted to ensure that I was there, for her, er legendary acknowledgement on Zedius.

"As you all know, Thelda has been important in helping Zedius with a perspective. Her natural ability to create has brought Zedius out of its self-imposed reclusion," Bren announced to the crowd that cheered with delight.

"When creation becomes at will, purpose is sidelined. When purpose is sidelined, then creation becomes a curse." Thelda placed her hand on the drum and put her weight on one foot and spoke. There was a dead silence in the stadium, a silence that rang with realization. The answer was so evident, but when one has the problem so close to one's face, one cannot see the evident and the obvious.

Zedius was suffering the same misery of my rich aunt. She had all the money, the cars, and the diamonds. Ahhhh! She had the life I could die for! Those were the things, the luxuries and comforts that I wanted. Those were the exact things that I spent my days at work in toil to achieve. And it was extremely strange to me that even though she had everything at the push of a button, she was not happy. She looked depressed and old in her expensive robe adorned with crystals. I never understood it. I felt that if I ever had all the things she had, I would be happy. Happiness is not in acquiring things. True happiness is in creating realities. If only my aunt could step out of her self-imposed imprisonment of 'luxury' and 'things' and if she could just actively participate in creation and contribution, she would discover happiness.

I wondered how the beings of Zedius never had this realization earlier? I guess when the arrogance of perfection and power clouds one's soul, then one cannot see clearly. One then seeks help from outside. The answer lay within Zedius all the time.

I focused my attention back on Thelda. Her perspective was bringing to me lessons that I needed to learn the most.

"The power to be, do and have is no power at all. It's a fantasy, it's not a reality that the universe supports. Real power is in creation with our hands of what the mind creates in thought. Real joy and real happiness is in what you created here with the music of this humble being from planet Earth." One being flew in centre-stage and spoke. I squinted to see if it was the same being of Zedius who had created the drum for Thelda.

A loud cheer broke out for Thelda and for every other being that had participated in the creation ever since we had landed on Zedius.

"Zi gave up his life and his soul to watch over us. Our ignorance cost us one life. As much as that is a great record considering the evil that prevails on other planets, we are in debt to Zi and his kind." Bren took over.

A loud cheer broke out in the stadium.

"Three cheers for Zi!" The beings of a new Zedius sang in chorus.

"We need to stay on guard henceforth to protect our planet from any evil force that may set their intention towards us, even if that means questioning the misplaced results of our actions. Our purpose will not be to destroy evil but to transform it." Bren announced and a rejoice broke out with his words.

"We cannot live in isolation, that is the height of arrogance, a disease called perfection. We will co-exist with others who would like to join us in our glory. We will request Waldon that Zedius open its doors to the universe and open it to any and every being whose purpose matches ours. We will open our doors to adventure, to learning and to spiritual growth. Zedius will be the home for anyone who seeks to build one on goodness and co-creation with a collective purpose!" Bren continued with his address. The beings of Zedius gasped at his declaration. This was never done in the lifetime of Zedius. After living in isolation, for so long, Bren was declaring that the rules be changed. The entire stadium came alive with waving arms and wings signaling their consent. A dance broke out in the sky. The beings of Zedius darted towards the starry sky and put up a spectacular show of jubilation.

Thelda walked towards me, pushing her way through the ecstatic crowd. Her aide was carrying her drum. Thelda had a different energy and charm about her. She still had the sagging eyes and the grey hair, but the energy about her was much, much younger. Her old body was totally deceptive about her youthful spirit.

"Did you like my music?" She danced as she approached me.

"I loved your music," I said, delighted. Thelda held my face in her hands inspecting if I was well.

"You look blue and dead," she joked and then burst out laughing. "I can't wait to tell you about all the adventure that happened with this drum from the Cannibals. You will be amazed at my story," Thelda's face lit up at the thought of filling me in with her adventures, that I had secretly been witness to on our journey back. I was genuinely happy to be able to hear her version of what I had already experienced. I would grow twice with her story, I knew that.

"Our term together on Zedius comes to an end," Bren joined our conversation.

Bren and Acrodorf followed Thelda, as she walked towards the hammock for one last nap, I guess. I stayed by the tree, resting my hand and my body against it. I had this funny sensation, a dizzy feeling, not out of weakness but out of euphoria maybe.

"We no longer have the promised powers where you can be, do and have anything you want at will," Bren said apologetically. Since the rules on Zedius would be changed, the old powers would no longer be in force.

"But what I can give you is our assistance if you ever need us, at will," He kept his hand on Thelda's shoulder quite expecting a disappointed outburst. Bren had brought Thelda to Zedius on a promise, and now when the time came for fulfillment he was breaking it.

"That is a bigger offer than before," Thelda said, to a relieved Bren.

"So you mean, if I so want, I can call for you from planet Earth, from two light years away?" Thelda enquired, plopping on the hammock with so much force that it rocked violently and toppled the orange bundle of enthusiasm over.

Bren roared with laughter. This was the first time I had seen such an open expression of joy from Bren. He was usually the one with the most reserved responses and emotions. I guess Acrodorf joined in the laughter more on Bren's reaction than on Thelda's fall.

"Yes," he said, coughing with laughter, "I will come to you in assistance, should you ever need me."

I guess the greatest gift one can give another is the promise of his presence. Acrodorf probably didn't know this but in breaking his promise he had given me the greatest gift of all, a promise of his presence in my life should I ever need him. If I really could tell him, I would tell him that I would need his presence in my life, forever.

Thelda did not dare to sit on the hammock again. There were hugs and kisses and goodbyes between the remaining beings of Zedius and Thelda, and soon we would be on our way off, two light years into the universe.

I had a funny feeling. Even though Acrodorf and Bren were standing with their backs to me in the distance, I could see their faces as if I was standing in front of them. I could feel their emotions as they spoke. I could feel the intention of their souls. I could see Thelda as she lay on the hammock, as if I was standing above her. What kind of feeling was this?

Thelda sensed my presence and immediately turned towards me and frowned.

I closed my eyes, I could see the beings of Zedius behind me, walking around helping clear the stadium and excitedly discussing their future with each other. I opened my eyes and pinched my hands. I was alive. I felt fine. I had this spiritual state of awareness similar to what I had when I was dead. When I was no longer in my body, I had this state of awareness where I could see and understand everything from a spiritual perspective but every time I became a body, I lost that. Right now, I was in my body and I was alive, but I had a total spiritual awareness. This felt strange.

I looked up at the sky with the two moons. They really shone bright.

Danny! I whispered suddenly.

I could see Danny sitting on my bed. He looked thinner. His jaw line was sharper and he had little puffs under his eyes. His blue eyes had a pink hue around them. He hadn't been sleeping. Danny's tall frame was seated on my bed. His hair was disheveled. I had always liked it that way but Danny would gel them back neatly and I hated it. Danny had come back. He had come back every night. He still had the keys to my house. He was sitting on my bed holding a picture frame in his hand. It had a picture of us that he had taken in the forest.

"I'm sorry," he kept whispering to my essence in the picture.

"You are not like me and I am not like you. I made a mistake. I wanted you to be like me. But," he hesitated and his eyes moistened, "If you became like me, I would not like you then! One me is enough. I love you for who you are. You are not like me and I love that about you."

"Come back, Niki." He looked at the ceiling and then lay down, keeping my picture on his chest.

I could see Danny. This was not a conjured up reverie. This was not something I was making up. This was something that I could see for real, two light years away from where I stood. I shook my head in bewilderment. I wondered if it were true. This was the last thing that I had expected from Danny. Maybe we did have a chance. Realization opens the door to another chance at happiness.

I closed my eyes and sighed.

I saw my boss, as stressed as ever, releasing his frustration on the keyboard of his computer. I saw the words roll out on the screen: "Your services are no longer needed at work and we wish you luck in your career ahead." The letter was addressed to me. My absence at work had pushed Louis over the edge and he had taken an emotionally rash decision of firing me. I think my time at my job had been up for a long time. Like my dead body, I had been failingly trying to pump life into it. I smiled. I was free. I was free to create out of my own choosing.

I saw him behind me. Even before his hand touched my shoulder, I spun around to face Acrodorf.

"You are The One," Acrodorf spoke kindly, as he put his hand on my shoulder. The whole universe must have come to a halt with his words because I felt that jerk in my heart. I felt a piercing energy with his touch and my soul sprang up with joy.

"I'm not the chosen one, Zi was….." I was interrupted by Acrodorf who grabbed my shoulders before I completed my sentence.

"I know that." Acrodorf smiled and I could see his shining white teeth. He held both my shoulders firmly.

"You are a superior soul," he said and was I stumped with his words. "You put everything together and yet you felt no need to claim the credit. You were Zi's aide. Your actions and your spiritual strength brought Zedius to this point where it has another chance, and yet you had no need for the limelight or even so the acknowledgement. When you move beyond the attachment to that which you created, you have moved beyond the bondage of matter. You are a superior soul." Acrodorf melted my heart. He read my soul. I was just behaving out of my instinct. I really had no need to go onto the stage and give a big speech. The point was made, the realization had been brought home, and there was no need for me to make claims of that which really did not matter.

"Your energy has brought a shift in the energy of Zedius and its impact has brought it the realization that was much needed." He spoke as I shuddered.

I had not meant to do anything spiritual with my actions. I was only doing what needed to be done for the highest good of everyone.

"That is the opportunity every soul has here on Zedius and in the universe. That is the opportunity very few take!" Acrodorf exclaimed. "For people mistakenly believe, that if they consider the good of all, then they will have less. 'All for myself' is not only a waste of energy, it is also bondage to matter."

"We have the perspective we need. It is clear that the beings of Zedius need to clean up their act." Acrodorf said, looking around to a new ignited spirit in the beings of Zedius. "You influenced this change, Niki. This is not ordinary. Your actions emerge from a superior intention."

Why did I have this nagging suspicion that Acrodorf was saying this, not with the intention to praise me but to nudge me to acknowledge my own greatness.

"I have personally learnt that The Perfect World is built every day. It is built in being honest with myself, even if that means to accept that I missed seeing a point, even if that means that I need to change my rules and my thinking to suit the higher good. Honesty means that I look for the consequence of my action and then decide if that is in accordance with my vision; if it is not, then to change my action and my thinking. Perfection is a result of change and constant improvement. In the ever expansive universe if I don't expand my vision and my thinking, then I will succumb to the evil that is resultant from that resistance!" I added in hindsight.

"And you know what the real power is? The more you become, the more you do, the less is your need to have. And the more you become and the more you do, you will always have more than you will ever need." Acrodorf placed his hand on my back and led me towards the others.

"Here is the mistake we made; our planet granted us the freedom to be, do and have anything we wanted. But when that power was narrowed to only creating material stuff, then we buried our own spirituality under slavery to that matter. It's like you give someone a billion dollars and he takes that money and buys a lottery ticket with it." Acrodorf said and I burst out into an unexpected laughter. I laughed and I laughed and Acrodorf occasionally laughed along.

He had struck home. That is exactly what I wanted to do with my powers. That was exactly my plan for my life back home. And I could see the naiveté in it.

I saw Thelda running behind me. I turned around and watched her trip over her robe.

"We can no longer have the power to be, do and have Niki for the rules of Zedius have changed but...." Thelda explained to me Bren's offer, that he and Acrodorf would come to us, should we ever need them. Thelda did not know that there was no greater power than that I could ever ask for, to have an assurance of Acrodorf's presence in my life forever.

Acrodorf looked at me and smiled.

"You were the most instrumental person in the transformation of Zedius," Bren said, joining Acrodorf.

"You don't have a natural affinity for disaster. That was your cover up for your natural affinity for greatness." Bren continued. "Zedius will always be indebted for the help that you brought us, by virtue of your own greatness."

I smiled and bowed my head, humbled with the praise from an evolved soul like Bren.

Thelda wriggled between Acrodorf and me.

"I can't wait to get home!" She announced and Bren beckoned that we all should be on our way.

Getting out of Zedius, was a much easier process than getting inside. Departure from the magnetic field symbolized the reclaim of all the abilities one had temporarily forfeited. In my case that did not apply though. I felt a release from the magnetic field and I paid my respects to Zi. I had liked Zi from the start. He was rightfully the chosen one.

Zedius zoomed away. It was still emanating light rays and sparks like it had done so earlier. But it did so now with different colors. Zedius was no longer hidden or obscured. It was radiating with colors that would make any being stop in his journey and take notice. Zedius had opened its doors to the universe.

"So, after you all left me at the stadium......" Thelda abruptly started her version of her experience on Zedius. Departure from Zedius was a very emotional moment, but the mood was totally broken with Thelda's excitement to fill us in with her concert. Acrodorf and Bren listened with full interest and I took delight in her exaggerated truth. I learnt that reality and experience are two different things. There was one reality that occurred but Thelda and I had different experiences of it. My version was colored with my urgency to save Zedius and Thelda's version was colored with her passion to create music. Thelda was right, in her version of what happened, I doubly grew.

Perspective is a powerful thing. Perspectives provide a chance to see the whole truth. I would never know what Thelda knew, if she didn't share her perspective. I would never be a drummer, but I became one as a part of her narration. Listening is an art; a creative art. When you listen creatively participating in the person's narration, you doubly learn, your perspective expands and your soul grows.

"So what was up with your dying thing?" Thelda chuckled, after she could not make up any more exotic and exaggerated instances.

I dryly narrated my experience with Jini and the fetching of Acrodorf. I conveniently left out the part where I was trying to reach Thelda and was an audience to her legendary performance.

"Wow!" She exclaimed in the end. "That is some story. I am glad I chose to stay and play the drum. I wonder what effect the coma would have had on my ability to play music," was her only comment.

I laughed. I laughed at the ability Thelda had, to look at the funny side of life. No wonder she was happy. She dug out humor in the gravest of situations, and while she did, she made others happy too.

"So where did Acrodorf find you?" She enquired, curiously.

"Outside your stadium!" Bren chuckled and we all had a hearty laugh for half the distance that we traveled together.

There was a dense silence and it prevailed for long. The thought of going back to planet Earth made me queasy. It was the same feeling of being ripped apart, as I had felt in leaving from planet Earth. Zedius felt like home. Zedius had Acrodorf.

"Your energy feels different, more powerful," Acrodorf said to me.

"My energy feels different too." Thelda butted into our conversation, "Though I would still have liked to have the power to be, do and have anything I want." She grumbled.

"You gave us the answer, Thelda and now you pose the same question? You brought us to realize that the power to be, do and have, is a power that is inherent to a soul. No matter where you are, no matter who you are, no matter what the condition of the world is around you, you can't deny that you have the power to be, do and have anything you want. You don't need to be on Zedius to be, do and have your heart's desire. You have that power already and it is at your disposal anywhere you go." Bren answered to Thelda's dismay.

"You chose to be a Sorceress on planet Earth. You chose to do what a Sorceress does. You had the glory resultant from that being and doing. Don't you get it? You did have the power to be, do and have, but in not using that power for what you really wanted, it didn't serve you!" Bren concluded.

What had started as a journey to gain extraordinary powers, ended with the realization that I had those powers all along. It ended with the revelation that I was even using those powers all along. The Maya that I wanted to escape from was a result of power gone astray. The illusion that I wanted to shatter, found its source in my lack of purpose.

I guess my hand was too close to my face to see that I was a powerful, immortal, indestructible soul. My hand was so close to my face that I had led my life half-blinded. I saw half the truth, I had half the vision, I did things with half a heart, I loved with half the passion, I trusted with half the faith, I lived with half the awareness and I thought with half a mind. And despite seeing only half, I never questioned the blindness of the other eye that my hand was covering. It took a journey of two light years into the universe to get my hand off my face and see the truth about my world and myself.

"What would you like to be, Niki?" Thelda tried to take the attention off from herself by putting me on the spot.

"I want to be a writer. I want to create stories about freedom and about infinite possibilities. I want to create such beautiful stories that when people read them, their soul will grow. I want to create energy, hope, greatness, abundance and boundless joy through my words. I will be a writer, Acrodorf! I will be a creator of stories that would have the power to liberate your soul," I spoke from the depths of my soul. And I felt Acrodorf's delight in my space.

I heard Thelda sniff.

"I want to read your stories, kiddo," she sniffed again.

I was happy with that thought. Finally after thirty years of drifting astray, I was finally going home, with a purpose.

Danny crossed my mind again. He was still in my house. He was talking to someone on the phone. It was Louis, my boss, er, now, ex-boss. Danny was worried that no one had seen me and that I had gone missing. He hung up the phone and sat at my writing desk. He dug his face in his hands. He looked up and pulled out a file and began to flip through the pages. That was my writing. It was a lousy story that I had written between my bouts of frustration and despair.

"Don't read that!" I muttered.

"Niki!" Bren and Thelda exclaimed together.

I sprang out of my thoughts.

"How did you do that? How can you move beyond space and time and connect with Danny in this present moment?" Thelda asked in disbelief.

"I... I don't know," I blabbered. I had forgotten that they were connected with me and they could pick up my thoughts and intentions.

"You are moving beyond space. So you are here two light years away from planet Earth and yet you can connect with Danny." Bren said, excited.

"I don't know, but I can see him. I don't know if what I see is for real." I tried to ward off any interest towards my personal life on planet Earth.

"You are a superior soul." Bren stated to Thelda's dismay.

Acrodorf was silent. He had told me this too while on Zedius.

"In this universe there are superior souls. They are creators. They move beyond the boundaries of matter, space, energy and time. Time stands still when they create. They move beyond space and they can see that, which others cannot. They create energy in all they do and matter does not define them. All souls aspire to touch that freedom." Bren explained and I hung on to every word he said.

"You," Bren said and I wanted to cover my imaginary ears. I didn't want to hear what followed, "are reclaiming your power. You are a superior soul."

Bren's words shattered the illusion of weakness that had served me well on my term on planet Earth.

"Planet Earth is about to witness a revolution, a new world, because Niki Sanders, the superior soul returns to inhabit it." Bren concluded.

I was silent. Silence is sometimes a very potent state to be in, especially when that silence is filled with the truth that you had been denying with the loudest noise. I was silent. I was gathering in me the courage to face the final truth about myself.

Acrodorf was awfully silent.

I could never have imagined this reality just a few days ago, when Acrodorf had asked me to come to Zedius. I could never have believed that I was a superior soul living in total oblivion of my eternity when Acrodorf…….. My thoughts came to a sudden halt. An imaginary thunder cracked in the space and an imaginary bolt of lightning struck my soul.

"Acrodorf!" I screeched. "You knew." I gasped with a sudden realization.

"You came to the forest for me, didn't you?!" I stammered. My presence in the forest was not an accident. I was meant to be there. Like Thelda had said, it was my destiny to be there. An avalanche of realization came smashing over my soul. If only Thelda was meant to be here, then Bren would have come alone for her. Acrodorf didn't need to come. Acrodorf was there for me! Why didn't he tell me that?

"You came for me, Acrodorf!" I exclaimed with certainty, "Why didn't you tell me?" There was silence. I could not sense anything from Acrodorf except his silence.

"Why did you come for me, Acrodorf?" I needed an answer.

"He came for you because you called him, Niki!" Thelda broke in.

"Tell her Acrodorf!" she scolded him, quite frustrated with this game of silence that she accused Acrodorf of playing.

"I called you?" I repeated Thelda's words, stunned by her comment.

Acrodorf was silent. As much as my soul was aching to hear the truth, I allowed him his silence.

"A long time ago, when I sent the communication to planet Earth, I got your connection." Acrodorf finally spoke his words laden with kindness.

"When a soul sends a communication out to another planet, then in most probability, it is a like-minded being that responds to the connection." Thelda interjected. She had not lost her habit of butting into other people's conversation.

"I never got an offer from you, it was just a connection. We get many connections from across the universe and then we lose them. Some souls temporarily connect with us and then go away. It's the same way you stop and greet a stranger and then walk on, never to meet him again. What makes the communication complete is a response, an offer to co-operate. Though I did not get a response from you, I also did not lose your connection. Strangely the connection only grew stronger and thicker as time passed. It made me curious. It drew me to you....." Acrodorf paused.

I felt Acrodorf's energy stir. I had felt this energy before. I had felt Acrodorf before. I had felt his strength when I was lost. I had felt his reassurance when I was beat. I had felt this presence that was watching over me, that did not let me fall, that kept me going in hope.

I had yearned for him. I had been seeking him in the people I met. I went to the forest every single time in search for him. It was Acrodorf.

"I could feel that you are a superior soul, trapped in the illusion of mortality on planet Earth. I could feel your spiritual unrest. I could feel your soul."

"As time passed by, Bren sent out a communication to planet

Earth. Thelda connected with Bren and volunteered to come to Zedius. When The Channel was being made, I risked everything in the universe to come here, to take a chance to bring you back to the glory and greatness you had surrendered to The Maya. I risked everything in the universe to allow you a chance to set yourself free." Acrodorf continued.

"Though we were on a mission to save Zedius, Waldon granted me the permission to follow my instinct. He said that when you free one soul, you also free a portion of the universe that is burdened under the weight of its ignorance."

"I had permission to come to you. I had permission to meet with you. And I am so elated that I did. I however did not have the permission to take you away, especially if that is not what you wanted. Our journey together rested on mutual agreement and I am so happy that you agreed to come to Zedius. The Game posed a threat. But I knew in my gut that you are a superior soul and that you will make it past The Game. Though Bren thinks that I took a big risk with you, I was only following what my heart knew to be true."

"I didn't think you would see this in this lifetime. But you did!" Acrodorf said, relieved.

I was stunned. This whole journey was not an accident. It was not a co-incidence that I was in the forest when Acrodorf arrived. I had led myself there, knowingly. I had led myself there every single day, in wait. I knew that there was more to life than what I was living. I had an inkling of a greater power, a greater force; I had just not suspected that it was within me. I was here with Acrodorf because this is where I was meant to be, in freedom and in greatness. Acrodorf was a superior soul. For only a soul that evolved would reach out to free another.

I remained in Arcodorf's silence. I shared his space. I shared his soul. I could feel that connection and I could feel it had grown into a thick bond. I remained in Acrodorf's silence, for when all was said, silence spoke a language only the soul could comprehend. Even Thelda dared not intrude.

It had to be Bren who finally spoke up, "We are close. The end of our journey is near!"

The Path to Purpose

I could not believe that my time in 'outer space' was up. I could not believe that it would end like this. I was not going to go anywhere without Acrodorf. I had connected with him and I did not want to let him go.

Acrodorf spoke to my rescue.

"We now come to the point, The Path," Acrodorf eased my soul with his words. So my time was not quite up.

"What's The Path?" Thelda asked curiously.

"The journey from here will be an individual journey. We will part ways and meet you at the magnetic field of planet Earth. You will be traveling on The Path that will lead you to your purpose!" Bren explained.

Before I could react to Bren's words, I felt a release, a release from Acrodorf's space. In the next instant, we had snapped into our forms. Thelda was as excited as always.

I stared at Acrodorf. Tears filled my eyes. I could see the whole universe in his eyes. I had traveled two light years into space with him, only to recognize him at the end of my journey. I wanted to talk to him. I wanted to thank him for taking a chance on me. I wanted to tell him that I wanted to stay connected with him forever. I wanted to tell him that I wanted to roam free in the universe with him, like we had done in our journey together. I wanted to tell him that I could not bear to let him go. Acrodorf did not shift his gaze from my eyes.

"So!" Bren exclaimed, rubbing his hands together. I don't know if it was to bring my focus back on to the purpose or it was for the delight that I was a superior soul.

Thelda was holding on to her drum with her life. A bluish horizon formed in front of us.

"Here from, we journey as individuals. Your path will be assigned to you." Bren said, pointing towards the blue horizon, which marked the line beyond which lay our freedom to choose our paths back home.

"We will be waiting for you at the magnetic field," Bren concluded.

I looked at Acrodorf. He seemed solemn and I could feel the restlessness in his soul. Why won't he say something?

"Let's go before the horizon dissolves," Bren left no room for my imaginary conversations with Acrodorf.

"Hoi won't wait." He urged

Bren darted towards the horizon and flung himself across and we all followed suit. Acrodorf was next to go. He turned back reassuringly before he leapt off the horizon and a tear rolled down my eye. Thelda hopped on dragging her drum, looking at me with compassion.

"Your purpose will lead you to Acrodorf. It has served you so far. Let's go, kiddo," she smiled.

I was the last to leap off into the bluish hue that seemed to lead into nowhere.

I felt like I was suspended in the ever-expansive universe, alone and clueless. I did not have the reassuring feeling of Acrodorf anymore.

"Niki?" I sighed with relief at the sight of Thelda.

"Where are we?" I asked. It felt weird to be on my own all of a sudden. I would have really preferred Acrodorf's company at least at this critical stage of our journey back home.

My question was answered with another presence. I felt a strange vibe close to me. Who was it?

"Welcome to The Path!" A humanoid creature emerged.

"I'm Hoi," he said. It had a humanoid form, but his hands and feet seemed to dissolve and then emerge in fumes. It was a very startling form. Though the human form is a great prototype, I don't think Hoi had got the purpose of the limbs very clearly.

"I'm Niki Sanders, from planet Earth," I introduced myself. I put my thoughts about Acrodorf aside. Thelda was right. My purpose would lead me to him. It had done so, so far.

Hoi's eyes were deep and absorbing. His hair also dissolved in fumes and I noticed that as he spoke, he also emitted vapors from his mouth.

"I'm Thelda, The Drummer," Thelda chuckled as she stretched out her hand to grasp the fast dissolving hand of Hoi. Hoi refrained from shaking hands, er, vapors.

"Your journey from here will equip you with the abilities you will need to fulfill your purpose," Hoi said and he began to float forward. Two rays of light extending into infinity emerged from where he stood.

"Your path," he said, pointing his hand towards the rays of light, "will test you and challenge you to hone your abilities and character that will be needed in the ultimate manifestation of your purpose!" He exclaimed, pleased.

Wow. This would be something! I had a purpose on planet Earth. I was clear in my vision that I wanted to be a writer, but I had this nagging doubt if I really had the ability to make it happen. When purpose is backed up by ability, then victory is a guaranteed result. I have seen so many people who do have a clear purpose, but fail because they did not invest in developing the abilities needed to get there.

"Exactly!" Hoi commented on my thoughts.

"You journeyed into the greater universe. You realized your eternity and immortality. You have a taste of freedom and creation. But when you collapse your intention on one purpose, then you need a certain set of abilities to get you through. Many drive themselves into disappointment not on lack of clarity of purpose, but on lack of the abilities necessary to drive them." Hoi exclaimed.

"That would be awesome!" Thelda burst out. "I could use some extra abilities to launch my new career as a musician with a bang."

"Tell me your purpose," Hoi said. A large white cloud seeped out of his mouth, "and I will assign you a path that will help you discover the ability to fulfill it with the glory it deserves."

"My purpose," Thelda went first, "is to create music that will take the listener on an adventure into the infinite. It will make him fall in love with himself and wake him up from his pretended misery. My music will heal!" Thelda declared proudly, tapping gently on the drum as she did.

One ray of light became thicker and turned pink. It became so thick that it resembled a tunnel made of light, stretching out into infinity.

"Your Path, is The Path of Noise," Hoi declared, pointing towards the tunnel of light, motioning Thelda to step into it.

"What? Path of Noise???" Thelda screamed, tapping her head gesturing that Hoi had lost his mind.

"Did you not hear my purpose? My purpose is to create music and you are putting me on The Path of Noise? Are you crazy, Vapor Man??" Thelda said angrily. Actually I quite agreed with her. If her path was to create music then she should be on a path that was in sync with that. The Path of Noise was the exact opposite of her purpose.

"Maybe your brains are dissolving in the vapor too!" Thelda spat out enraged.

"If the tunnel closes, you will be suspended here for eternity. I suggest you be off on the path or stay hung in time forever," Hoi said calmly to a much-worked-up Thelda. By the looks of it, it seemed that Hoi was quite used to this kind of mutiny.

"You will be damned, Vapor Man!" Thelda cursed. She raised her fist and dragged her drum into the pink tunnel of light that collapsed into a dot the minute she set foot into it.

Hoi turned towards me, "What's your purpose, Niki Sanders?"

"Er," I stammered. I had a growing doubt on Hoi's ability to assign the correct path to people.

"My purpose is to be a story teller, to tell stories that will liberate people's souls, that will ignite them towards their own immortality and their innate power to create and choose from infinite possibilities. My writing will free their souls from The Maya they create out of their ignorance!" I had a great purpose and I just hoped that unlike Thelda, Hoi would put me on the path that was worthy of my purpose, maybe towards Acrodorf.

"Acrodorf told me to take special care of you," Hoi smiled. My heart skipped a beat. My soul lit up at his name.

The ray of light became thicker and turned green. In no time, it formed into an infinitely long tunnel. I shivered looking at it. Soon I would step into it and only time would tell what abilities I would find in myself.

"Your Path is the Path of The Lost Souls," Hoi declared. He stretched out his hand motioning that I step into the tunnel without protest. I wanted to protest. What kind of path was this? Should he not be putting me on the path of creative writing or innovative thinking or how to find a publisher or ten ways to create a best seller? Hoi had strange ways and allowed no negotiation. I had to trust him and Acrodorf. I had to find out for myself what my path held for me. I took a deep breath and I stepped into the tunnel of light.

Electric energy pierced into me and radiated from every cell of my body to the point that I was consumed by the light. I became the light radiating in every direction and then it collapsed. I collapsed.

I found myself laying on a blue cloudy expanse. The whole universe adorned this gigantic blue cloud that was moving into space, towards planet Earth, I suspected. The cloud was solid and I sat up on it and looked around. I was alone. The blue cloud had little protruding mounds like the clouds on planet earth except that this one was solid. I stood up, stunned with the magical view around me. Planets, meteors, stars and galaxies moved by as the cloud moved through space. This is how I had wanted to travel in space. This is exactly what I had expected and desired when I was traveling with Acrodorf towards Zedius. The journey as a spirit was totally different and this journey with the body and traveling through space was something else. It was like traveling in space in a convertible. I loved it.

I opened my arms and looked around in delight. This was amazing. Acrodorf had told Hoi to take special care of me, and this is exactly what I had wanted. And then I heard a strange sound and spun around to see who it was.

"Help me!" I heard a wail but there was no one there. I could not see anyone, but I could feel a very weighty and heavy presence in the space around.

"Where are you?" I spun around looking in all directions.

"Help me!" The wail grew louder and then it appeared, a dark grey ink drop-like er, creature. That's all. It had the shape of a drop of ink that was dropped into the vast universe. All through my journey into the universe, I had observed that the humanoid was the most preferred prototype for a form, but this was just the form of a drop of ink, a weird life form.

"What's wrong?" I enquired. I was on The Path of The Lost Souls and maybe I had to discover my ability to help this soul free itself.

"I come from The Planet of Alternate Realities," the ink drop wailed as it sped towards me, bringing with it this heavy and depressing energy.

"And then I had to choose........I couldn't decide... I didn't know what was right...." The ink drop continued and came close to my face, as the energy around me tensed up. I could no longer hear his words. All I could feel was a negative energy sapping my own.

"How will I ever get home....." It continued its grievance and to my dismay placed itself on my left shoulder. I staggered under the weight. The ink drop continued speaking oblivious to my shock. I was overwhelmed with the weight that every word was putting on me that I could no longer focus on its story.

"Help me!" I heard another voice.

I turned my neck around with a lot of effort and soon another ink drop emerged. The space around me grew tighter.

"I come from the Planet......" The ink drop started with his sad story that he expected me to turn to light. The first ink drop had not yet finished his misery-loaded story and now the second one was fast approaching me with his. I didn't know what to focus on, my discomfort with their negativity or on their agony. I wanted to interrupt and I wanted to stop the ink drop, but the weight was pulling me down. The second ink drop settled on my head and I staggered. The two stories were getting mixed up and their combined force was growing.

"Help me!" I heard chimes and two more ink drops emerged a few meters away.

I heard jumbled words and wails and cries emerging from the ink drop creatures on my body and from the two that were speeding towards me. I felt suffocated and I could not breathe. I was too shocked to understand what was going on. The ink drop creatures settled on my shoulder and my back. I bent forward with the weight. There were so many voices, there was so much sadness and grief. A world full of failure and misery had broken loose upon me. I tried to get my balance and I tried to stop them, but their outburst was so loud that my cry for help did not even matter. To my dismay, one more ink drop formed around me.

"Help me!" The shriek echoed from around me and the ink drop creature settled on my chest. They were all clinging to me like parasites till I could not stand anymore. I collapsed onto the cloud under their weight. They were draining my energy with their problems that I could not understand, let alone solve.

"Help me!" The shrieks were deafening and were filling my soul with pain and sorrow. The weight of the ink drops kept growing on me. I not only could not help them, but I was going to lose myself under the weight of their unresolved angst.

The weight was pinning me down. I was fast losing myself. What had I brought myself onto? How was I ever going to fulfill my purpose of liberating people from their own Maya? These lost souls were wailing non-stop about how lost they were, about how they did not know which direction to take, about how they were confused if they were doing the right thing, about how they were afraid to make decisions.

They wanted me to decide for them, they wanted me to show them the way to their destiny, they wanted me to tell them what was right.

"Please stop!" I sobbed. I had lost. I had no ability to help. I was going to succumb to failure on my own path towards my own purpose.

"Please stop!" I whimpered under the weight that was wrenching my soul. If this was a test, I was failing miserably. The purpose to liberate others is a big purpose. I had a swelling feeling of doubt if I had the ability to fulfill it.

"Please stop. You are killing me," I tried to whisper to the ink drop creatures whose burden was making it difficult for me to speak.

"Stop?" The creature asked surprised.

"Stop?" Another creature shouted.

"Stop?" All the ink drop creatures shouted at each other and in moments, there was silence.

"I will die under your weight," I begged in whispers, "Please get off me!" I pleaded. And then I said the words that would spell my own doom on The Path that would supposedly lead to my purpose.

"I cannot help you," I sobbed. I really could not help these creatures. No one can tell you what is right for you, only you can. No one can show you the direction of your life, only you can. For if you are lost, then it is you who must find out the way.

I could feel the shock in their souls. I could feel the heart shattering agony that emerged from each and every soul.

"I cannot help you. Please don't kill me with your weight," I begged in my last attempt to make them understand that I was not the answer to their problems.

I felt the weight lighten around me until the last ink drop lifted. I sat up carefully. Above me was a thick grey cloud of the ink drops that were slowly retreating.

The ink drop creature's cloud retreated further to my relief.

"But we are lost souls!" Two voices echoed together.

"Help me!" Another thundered in.

"I cannot help you," I begged for them to understand.

"I was also a lost soul!" I could not believe my own words.

There was a loud gasp from the ink drop creatures, the lost souls.

"You were a lost soul? Really?" There was total disbelief that erupted.

"Yes, I was like you, a lost soul, trying to find my path that would lead me to my purpose." I hung my head low in reflection of my life term on planet Earth as I spoke.

The cloud of ink drops retreated further in disappointment.

I folded my legs and held them close to my chest. I rested my face on my knees and I looked at the retreating creatures.

"I was a lost soul too," I whispered to no one in particular, half expecting my body to turn into an ink drop as I declared that.

"When I met these powerful creatures from Zedius, The Perfect World with Thelda on planet Earth, I was a lost soul. I had no idea what choices to make when Acrodorf offered me a chance to come to Zedius." I raised my head and spoke to the ink drop creatures and they stopped in their retreat, curious about my story.

"But I made the right choice. I chose to come to Zedius over the predictable misery that awaited me, had I turned back. There was certainly no power if I stepped backwards, but the step forward to come to Zedius had potential and hope. And in making that choice I found some power. I found power in moving forward in trust. I was lost because I was constantly moving further back into the cave of doubt."

"And then to leave planet Earth, I was thrown into The Maya and I felt lost yet again. Heck, I felt so lost that I forgot the purpose of my journey. I forgot my power that I had felt just a few moments ago. But in connecting with Acrodorf, I found the reality behind the illusion. I broke free from The Maya and I felt powerful. I felt so powerful that I could conquer the universe."

"And then my term was decided on The Game and I felt really lost all over again. In the Land of the Cannibals, I felt so lost that I abandoned those who helped me to save my own life. And then I found in me the courage to face fear and to move beyond it. And in doing that I liberated myself and those who were misunderstood. I felt powerful and happy. But when I was faced with the saber-toothed lion in the next level of The Game, Jesus, I felt lost again!! I felt I had lost my ability to trust and my ability to allow people to be themselves. I felt lost that I could not find a way to survive the threat of a predator, whose sole intention was my destruction. And then I found in me the ability to connect with my opponent, to understand it, to liberate him from his misled purpose. And when I did that, I felt powerful. I was granted the freedom to travel the universe. That was a big victory for me."

"And then on the Planet of Truth when I had to walk on water, I felt lost. I had no clue on how to walk on a fast moving stream. I could not understand how others were doing it and could not figure what I was doing wrong. Then, I found the importance of holding onto a vision and I felt powerful. I made it to the mountain, The

Great Realization and in blindly following Zi, I lost the way of my purpose. In meeting Saga, I found the disaster I was creating by repeatedly going astray and not walking on my purpose. That cognition brought me power. And when Saga implied that the clouds that hid the sun when it was my turn to make fire was my fault, I felt lost. I could not make the clouds go away. I felt lost on how it was me who had obscured the sun behind the clouds in the first place? And then I found my truth that I was denying my purpose and tagging along with other's. I found my truth that I was the creator of all the clouds of disaster that loomed over my career and relationships and in finding that I could make them go away. I felt very powerful to be in the light of the truth."

"And when I reached Zedius and I was confronted with Jini, I was lost on how I could stop her from her evil intentions to destroy Zedius. I felt lost and beat that I was responsible for the disaster that lay ahead for all the beings of Zedius. And then I found in me the valor to stake my life in an attempt to safe-guard a million others. And when I got Acrodorf to get help for Zedius, I felt powerful. I felt so powerful that I felt that now I could go back home and conquer my world with my purpose."

"And when I reached here, confronted with your burden and pain, I feel lost once again for I don't know how to help you," I paused. I could swear I felt the space around me lighten up. It was not as heavy and negative as before, but the ink drop creatures had stayed where they were in a cloud. Their presence was there, but their weight had lessened.

"All I can tell you is this; every time I have felt lost, it only meant that there was more that I had to find of myself. When I look back and see every situation that I have felt lost in, it only gave me an opportunity to search the truth that I had been hiding from myself. And when I found that truth, I found my power, I found myself and I was not lost anymore," I said. The space around me felt light and I could breathe without constriction. The heaviness in my body was lifting and I could feel a sense of relief building up.

"I know that one day, some day, I will fulfill my purpose, and I also know that on that day of fulfillment, I will feel lost once again, for my universe would have expanded beyond that purpose. And I know that day I would have to find in me a higher vision. I know I will feel lost and doubt my abilities to reach it, and then I will find in me exactly that strength that will lead me there." I stood up and felt a joy stir in the depths of my soul.

"I cannot help you and I need to find in me the ability to forgive myself that I can't," I folded my hands before the souls, who felt so lost that they had shrunk their beingness to that of an ink drop and asked for their forgiveness.

"I was lost too," one ink drop broke loose from the cloud and floated towards me. It grew bigger and bigger as it did, until it was a monstrous ink drop and then it exploded with a spark of white light and snapped into a beautiful form with an outline of a very beautiful humanoid. I heard gasps emerge from the ink drop cloud and it began to tremble and rumble.

"I was lost too," The beautiful outline creature spoke rapidly from the invisible interior, "But I remained lost. I stood there. I refused to move further. I waited for someone to help me. I waited for someone to cover me up. I waited for someone to show me the way and decide for me. I stood still in wait for that help, that I should have found within me. I remained lost because I sought my freedom in the answer of another."

"I remained lost." A sudden intrusion startled me. It was another beautiful creature that came close, "Because I equated feeling lost with feeling small and unworthy."

"I thought that because I felt lost, there was no hope," another ink drop transformed into its form and approached me.

"And I thought I was the only one who was lost!"

"I never understood that everyone feels lost temporarily when they want to change their world and the state of their life."

"If I only knew that being lost was a clue to finding within me the courage and greatness to keep moving forward, I would never have lived small."

"When I felt lost, I shut myself down. And when I did that, I sealed myself from any progress that potentially awaited me."

All the ink drop creatures had snapped into their forms talking to each other, telling each other about how they had misunderstood and underestimated their own greatness on the first sign of feeling lost.

I feel that change brings the illusion of doubt. I feel that when our vision and perspective expands, it creates a temporary feeling of being lost. When we leave our familiar ground and move on to explore a higher awareness, it is natural to feel a momentary loss of familiarity and comfort. But growth lies beyond that line of uncertainty. Great souls made it to greatness not because they knew everything from the start, they made it to greatness because they found in themselves the courage to learn and grow each time they felt lost.

"Feeling lost is an illusion that brings your fears and confusion to life. We began to live in the illusion and we stayed forever, lost souls." One divine creature moved up to me and held my hand in hers. She had an aura of purity around her.

"Thank you for liberating us." She looked back at the others who had liberated themselves from their self-imposed imprisonment of being lost souls.

"I didn't do anything," I looked over to a totally transformed lot of beautiful creatures.

"When one tells one's own story of liberation with absolute honesty, not only about the glory of victory but also about the shame of feeling lost, that story has so much power that it can't help but liberate others.

The story of one soul is the story of another. And when one soul frees herself from her self-created illusion, that story in turn frees a million others," Hoi made his way from the commotion.

A swirling energy began to build up and the beings began to move into circles around me like an outward flowing whirlpool.

"Thank you,"

"You liberated us,"

"You are an inspiration,"

"I found myself,"

"I will never be lost again."

I heard their combined voices, as they quickly passed by me in acknowledgement of my act of greatness in liberating them through my own story.

I stayed still, delighted. There is no greater satisfaction, there is no greater joy in this world than knowing that you contributed to the growth and evolution of another soul. I don't know how long I stayed there on the blue cloud until the last being thanked me and disappeared. Gratitude has energy, an energy so potent that it cannot but humble the receiver. I knew that I would write the story of The Perfect World, that it was built not because there was certainty and clarity, it was built because there was doubt and confusion. That would be a story of liberation, story of a lost soul who found her eternity and her power within.

I was so immersed in my thoughts that I did not notice that the cloud was fast shrinking. A large star was shining onto the little island of blue that I stood upon and I could see in the distance, a green dot that grew bigger and bigger, exposing the mouth of the same light tunnel that I had entered from.

In a few moments, the blue cloud stopped right at the brink of the green tunnel made of light.

"You liberate a lost soul, when you tell the untold story of your own liberation. For that, you have to admit to your own weakness before you can take credit for your strength. You liberate a lost soul when you tell the story about your journey to greatness and infinite possibilities that started from the point of being lost." Hoi smiled at me and the vapors dissolved in the space around us.

Hoi was right. I needed this ability, an ability to tell my story as an answer to another's pain. I cannot write another's story and I cannot help solve another's problem, but I sure can tell how I overcame mine. And in doing that, I allow the reader to understand and find out for themselves what they need to know.

Hoi pointed at the tunnel with his hands dissolving into vapors.

I was more than delighted to step off and heaved myself into the tunnel. With a few electric spurts of radiating light penetrating through my body, I shone so bright I could have lit a thousand suns.

I rolled out from the other end of the tunnel into the arms of a very excited Thelda.

"I have the ability to make soulful music," Thelda squealed in delight. "My Path served me well, it was amazing!"

Thelda spoke in one breath non-stop about how she realized that music and noise were composed of the same energy of sound. When sound energy finds its source in the soul then it creates music. She said that she found the ability to bring music where there was noise, by silencing her own soul of the noise first. She said she found that when her soul became silent, it came alive with music.

"What did you find on your Path?" She finally ended her story with the question.

"I found the ability to liberate another through my story. I will write about the Perfect World once I am home....." Thelda interrupted me before I could complete my sentence.

"Will I be in it?" She raised her eyebrows and giggled.

"You are the main lead in the story," I laughed and hugged Thelda. We spoke and laughed and giggled, alternating between our plans on what we would do, once we get back home.

Planet Earth was becoming visible now; the bluish green ball of illusion that was guarded by The Maya; The Maya we created in our daily denials of our own power to be, do and have anything we wanted.

Two familiar figures ahead made my heart leap with joy. I sped towards Acrodorf and hugged him tight.

"We are approaching the end of our journey," Bren smiled, looking at Thelda and me.

"We must part here, and be on our journey to create spiritual freedom," Bren continued, oblivious to my disappointment.

I did not let go of Acrodorf. I was not going to let go of Acrodorf.

"If you cling on to him like that, you will grow wings too," Thelda guffawed.

Acrodorf let go of his arm from my shoulder and caught the tear in his palm as it rolled down my eyelashes.

"In bringing you to Zedius, I have found more of myself. Your presence has expanded mine. Your energy has added to mine. When I first saw you, my whole soul inhaled your presence and your beauty. I felt that I met a long lost friend in this ever-expanding universe. I just hoped for my sake that you would agree to honor me with your company. I don't know how you did it; not see who you are. How could you have escaped your own greatness for so long?" Acrodorf held me close, speaking to my soul and I smiled through my tears.

"I was set on The Path of Letting Go, for the hardest thing for me to do would be to let go of your presence. In my life term, I had sought your company just like you had sought mine. Our connection was long pending. In finding you, I have also had to find in myself the strength to let you go," Acrodorf said and pulled me into his arms. His hair crept onto my neck joyously and I saw his wings unfold and span and then fold up over me.

"There is no greater joy for me than in knowing that you exist for real…. Even if it is two light years away." His hair danced around his neck and I reached around his neck and touched it. The strand spun around my finger and held it tight.

"You are a superior soul. I saw that in you. I know you see it too." He whispered, as he let me go from his embrace. I could see the reflection of my face in his greenish blue eyes and I wished I could stay in them for real, forever.

"Your purpose is not ordinary. You trusted me, you trusted yourself to give yourself this chance. Zi gave up his life and stays a part of Zedius. You gave up your life to give him that chance. Your act leads to the fulfillment of his. Your essence, your sacrifice and your love will always reverberate in the soul of Zedius. I am grateful that you allowed me to bring you here and I am grateful that you saved our planet," Acrodorf said, holding my face in his hands.

I saw my face in his eyes and I saw tears roll down my eyes in his.

"You gave me a new life, Acrodorf. You are the superior one!" I sniffed.

"You both are superior!" Thelda brought our emotional argument to an end and gave us both a tight hug. I laughed. Acrodorf laughed. Bren laughed, brushing aside a tear.

I knew that I would carry a part of Acrodorf as I knew he would carry a part of me.

"I got concerts to organize!!" Thelda giggled, "Thelda the Sorceress is coming back in a new avatar." Thelda began to rumble the drum.

Acrodorf did finally let go of me and he held me up for Bren. Bren was waiting behind us for his turn to say goodbye.

Bren took my face in his hands and spoke to my soul.

"Be the best writer your world has ever had. Be the truth, do out of that truth and have the truth prevail, that you are immortal, indestructible and powerful enough to create infinite possibilities to have any life you so choose. I will be there with you and for you. Will me, and I will be there!" Bren held me tight and squeezed the breath out of me.

Bren had been instrumental in my evolution. I owed him a lot. Though I had had my reservations about him in the start, he played an important part in my purpose. Bren held me back and gazed into my eyes.

"Thank you. In knowing you I have grown, Zedius has grown. Our paths will cross again soon." He winked at Acrodorf.

I didn't want this moment to end. I didn't know how to end this moment. I didn't know what to say. There were no words that could express the way I felt right now. I was overwhelmed with gratitude, with love, with sorrow, with power - all at the same time.

"You will come back, right?" I turned to Acrodorf. "You will come back when I need you?" That was the promise that Bren had made in exchange of the power to be, do and have anything we wanted. "I will not come back," Acrodorf spoke and my heart dropped to my feet, "because I will never leave your side," he smiled from ear to ear. I ran to Acrodorf and he caught me before I flung myself on him.

We laughed and we cried and then we laughed again. Thelda added some music to the total bliss that I felt in the company of my long lost friend.

"Our time is long past up, you have to leave before The Game reprimands you for trespassing again," Bren sighed. Thelda was pulling at my arm and I was holding on to Acrodorf's, with all my might.

"Niki!" Thelda held my arm and waist and Bren laughed behind us. "You went on The Path of Letting Go," I shouted to Acrodorf as a very persistent Thelda dragged me away from him, "I didn't go there. I am not letting you go!"

Acrodorf smiled and crossed his heart with a promise to return when I needed him.

Acrodorf and Bren disappeared with a bow. I kept staring at the spot where they had stood a moment ago. Thelda grabbed my shoulder and pulled me towards her. This Sorceress had become my best friend for eternity. Who would have ever thought that magic would find its peace in music and that doubt would find its peace in power.

I looked at my planet, The Maya laden abode of illusions. Just a few days ago, I was just another person walking around, clueless, of my spiritual eternity and my innate powers. All I had was a nagging suspicion that there was more to life than I was living. I was right. There was a universe full of adventure and intelligence. I traveled across the universe reclaiming my own identity, an identity that I had surrendered to The Maya, so that I could justify my mortality. I started my journey with the intention to acquire powers so I could live a better life back home, and in completing my journey, my intention was now to contribute towards the lives of my fellow beings, so that they could have their share of the universe too.

I started out as Niki Sanders, the lost soul, failing, at work, at relationships, and at her purpose. I was stepping back as Niki Sanders, the superior soul, who would build a new world, for herself and for others.

"Are you thinking what I am thinking?" Thelda, The Drummer pried into my thoughts. Her face was inches away from mine.
"Stop intruding in my thoughts," I pushed Thelda away.

"I want to meet The Creator of this darned Planet governed by The Maya," Thelda spoke spitefully.

"And I want to meet Acrodorf again," I spoke carelessly.

"Ow," I yelped as Thelda pinched my arm.

"I want to create a better world, Thelda. I don't care who created this planet because I still can create my world in it. The illusion cannot exist without my permission. The illusion, The Maya is an excuse. I am not going to make any excuses for my life anymore. Either you can have excuses, or you can have power. You can never have both. I have reclaimed my power and I am going to create magic with it." I beamed.

"You are right, Niki," Thelda cheered up.

"I got concerts to organize, kiddo. I got music to create. The planet will celebrate, for Thelda, The Drummer sets foot to create magic with music." Thelda rumbled her drum to emphasize her point.

"Thank you, Thelda, for bringing me here. I owe you a lot. You are instrumental in all that I have gained, including my own self." I held Thelda's hands in gratitude. I could not end this journey without acknowledging Thelda's role in who I had become today.

"I told you, it was your destiny to be here. What I did not tell you was, that your choices held the destiny of our planet. You are a superior soul." Thelda squeezed my hand and gently touched my head.

"I will use my powers well, Thelda. I will be the influencing factor that will wake up lost souls. Everything that I do, will be intended towards spreading the truth, the truth that we all are superior souls, making excuses of mediocrity. I will settle for nothing less than a better world, a spiritually enlightened world. I will make my planet a worthy abode for all the special beings that inhabit it, so that one day, some day, we can invite other evolved souls in the universe, to take notice, and join us in the discovery of yet a better self."

"Your destiny awaits you, Niki Sanders," Thelda smiled.

"You better get to my concerts from the start. I want to see you on the front seat this time," Thelda joked.

"I promise," I crossed my heart.

"These jewels could be worth millions," Thelda ran her fingers on my bracelet and then cast a sorry glance on her drum.

"These jewels are worth millions, Niki!" She yelped, her eyes turning wide.

"It was my destiny to have them," I winked and pulled my sweater over the bracelet. "Let's get to work, Thelda. Let's create a Perfect World down there!"

We held hands like school girls do, rejoicing in this new state of power and happiness that we felt.

"Let's create a Perfect World then!" Thelda's words faded.

I felt a nasty pull downwards and we went speeding into planet Earth. A nasty knot built up in my soul, like that jerk you feel in your heart when a loved one is in trouble. The magnetic field emerged above us as we headed downwards. The Maya made a secure ring around the planet to ensure there would be no further escaping from its trap. It would only be a few seconds, soul crashing through half a dozen aircrafts before we reached the forest in the Canary Islands where we had first embarked on our journey to Zedius, The Channel in wait to snap us back to humanity.

The Earth shook or maybe it was my soul that shuddered, before I heard the thunder of Acrodorf's voice.

"You can't go back Niki!" A horrified Acrodorf was screaming, speeding towards us with a trail of lightning behind him.

"The Channel has been removed!" His face spelt alarm, disaster and horror.

.... *a further journey awaits.*

My Perfect World

I have learnt that the real meaning of success lies in questioning myself – am I happy? Did I contribute? Did I grow as a result of my experiences? I am as successful as I am happy. I am as successful as I am contributing and growing, constantly.

I left 'him' a long time ago. Since I didn't know how to be happy with him, I let him go, to explore and embrace his own happiness. Today, I am wiser and I am happier, and I can't wait to share my happiness with 'him', the one that I have not yet found.

I quit on distractions that I called 'work'. I realized that I was working very hard, but I was not really getting anywhere. Money was always scarce and so was my attitude. But by focusing on what I love to do, I am happy, mostly. I smile, I laugh and I even sing, easily, naturally. Money still doesn't flow easily, but my ability to be patient, to be helpful, to be rational, emerges from the love that finds its expression in my days work.

I don't know if my writing will touch the world. I don't know if my book will make it as an international best seller. And in this moment, I don't really need to know that. I created it out of love and I sent it out to the world. Now 'others' have the choice to create further with my book, or to create that which makes them happy. And when they do that, my book is relieved of its responsibility.

I take a chance when life offers an opportunity for greatness. Sometimes that chance is to go to Zedius, the unknown. And sometimes that chance is to leave planet Earth, the familiar. I leap into both, excitedly. In exploring I learn. Spiritual grandeur is not just about playing the same game, living the same life, at higher levels. Spiritual evolution is about playing new games, creating new possibilities, living a new ignited life altogether.

My eyes are open. I see people for who they really are. I see life for what it really is. I see beyond the obvious. Life, like people sometimes projects illusions of hatred, insecurity, scarcity and weakness. I can see the truth – the unchanging constant – that we are all powerful, immortal, indestructible souls. I treat people out of that respect and I expect them to behave out of that power. And when they don't – I accept their disguise with a smile. I know that the villain is as much as an actor as the hero. They both are a part of the same story, an important part. And when the story ends, they both go home, to the perfect world.

I am aware that I in living my life I am serving term in a bigger game than most realize. I earn my freedom, my salvation, my redemption, when I grant others of their share first. I don't know how to get into your heart so you can set me free of the pain I caused you, but I sure can free my need to hold you responsible for all that I should have been. My purpose and my intention starts with me and it ends with me. As long as I play fair, as long as I play to love and liberate, in the end, we all win. I cannot predict how people and life will play, but I can guarantee that I will play with honor.

My focus is my greatest strength. I can create fire, literally, with the amount of energy and passion that I put towards my purpose. Where I see lack of purpose and lack of passion, I find lack of focus. When I catch areas that are falling and failing, I know that I can set them right with my attention. I don't drift anymore and I don't allow distractions to sway me. But I still do stop to smell the roses, and when I do that, I carry their fragrance into my purpose.

My world is not perfect, but I am the chosen one to set it right. In knowing that I have embraced the responsibility to create a better life than yesterday. To do that, I have to think beyond myself, and in doing that, I become bigger than I was.

We are all connected - by a common purpose. If we haven't made the connection yet, it is not because our purposes don't match - it is because either one of us hasn't tuned in yet. We are ALL connected by a common purpose. I sometimes wish that people I love would hurry up and get on track. I did, and I wait for you to make the connection too.

My purpose is to tell stories that I need to learn from. My purpose is to put on paper that which sometimes gets lost in the noise in my head. In writing this book I have fulfilled that purpose. I can now read and acknowledge and rejoice in all that I always knew but missed to see in my daily life. My purpose has saved my life. My purpose has liberated me, and that is one big load off the world. That is one lost soul, less.

I stand at the beginning of a new story. I stand at the beginning of a new life, a new world. The world need not offer me anything anymore, for I have a new world to offer.

Love & laughter,
Priya

Also by Priya Kumar

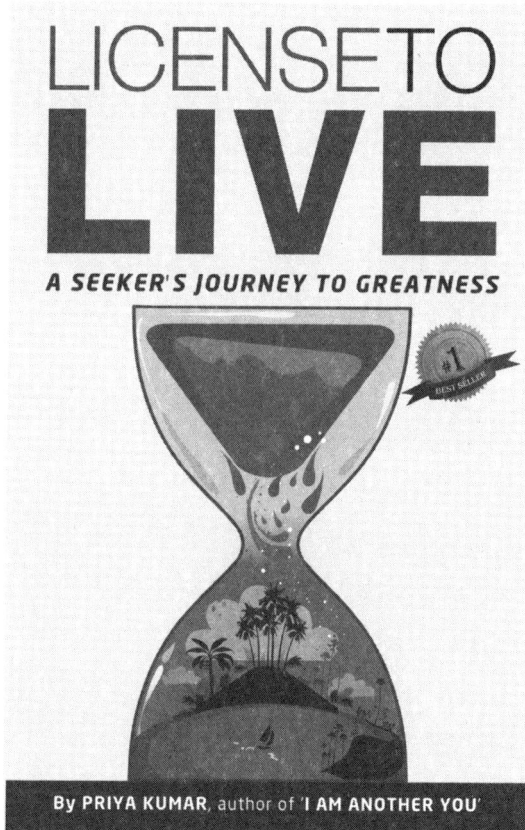

LICENSE TO LIVE

A SEEKER'S JOURNEY TO GREATNESS

#1 BEST SELLER

By PRIYA KUMAR, author of 'I AM ANOTHER YOU'

License to Live is a seekers journey towards finding greatness within. This wonderfully crafted fable is about finding the direction you are destined to head in and creating the life of your dreams. **License to Live** tells the tale of a successful corporate guru who enrolls herself in a seminar by one of the finest success coaches in the world. His radical training methods take her on a life-changing odyssey.

Full of wisdom, wit and spiritual insights, you find lessons here that will change the way you lead your life forever.

Also by Priya Kumar

"A Journey to Powerful Breakthroughs"

#1 BESTSELLER

I AM
another
YOU

by priya kumar

A Book of many lessons, many insights and many truths, it has the power to awaken you to your best self. This book will urge you to take that path you always knew was right but never had the courage to follow. It will guide you, humour you, inspire you, touch you and above all lead you to – your own breakthroughs.